MW00653927

The Incident of the Book in the Nighttime

Sherlock Holmes Bookshop Mysteries

The Sign of Four Spirits
The Game Is a Footnote
A Three Book Problem
A Curious Incident
There's a Murder Afoot
A Scandal in Scarlet
The Cat of the Baskervilles
Body on Baker Street
Elementary, She Read

Lighthouse Library Mysteries (writing as Eva Gates)

The Stranger in the Library
Death Knells and Wedding Bells
Death by Beach Read
Deadly Ever After
A Death Long Overdue
Read and Buried
Something Read, Something Dead
The Spook in the Stacks
Reading Up a Storm
Booked for Trouble
By Book or by Crook

Ashley Grant Mysteries

Coral Reef Views
Blue Water Hues
White Sand Blues

Year Round Christmas Mysteries

Have Yourself a Deadly Little Christmas
Dying in a Winter Wonderland
Silent Night, Deadly Night
Hark the Herald Angels Slay
We Wish You a Murderous Christmas
Rest Ye Murdered Gentlemen

Constable Molly Smith Mysteries

Unreasonable Doubt
Under Cold Stone
A Cold White Sun
Among the Departed
Negative Image
Winter of Secrets
Valley of the Lost
In the Shadow of the Glacier

Tea by the Sea Mysteries

Murder Spills the Tea
Murder in a Teacup
Tea & Treachery

Catskill Summer Resort Mysteries

Deadly Director's Cut
Deadly Summer Nights

Also Available by Vicki Delany

More than Sorrow
Burden of Memory
Scare the Light Away

The Incident of the Book in the Nighttime

A SHERLOCK HOLMES BOOKSHOP MYSTERY

Vicki Delany

NEW YORK

This is a work of fiction. All of the names, characters, organizations, places and events portrayed in this novel are either products of the author's imagination or are used fictitiously. Any resemblance to real or actual events, locales, or persons, living or dead, is entirely coincidental.

Published in the United States by Crooked Lane Books, an imprint of The Quick Brown Fox & Company LLC.

Crooked Lane Books and its logo are trademarks of The Quick Brown Fox & Company LLC.

Library of Congress Catalog-in-Publication data available upon request.

ISBN (hardcover): 978-1-63910-926-5
ISBN (ebook): 978-1-63910-927-2

Cover design by Joe Burleson

Printed in the United States.

www.crookedlanebooks.com

Crooked Lane Books
34 West 27th St., 10th Floor
New York, NY 10001

First Edition: January 2025

10 9 8 7 6 5 4 3 2 1

To Alex, who loves London.

Chapter One

I have to admit, it was a lovely wedding. The bride was beautiful and radiant, the groom handsome and beaming with joy. The guests were well turned out, everyone clearly delighted for the couple. The service had been a short, no-nonsense affair held in a no-nonsense registry office, but the reception was held at an excellent restaurant in one of the city's best hotels. Wine and cocktails flowed freely, the food was extraordinary, the ambience perfect, the service unobtrusive and discreet.

When the groom tapped his glass and rose to his feet to speak, he choked up for a moment and I wondered if he might cry. Instead, he swallowed and then simply thanked everyone for coming, some of us a long way, and mumbled a few words about how delighted he was that this amazing woman had agreed to spend the rest of her life with him. Pippa, my sister, gazed at her beloved in sheer adoration.

To my considerable surprise, she hadn't so much as glanced at her phone since arriving at the registry office at Mayfair Library, as far as I could tell anyway. The perfect place for this marriage ceremony, I thought, considering the groom is a dealer in rare books, as it is in a real library and the Marylebone Room is full of antique books. Formalities over, Grant and Pippa had taken a cab to the reception venue at a hotel on the Strand in central London, so it is possible she checked in with "the office" as the newlyweds wound through the crowded streets of a Saturday evening. Then again, my sister could be mighty discreet. When she wanted to be.

Perhaps she truly had taken an entire day off. They were supposed to be going on honeymoon eventually, but no definite plans had been set. A vacation for my workaholic, high-achieving sister? Perhaps. She'd changed since meeting and falling in love with Grant Thompson. She sent me the occasional photograph of the two of them enjoying dinner in a nice restaurant or touring the sights of London and the South of England together. They'd gone hiking in Wales for an entire three-day weekend, Pippa's hiking gear so new, I could hear her boots squeak above the sound of the wind in the video on my phone. She'd put on a bit of much-needed weight—not too much, mind—and she smiled in a way I hadn't seen since . . . since ever, I suppose. She was seven years older than me, and even when she was a child, Pippa had been more of an adult than many adults I knew.

Pippa was next to stand up, her smooth, sleek cream satin gown flowing like a river as she did so. She also made a short speech thanking us for coming and thanking Grant for coming into her life, before raising a toast to him, to which we all responded with enthusiasm. She was about to sit down when she hesitated, took a breath, and lifted her glass once again. "Last of all, I have to give my heartfelt thanks and all the love in the world to my darling sister."

That was unexpected. I refrained from glancing around to see if a previously unknown sibling had suddenly put in an appearance.

"To Gemma, for bringing Grant into my life."

"To Gemma!" Everyone drank my health. I smiled stiffly and waved in acknowledgment. I might have even blushed. I try not to make a habit of doing such a thing.

"That was a nice gesture." Jayne Wilson leaned across her own fiancé once conversation resumed. "Thanking you, I mean."

"It was," I said. "Surprisingly so."

On the other side of me Ryan Ashburton, here as my date as well as a friend of the groom, pushed back his chair. He laid one hand lightly on my shoulder. "I'm going to grab the chance to corner Grant while he's momentarily alone. We haven't had the opportunity to catch up."

I watched Ryan thread his way across the crowded room to the head table. My sister thanking me was unexpected but entirely warranted. Grant had been my friend before he met Pippa and subsequently being swept off his feet. I'd come to London to attend a Sherlock Holmes convention in my home city. Grant had accompanied me hoping to find some good deals on Sir Arthur Conan Doyle first editions. Instead, he found Phillipa Doyle. By the time we returned to West London, Massachusetts, where I now live, he and Pippa had made plans for him to move to England to be with her.

At the time, I'd had my doubts as to the wisdom of that, but it clearly worked out well. For both of them.

In addition to Grant, Ryan, Jayne, and our friend Donald Morris had come to the convention with me and found themselves caught up in subsequent unfortunate events. Thus they'd all been invited to the wedding. Jayne had brought her own fiancé, Andy Whitehall.

Andy had never been to the U.K. before, and normally I love nothing more than showing off my beloved city to American visitors. Unfortunately, our arrival had been severely delayed. A flight that didn't take off, for reasons still unknown; another having to turn around over the Atlantic and return to Boston; overnight in an uncomfortable, hugely overpriced airport hotel; yet another delayed flight. All the joys of modern air travel.

We finally arrived at Heathrow, tired, hungry, grumpy, late in the morning of the wedding. At least we made it in time, although one bag had not—mine. As I couldn't go to the wedding of my only sister in nylon trousers with numerous zippers and big pockets, a beige T-shirt on which coffee had been spilled while waiting for the first (which never happened) flight, and a baggy cardigan, all of which had been worn several days in a row, I had to spend the day shopping while my friends slept. My mother, Anne, accompanied me to Harrods to get something suitable. The dress we chose was far above my regular budget, but I did love it. Navy blue, tea dress length, boat neck, sleeves to the elbow, wide chiffon skirt with a lacy overskirt dotted with sequins, thin belt. Not only expensive but far fancier than I would normally wear. But this wedding was a grand affair, and everyone dressed in their best finery. Grant and my father wore morning suits; the other men, including Grant's father, were in suits and ties. Fortunately for Donald, Sherlockian to his core, men's evening wear hasn't changed all that much in the last hundred years, so he wasn't entirely out of place in his gray three-piece suit, gold watch chain, heavily starched white shirt worn without a tie, Ulster cape, and sturdy black umbrella. I still have no idea how he got the umbrella through airport security.

At my request, I'd been seated at the dinner with my American friends, rather than my distant, largely unknown relatives. When the toasts and speeches were over and the guests up and mingling, Donald leaned across the table toward Andy. "Fortunately you have a free day tomorrow before heading off on your fishing expedition on Monday. I spent some time earlier today rearranging our plans. I was able to get us places in the Sherlock Holmes walking tour for ten thirty tomorrow morning." In his fifties, Donald had given up his law practice to devote his life to the study of the Great Detective and his creator. Whereupon he found being a Sherlockian expert doesn't provide much of a living. But he was a happy man, nonetheless, and a faithful patron of the Sherlock Holmes Bookshop and Emporium.

"Ten thirty's a bit—" Andy began.

Donald paid him no mind. "It's a different tour than the one I went on last time, specifically recommended by some of my illustrious colleagues, so I'm looking forward to new sights and a new perspective. After the tour, we'll have time to fit in . . ."

I tuned Donald out as he continued laying out his well-planned schedule. On our previous visit to London, Donald's first time in the city of which his idol had "an exact knowledge," he missed many of the Sherlockian highlights, as he'd been caught up in helping me clear my father of a false murder accusation. He was determined to see absolutely everything on this visit. And equally determined that the rest of us would as well, whether we wanted to see the highlights of Holmes's London or not. Which, judging by the look on Andy's face, was a definite "not." Before leaving West London, he told me that as well as the planned fishing trip with my father and Ryan, he wanted to see the great art galleries and museums. I hadn't known until this week that Andy was enraptured by the Pre-Raphaelites. While Jayne scoured guidebooks for the best places to see the work of Millais, Rossetti, and their fellows, Donald consulted schedules and locations of the most touristy of tourist traps.

I left them to their plans and found my mind wandering. I'd had a wedding once. I'd been young, too young, and my parents hadn't entirely approved of my choice of groom or of me leaping prematurely to the altar. But they'd forced out smiles and congratulations and gave us a nice celebration. We'd been married in the Church of England, all flowers and hymns, and had our reception at a swanky restaurant in South Kensington. As I recall, to my extreme embarrassment, I wore an over-stuffed, over-decorated, overly large white dress. I must have looked like an idiot. On the termination of the marriage, I tossed every picture of that bad memory I could find. I still don't know what had come over me, other than, I suppose, youthful romanticism. Then again, Paul could be quite the charmer.

And not only to me, as I later found out.

To avoid thinking any more about that unpleasantness, I glanced around the crowded room. Ten round tables for eight plus the head table for Pippa, Grant, Grant's parents, and mine. Meaning eighty-six guests. Other than a few distant relatives I vaguely remembered meeting once or twice, I didn't know most of the people here, but that came as no surprise. Not only is the age difference between my sister and me considerable, but we've always moved in completely different circles. I'm a bookstore owner. Paul, my ex-husband, and I had owned a mystery bookstore near Trafalgar Square, but after I divested myself of both the marriage and the business interest, I moved to America to help my great-uncle Arthur Doyle manage the Sherlock Holmes Bookshop and Emporium he'd foolishly opened on a whim because he liked the address—222 Baker Street, West London. We'd later gone into partnership with Jayne Wilson to establish Mrs. Hudson's Tea Room, located at 220 Baker Street.

Uncle Arthur hadn't made it to Pippa's wedding. He hadn't even made it as far as the airport. A few days before our scheduled departure, he sprained his right ankle. Nothing terribly serious, except that most things are serious for a man in his eighties. Rather than struggle on and off airplanes, in and out of subway and railway stations, and try to maneuver his way around my parents' multistoried house, he declared he'd stay at home and nurse his injury. Besides, he assured me, someone had to keep an eye on our dogs and our businesses. I wasn't entirely comfortable with that. Arthur was strictly a silent partner in our affairs. There was a reason he needed me to run the shop. And that reason was because he sometimes forgot that to stay in business we had to sell things to people. Fortunately, it was late October, a slow time in our tourist town, and my assistants Ashleigh and Gale were more than capable of the day-to-day running of the shop. Same applied to Jayne's tearoom, where she'd convinced a retired baker friend by the name of Mikey to handle the majority of the baking in her absence.

Fortunately, Uncle Arthur had no interest in "helping" to run the tearoom.

While Ryan and Grant talked, and Donald regaled Andy and Jayne with details of his plans for the trip, I amused myself by studying the room. No one had been introduced to me as a friend of Pippa's. My sister didn't have friends. She had her "office" and she had "people." But not friends. I don't know exactly what Pippa does for a living, but I have my suspicions. She was, she told everyone who asked, an admin assistant to a midlevel manager in the Ministry for Transport, a "minor functionary in the British government."

She was a heck of a lot more than that, but there was no point in asking her for specifics. As I said, I had my suspicions. A couple of people here, I thought, might be her coworkers. Men in exceptionally good suits with school or regimental ties, women in high heels, well-fitted dresses, and discreet but obviously expensive jewelry. Maybe the older woman, the one with sharp eyes, gray hair in a perfect chignon, designer suit, diamond necklace and matching earrings. She saw me looking and gave me a tight nod.

Yup, that one for sure. I considered going up to some of the younger people and casually asking what they did in the "Ministry for Transport," but I knew they wouldn't slip up. That sort never did. They wouldn't work for the "Ministry for Transport" if they did.

The three other people seated at our table were a teenager, who said she was Millicent's daughter and spent most of her time typing on the phone on her lap. I didn't know who Millicent was or why she'd brought her daughter, and polite inquiries had been returned with nothing more than a tight smile and a comment on the bride's dress, so I went on to introduce myself and my friends to the others. A solicitor from my mother's chambers—her law office—and her husband, a ruddy-faced man with a strong East End accent and belly-splitting laugh, who owned a construction company.

"Sherlock 'olmes?" he said on meeting Donald. "You lot have come all the way from America and you want to see Sherlock 'olmes rubbish?"

I thought Donald might choke.

"I've got two tickets for tomorrow's match," the solicitor's husband said. "For me and my mate. I'll see if I can get one more. Nothin' like a good rugby match to show you Yanks how we live over here."

At the moment, Pippa was chatting with a gentleman I did recognize. Alistair Denhaugh, the eighth Earl of Ramshaw, my mother's second cousin once removed. His distinguished title in no way matched the state of his finances. "Virtually destitute" was my mother's usual comment on the aristocratic branch of her family. "Only managing to hold on to that pile he inherited because of his wife's private income." When you're the eighth earl of anything, you can dress pretty much as you like. His suit was at least forty years out of date, and I could smell the mothballs from here. He was accompanied by a well-preserved lady a few years younger than his mid-sixties, his wife, Genevieve. Her dress was not new, although well cared for, likely chosen for its longevity and bought at an end-of-season sale. Tiny stitches attempted to repair a rip on the hem of her sleeve, and the heel of one shoe was worn on the inside, giving her a slightly lopsided tilt when she walked. Her necklace was a long double strand of pearls, matching her earrings. Imitation, obviously, copied from what had had to be sold off long ago. The younger man with them showed every sign of having come to this dinner only for the free meal. And drinks. He'd had plenty of free drinks. He'd been introduced as their son, Lawrence.

I met Grant's parents, Roger and Linda Thompson, for the first time at the registry office. I had no reason to think they weren't exactly what they appeared to be: a pleasant middle-class couple from Iowa, thrilled to be in England for the first time, and totally overwhelmed by their son's new bride and her parents. Not that my parents are at all stuck-up. Quite the opposite. But my mum does speak in the plummy vowels of an elite private school nurtured in the highest law courts of the land; my father, Henry Doyle, is a retired DCS, Detective Chief Superintendent, with the Metropolitan Police. They own an entire row house in South Kensington, which must be worth in the fifteen to twenty million pound range these days. Roger, a real estate agent, would have checked into what similar houses were going for. He'd know the value of the property but not be aware that the house where my sister and I grew up had been my grandparents' house, and once they died, my own parents worked very hard indeed to keep it.

Pippa, on the other hand, can be the very definition of English aloofness, but I noticed her chatting comfortably with her new mother-in-law over pre-dinner cocktails. Yes, Grant was mellowing her. Several of the guests were new friends of Grant, people from the book business. A couple of them pressed their business cards on me the moment he told them what I did for a living. I accepted the cards with a smile and slipped them into my tiny evening bag without saying that the Sherlock Holmes Bookshop and Emporium is strictly retail. We don't sell used or collectable books, with the occasional exception of a second or third edition or low-quality first, which might attract Uncle Arthur's interest.

I stifled an enormous yawn. I didn't stifle it well enough, as Jayne interrupted Donald in mid-expostulation to lean across Andy and say, "You must be beat, Gemma."

"You could say that."

While my mother and I grabbed a cab and ran around London looking for clothes for me, Jayne napped. She looked refreshed, bright-eyed, rosy-cheeked. Her blonde hair was washed and styled to fall around her shoulders in sleek waves, her makeup lightly but perfectly applied.

My mother offered to lend me some of her cosmetics, but we do not have the same coloring, so I reluctantly invested in a completely new set. Which was not cheap (nothing is) at Harrod's. We also had to shop for a casual outfit in case my suitcase never managed to find me. Fortunately, I'd kept my good jewelry in my carry-on, so I was wearing the earrings I'd inherited from my grandmother.

Grant moved on to visit with other guests, and Ryan and my dad found a table in a corner where they leaned close together, clearly exchanging police war stories. Ryan is the lead detective with the West London PD.

I yawned again.

Jayne began gathering her things. "Why don't you and I slip away? We have a good excuse, jet lag. We've been on the move for days."

"But Grant said there'll be a late-night dessert buffet," Andy protested. "Besides, it's only afternoon at home, and I'm still on that time zone."

"I haven't finished laying out the plans for Sunday and Monday," Donald said. He'd managed to politely excuse himself from attending a rugby game on the grounds of wanting to spend the day with his friends. Once dinner was finished and guests began to mingle, the solicitor excused herself to speak to my mother, while her husband wandered away, still mumbling about that "'olmes rubbish." Millicent's daughter continued texting.

I was beginning to suspect the young woman wasn't the daughter of anyone. Anyone here, that is. Her head was down, her thumbs moving constantly; she sighed or chuckled occasionally. She was seated on the other side of the table from me, so I couldn't see the screen of her phone. Her head was down, but her eyes were not totally focused on the object in her hands. She had a way of watching everything without appearing to be doing so that reminded me very much of my own sister. She'd nibbled at her food, and although she accepted a glass of Champagne with which to toast the couple, noticeably she did little more than wet her lips, although she had a regretful look on her face when she pushed the glass aside. At a hotel like this one, that stuff must cost in the hundreds of pounds a bottle range.

When a waiter dropped a tray and the sound echoed around the room, she was on her feet faster than anyone, with the exception of the bride. Even faster than the father of the bride, a former police officer, and the plus-one of the bride's sister, a currently serving police officer. When she caught me looking at her, Millicent's unnamed daughter gave me a shrug and an embarrassed giggle as she sat down again. She patted the vague location of her heart. "Goodness, but that frightened me."

"Obviously," I'd said.

"I'm going to take my leave," I said now. "You don't need to come with me, Jayne. I can find my way to Stanhope Gardens all by myself."

My friend looked dubious. Andy looked hopeful.

I stood up.

"If you're sure?" Jayne said.

"I am. You enjoy the rest of the party."

"We should leave at nine thirty to get there in time for the tour," Donald said. "Do you think Anne will have breakfast for us, Gemma?"

I glanced toward my mother. She'd joined the eighth earl and his wife and son at their table. A waiter arrived with a fresh bottle of Dom Perignon, and she signaled to him to fill their glasses. "Mum won't be up and making breakfast before noon," I said. "We're on our own."

"The tour meets near the Criterion," Donald said, "the very place where Holmes and Watson first met. I'll check to see if they serve a hearty full English Sunday breakfast."

"They don't," Millicent's daughter said, without looking up. "I mean, I think someone told me they've closed. Don't remember who."

"You can take that to the bank," I said to Donald. "I'll tell Ryan I'm ducking out."

Ryan and Dad had taken off their jackets and loosened their ties. They each had a glass of whiskey in front of them, and their heads were close in conversation. I put my arms around Ryan's neck and kissed him on the top of the head. "I'm off. Unlike the rest of you lucky travelers, I didn't get an afternoon nap. I can't keep my eyes open any longer. No, don't get up. Please. You stay. I'll grab a cab."

"Are you sure?" he asked.

"Am I sure I can get a London cab outside a hotel in the Strand on a Saturday night and direct the cabbie to the street where I lived for the first eighteen years of my life? Yes, I'm sure. If you're at all interested, and even if you're not, Donald is organizing a Sherlock Holmes walking tour, preceded by breakfast at a venue yet to be decided, departing at nine from the front door. I will not be joining you. We have dinner at Grant and Pippa's at six tomorrow. Consider that to be a command performance."

I kissed him again and left. I didn't bother saying good night to the newlyweds. Grant was introducing his parents to his bookish friends, and Pippa approached Jayne and Andy, so pointedly ignoring Millicent's daughter, I knew she was fully aware of exactly what the young woman was up to.

It would appear that Pippa hadn't entirely taken the day off work after all. None of my business.

I slipped out of the banquet room and headed for the cloakroom. I hadn't had to buy a new coat; my mother had a closet full of them. Unlike an evening dress, it didn't matter too much that the sleeves were too short, the shoulders too tight, and the hem fell about three inches above the bottom of my skirt. I buttoned the coat up as I crossed the lobby. It was raining hard, but the doorman would have no trouble, not at this hotel in this area, hailing me a cab.

It was shortly after ten o'clock, and the lobby was still busy. The sounds of conversation, laughter, and the clink of cutlery and glassware drifted out of the restaurant and the bar. Guests, dripping rainwater or shaking off umbrellas, came into the hotel after enjoying a night out. Outside, the streets were slick, and a stream of headlights moved slowly through the traffic.

Out of the corner of my eye, I noticed a man stand up as I approached the doors. I paid him no mind, until he said in a deep, low voice. "Gemma."

I stopped dead. I knew that voice. I turned and faced him.

He gave me a stiff smile. "Gemma Doyle. I was hoping to run into you."

His name was Paul Erikson, and he had once been my husband.

Chapter Two

For the briefest of moments, I wondered if my recent thoughts about Paul and our wedding had summoned him like an unwanted apparition. "You knew I'd be here?" I asked when I'd recovered my wits.

"I knew Pippa was having her wedding dinner here, so I took a chance you'd come for it. I found myself a comfortable seat and waited." He slipped a tattered, yellowing paperback of Raymond Chandler's classic novel *Farewell, My Lovely* into his jacket pocket. Paul had always had a weakness for the golden age of American fictional P.I.s.

"And how, precisely, did you know that?" I asked.

"My father's still a senior clerk in the chambers adjoining Anne's. Mothers talk about their daughter's weddings, and word got around. You know how tight clerks are in those law offices. Dad always hoped you and I'd get back together, so he pays attention to what he hears about your family."

That was how Paul and I met originally, a chance encounter in the lift when I dropped into my mother's office.

"I hear you moved to America. That came as a surprise; I always thought of you as a London girl. One hundred percent."

His eyes dropped to my left hand. Checking for a wedding ring. I'd already noticed he was not wearing one. Either he hadn't got one on his second marriage or the couple were divorced already. Likely the latter. I hadn't seen Paul for seven years. Those years had not been good to him. Stubble was thick on his jaw but not in a nicely trimmed, fashionable way, more as though he hadn't bothered to shave recently. His reddish-brown hair, now heavily streaked with gray even though he was only in his midthirties, badly needed a cut. The whites of his eyes were tinged red, and the skin beneath those eyes was as dark as fresh bruises. His fingernails were bitten to the quick. He'd made an attempt to look respectable, not wanting to be asked to leave this hotel, but his leather jacket was badly worn, his shoes tattered, and his trousers too tight. He'd put on weight recently and hadn't had the money, or the inclination, to buy new clothes. Paul was thirty-five, the same age as Ryan. He looked ten years older. Paul was the same age as me. I hoped he looked ten years older than me too.

Rain dripped on the floor around his feet. Either he hadn't been waiting a long time or he'd been in and out of the hotel, trying to avoid the stern gaze of the doorman and the concierge. Maybe simply restless as he waited. I'd never known Paul to have an ounce of patience.

"I left my sister's wedding early because I'm dead beat," I said. "My flight here wasn't exactly a short or easy one. I'm sorry," not really, "but I don't have time to chat. Good night, Paul."

His hand shot out, and he grabbed my arm. I froze in place and simply stared at it until he released me. "Sorry, Gemma."

"Good night, Paul."

"Everything all right here, madam?" the doorman asked me with a side glance at Paul.

I smiled at him. "I'll be fine, thank you."

"Yup. Thanks, we're fine," Paul said to the doorman, who didn't look all that reassured. "What's the hurry? Bar's still open. Can I buy you a drink? They have a great gin menu here."

"You most definitely cannot."

A few of the elderly wedding guests were beginning to leave the party, along with younger people likely to have small children at home, meaning they couldn't sleep off a night of indulgence. They nodded briefly to me in recognition but were more intent on pulling on raincoats and preparing umbrellas to be unfurled. The doorman slipped out to hail cabs.

"Okay, I get it," Paul said. "Not a good idea tonight. I'd like to catch up while you're in London. Just as . . . old friends. We were close once, right?" He gave me that crooked grin I'd once found so charming. Now I found it full of nothing but loneliness and regret. "I have something that might be of interest to you."

"What sort of something?" I have to admit, my curiously was aroused. Paul and I hadn't parted on good terms. I'd been away from England for seven years. He could have found me easily and written if he wanted to. But I hadn't heard a word since the divorce was finalized and our mutual business affairs settled. Entirely to my satisfaction, I must add.

Paul talked quickly, the words spilling all over themselves in his haste to get them out. "I know you live in America now. You own a bookshop with Arthur Doyle. One bookshop. You had plans to own several shops, as I recall."

"Plans change. One is fine for me now. Something about my original start-up store failing because of, let me think, what was it now? Oh, yes, ineptitude and mismanagement on the part of one of the partners." And blind stupidity on the part of the other. The latter had been me. "I also own one quarter of a restaurant and tearoom."

"For what it's worth, Gemma, I am sorry about how things worked out between us. Truly sorry."

"So you keep saying, but it's worth absolutely nothing, Paul. Shall I assume Sophie is out of the picture?"

"She is. We . . . uh . . . decided it wasn't working out."

"What a surprise." Paul and I had jointly owned that mystery bookstore. Sophie, young and pretty, worked for us. People say I have good powers of observation, but those powers sadly deserted me on that one occasion. Perhaps I didn't see what I didn't want to see. When I finally had seen—because Sophie shoved it in my face—I dumped the cheating man. I had no trouble getting him to buy my share of the store, and I walked away with a nice profit. The shop had, to no one's surprise, least of all mine, immediately gone into a precipitous decline. Which might have had something to do with the fact that the part-owner who did almost all of the work had left.

"I know it's a lot to ask, Gemma, but—"

"Not interested." I took a step toward the door.

"I'd give anything in the world for that foolishness not to have happened." Paul lowered his voice. "For us to get back together. For you to love me again. The way I love you. The way I still love you. The way I've always loved you."

"Give it a rest, Paul."

"Okay, that's not going to happen. Forget I said it. I need your advice, Gemma. That's why I sought you out. I have this book. It might be the real deal. I'd like you to have a look at it."

"A book? You mean a collector's item? I sell new books, Paul, not anything rare or valuable."

"You never know what riches can be found between the pages of old books, do you, Gemma? Come to the shop tomorrow. Have a look. That's all I ask. Please, Gemma. You remember where the shop is?"

I'd heard he sold the store for a bargain basement price. Perhaps my information had been wrong. Perhaps he still worked there, although he didn't own it any longer. I hesitated.

"Please, Gemma? Come to the shop. I ask nothing else."

Despite my better instincts, my curiosity had been aroused. I knew I'd regret it, but I said, "Tomorrow then."

"Great. Sundays we open at noon."

"I'm not coming as a customer, Paul. But noon should do."

"Let me give you my number."

"Don't want it." I walked out of the hotel.

Chapter Three

I stared out of the window of the taxi. A Saturday night in London. Despite the rain, the weather was warm and people were out in masses. Bars and restaurants were packed, drinkers clustered outside pubs, crowds streaming out of theaters. The cab edged forward. There were times I missed my city. Very much. I was more than happy with my life in West London. In love with Ryan Ashburton. Best friends with Jayne Wilson. Part owner of two successful businesses as well as two wonderful dogs. Not to mention a grumpy shop cat named Moriarty. But London . . . London was London. No longer the most important and exciting city in the world, but it still had a strong pull on my heart.

Ryan and I, as well as Jayne and Andy and Donald, were staying at my parents' house in South Kensington. I asked the driver to let me off on Cromwell Road and walked the remaining distance to Stanhope Gardens. The streets were wet, but the rain had stopped as I crossed town, leaving the air as fresh as it ever gets in the crowded metropolis. Away from the bright lights of the theaters and shops, the crowds outside pubs and restaurants, the residential streets were quiet, wrapped in darkness. I glanced up regularly, looking for the ubiquitous CCTV cameras. London, the most surveilled city on earth, was full of them. Most of the cameras were mounted on poles, highly visible. Many, I knew, were not. I refrained from waving as I passed beneath them.

My parents' house is in the center of a typical Kensington housing row. Three stairs up to the front door, painted a solid black. White pillars guarding the entrance, iron railings, set not far back from the pavement. Three stories tall, long and thin, with a terrace and a small garden in the back barely large enough for the shed where my father does his woodworking. A narrow twisting staircase leads down to what would once have been the servants' and tradespeople's entrance. Despite it being late October, flowers and ivy spilled from planters fastened to the railings by the pavement and the upper windows.

I'd been given a key to the house, so I let myself in. All the lights were off, save one over the front door and the chandelier, turned low, in the entrance hall. Off-white paint on the walls, white tiles on the floor. A chaise longue in soft cream and a glass-topped table on which sat a gold reproduction-antique clock. A sweeping staircase with a wide oak banister led upstairs, and a portrait of my mother, young and beautiful, hung on the wall. It had been painted in honor of her being called to the bar.

Horace, my father's schnauzer—named after Horace Walpole, one of Dad's favorite authors—was delighted to see me. I gave him a hearty scratch behind the ears, and he wagged his stubby tail in pleasure. He was solid black, with dense wiry fur, a beard, and small erect ears. He stood about two feet tall, weighed sixty-five or seventy pounds, and seemed to love nothing more than having people to stay.

I told Horace my parents and the rest of their guests wouldn't be too much longer and staggered up to bed. Ryan and I had been given my childhood bedroom, the one at the front of the house, overlooking the street. The moment I moved out, the room was redecorated so that not a single memory of that childhood remained. I didn't mind in the least. I'd had a pleasant, often happy youth, but I had little sentimentality about it.

I crawled into bed and there I lay, wide awake, thinking about Paul Erikson and our brief disastrous marriage. We must have had some good times together, although I had trouble remembering them now. He'd never been handsome, but he had that lopsided grin and sparkle in the eyes that appealed to me. And the charm, mustn't forget the charm. While it lasted, at any rate. Owning a bookshop had been his idea, originally. I hadn't yet decided what I wanted to do with my life, although I did know I didn't want to continue in the government job my sister found for me one summer. But when he suggested buying the shop that had just come on the market, I realized that would be perfect for me. As Paul had said, I then had the idea of eventually owning a bookstore empire. That idea died along with the lopsided grin and the sparkle, as well as the charm.

Paul wanted me to look at a book. "The real deal," he called it. What did that mean? A rare book most likely. I couldn't think of any other reason he'd want me to see it. I have a small amount of knowledge about collectable books, but I'm no authority. Uncle Arthur is vastly more knowledgeable than I am, but Paul hadn't asked me to bring Arthur. I hoped this book wasn't a ploy to get me alone with him so he could pursue his renewed quest for my heart. As if.

Perhaps he wanted to sell the book to me. That might be it. He knew I owned a Sherlock Holmes themed store. If he'd done his due diligence, he would also know we were strictly retail. Then again, if he was capable of due diligence, he wouldn't be in the financial mess he clearly was in.

I considered not going, but he'd hunt me down if I didn't show up tomorrow. He knew where I was staying, and I didn't want him rapping on the front door. My parents would not, to put it mildly, be overjoyed at a reunion. They'd not come straight out and warned me against marrying Paul, and neither had they said, "I told you so" when the marriage abruptly ended. But I'd always known they thought it.

I briefly debated whether to bring Ryan with me tomorrow, but eventually I decided not to. Paul had confessed he still held feelings for me, and he'd be instantly antagonistic toward Ryan. He'd likely come over all friendly while at the same time making snide comments about American men, full of inuendo and insults, which Ryan wouldn't understand. But Ryan would sense the hostility, and although he wouldn't return it, he'd be on guard and might even verge on being overly protective of me. Foolish man. I didn't care to find myself standing between two men butting antlers over me as though I couldn't make up my mind between them without them engaging in some sort of ridiculous courtship display.

As for my personal safety, I had no concerns on that account. I was meeting Paul at his place of business in the middle of London in the middle of the day. If I felt uncomfortable, I'd walk out. Maybe spend a bit of time at the National Portrait Gallery, which isn't far from the bookshop. Which reminded me that on our last visit, my mother planned to take Jayne to afternoon tea at the gallery. Like so many of our plans, that one had been scuppered as we raced around London searching for a killer. Perhaps I could dare to incur Donald's wrath by suggesting Jayne, my mother, and I have tea tomorrow afternoon after I'd been to the store. Just us girls.

No, Andy would want to come, and Jayne would want Andy to come. Jayne and I had tea together every day back home in West London, in what we called our daily partners' meeting although it was more of a girlfriend catch-up session. I'd suggest Andy take Jayne to tea. A nice romantic gesture.

Eventually I heard a car pull up outside, followed by another. Doors slammed. Someone laughed. The front door opened, and chattering, laughing people spilled into the house. Horace barked greetings.

"Shush, everyone," Jayne said. "We don't want to wake Gemma."

A full umbrella stand crashed to the floor. "Shoot. Sorry," Donald said.

"Shush," Jayne repeated.

"Tea?" my mother said.

"Nightcap?" my father said.

"Good idea," Ryan said. "I'll run up and check on Gemma first. Be right back."

"I'd like tea," Jayne said. "Can I help you, Anne?"

"All in hand, love. You take a seat in the library. Henry, it's chilly enough tonight for a fire, I believe. I'll have a dram also, as long as you're offering."

They clattered down the hallway. Ryan ran up the stairs. He hesitated at the door before opening it a crack. Light flooded in. He tiptoed across the thick carpet, the old floorboards beneath creaking at every step. I imagined him creeping up on miscreants in a Victorian-era opium den in Limehouse and tried very hard not to laugh. He sat on the edge of the bed. The springs squeaked.

"Awake," I said. "Did you enjoy yourself?"

"It was a great party. I'm happy for Grant. Can I get you anything?"

I rolled over and smiled up at him. The top button of his shirt was undone, and his tie was draped around his neck. "Nope." I had a sudden idea and said, "Grant asked me to go book shopping with him tomorrow. Want to come?"

"To look at books? No, thanks." He chuckled. "That sounds like Grant. The day after his wedding and he's got a line on a book so he's off on the hunt. Despite Donald's encouragement, absolutely no one wants to go on the Sherlock Holmes walking tour first thing tomorrow, so we're staying in until noon at least." He kissed me lightly. "Go back to sleep, Gemma."

I purred happily. When the door had shut behind him, I sat up and reached for my phone. I hoped Grant would be willing to look at books the morning after his wedding.

* * *

"Pippa's in bed with a tray bearing a pot of tea and a plate of toast and marmalade, like a proper English married woman of the upper classes," Grant said. "Although unlike Mrs. Bennet or Lady Grantham, she has about a hundred alerts set on her phone and is surrounded by binders containing what's probably her briefing notes."

"Do you know what she does?" I asked.

"Not exactly, but when I first moved in with her, the security clearances I had to go through were extensive. Probably helped I'd lived in England for a while when I was at Oxford, and I managed to keep myself out of trouble while I was here. We book dealers do have a reputation of being rather dull. Speaking of which . . . ?"

We were standing in front of the great church of St. Martin-in-the-Fields. Across the street, Trafalgar Square was busy, although considerably less crowded than it would be in the summer. People took pictures of themselves with Nelson's Column in the background, fed the pigeons, listened to the buskers, or streamed up the stairs into the National Gallery. A few people carrying placards and signs mingled in the square, likely preparing for a demonstration. Someone was always protesting something in Trafalgar Square. It was a lovely fall morning, cool and crisp. The sun shone in a sky of a highly un-English blue, and most of the puddles deposited by last night's rain had disappeared.

After I'd called Grant last night and suggested, in as few words as possible, the outing, I'd fallen into a restless sleep. I'd been dimly aware of the scent of a wood fire being lit, then the sound of others climbing the stairs, calling good night, the closing of bedroom doors, the rush of water in the pipes. Jayne shouting at everyone not to wake Gemma. All followed by the gentle sounds of a well-made old house falling into night and the distant hum of traffic from Queen's Gate, in a city that never sleeps.

Grant was coming from Isle of Dogs to the east of the City, where he and Pippa lived, and I was in South Kensington to the west, so we arranged to meet near the bookshop.

Jayne had been up bright and early, as is her custom. She's a baker, after all. She got the tea and coffee on and breakfast started. Despite the late hour everyone had gone to bed, the visitors emerged shortly after, all except for Andy who, Jayne informed us, was still firmly on West London time. My parents, always the proper hosts, rose when they heard their guests moving about. Jayne served a hearty breakfast of fresh croissants, scrambled eggs, sausages, and a mountain of toast. Conversation around the table in the morning room was all about the wedding and what a marvelous time everyone had.

Conveniently, my father had arranged to take Ryan for lunch with some of his longtime friends from the Met for an afternoon of talking policing. Jayne made Andy's and her excuses to Donald, saying they hoped to go to the Tower of London. Mum announced that she needed to spend a few hours preparing for court tomorrow. Donald attempted to keep a stiff upper lip as he abandoned his plans for Baker Street and another Sherlock Holmes tour and declared he might as well come with Grant and me. I couldn't think of a way of dissuading him without making it look as though I didn't want his company, so I said nothing.

We were all due to meet back at the house at five thirty to go to Grant and Pippa's for dinner.

No one seemed to think it at all strange that Grant and I would spend our day looking at old books. Last night, I hadn't told him the reason for the outing, so I filled him in now. "This isn't exactly an impromptu venture," I said as Grant, Donald, and I crossed the street in a stream of pedestrians. Before stepping off the sidewalk, I reminded Donald to look to his left and pointed at the warning painted on the roadway to that effect.

"Didn't think it was," Grant replied as Donald peered intently to the left. "What's up?" He looked very handsome this morning, I thought. Nothing like true love to make anyone look good.

"A man with whom I used to be acquainted contacted me last night saying he had a book to show me. Something he called 'the real deal.'"

"Meaning?"

"Meaning, Grant, I have no idea. This person and I were once . . . close, but we had a falling out. We've not had contact for a number of years. Judging by appearances, he's fallen on hard times."

"Appearances? You mean he did more than phone you? You saw him? Yesterday?"

"Yes. He sought me out about this book."

"Does he think you're a dealer?"

"It looks as though we're close to the Sherlock Holmes Pub," Donald said, peering intently at the map on his phone, using his fingers to zoom in and out. "I do believe we are. If we finish our business early, perhaps we can pop in for a quick one."

"It's a tourist favorite," I said. "As well as a good pub. They've got a substantial number of items on display, not to mention a reproduction of the sitting room at 221B. I used to go there after work on occasion when I worked near here."

Donald's eyes lit up.

"If you'd like to have a look," I said, "Grant and I can meet you there when we've finished."

For the briefest of moments, indecision crossed his face before he said firmly, "That pleasure can wait. I am here to offer what assistance I might be able to."

"As for Grant's question, I don't know why Paul wants to show this book to me. That's why I asked you to come with me. If this book is rare or valuable, you might be able to tell me. If it's a lure to get my attention, then we'll leave."

"A Conan Doyle first edition, do you think?" Donald said. "Perhaps a signed copy. A prize worth locating."

"No point in speculating. This person gave me not the slightest clue."

"Does Ryan know about this male acquaintance with whom you had a falling out?" Grant asked.

"Nope. That's the bookstore up ahead. On the corner." The store was on Villiers Street, between the river and the Strand, behind Charing Cross station. A narrow, brick-paved street of tourist shops, pubs, fast food emporiums, and vape shops that hadn't existed when I'd been here last. At this time of day, the street was closed to cars, and pedestrians strolled up and down. I stood in the middle of the street and studied the shop front. The awing was in dire need of a good cleaning, the front windows were dull under a layer of grime, the paint on the sign above the door chipped and peeling. Trafalgar Fine Books, it read. When I'd owned it, the business had been named Trafalgar Square Mystery Bookshop.

Long ago, I'd had my heart set on making a success of this store. Today, in the bright sunshine, amid the bustle of activity, it simply looked sad.

"It looks like a genuine bookstore," Donald said with glee. "The sort of place Sir Arthur might have browsed after a meeting at the College of Psychic Studies, seeking out the latest volumes of fairy lore or communicating with the spirits. Do you suppose they have some early editions of his works I might be interested in purchasing?"

"It wasn't a secondhand or used shop in my day," I said, "but things appear to have changed."

Grant hung back as Donald charged toward his goal. "In your day," Grant said. "I know you owned a bookstore near Trafalgar Square. Is this the one?"

"It is. The current owner is my ex-husband. He bought me out when we separated. I got the better of the deal."

"I didn't know you'd been married."

"I try not to think about it."

"Does Ryan know?"

"Nope."

"Don't you think he should?"

"Like I said, I don't like thinking about it, and I particularly don't like talking about it. So, I never do. I now realize that might have been a slight oversight on my part."

Grant opened the door, and we followed Donald into the bookshop. The feeling of neglect I'd sensed from the outside only increased inside the shop. The shelves were dusty, a spider had taken up residence in a corner, the display tables were piled with books, books stacked upon more books, with no sense of creating an attractive display or any notable attempt at arranging by theme or genre. The grimy windows didn't let in a lot of light, and the scent of dust and aging paper permeated everything. When I'd managed the place, I decorated it with signed posters of book covers from authors who made an appearance at the shop. These same posters were where I'd left them, the print faded, their edges curling. A wide staircase with ornate wooden railings led up to the first floor. I'd used that area for hosting visiting authors. A space for setting out chairs and refreshments, a couch where the writer could relax and chat with readers, a lectern from which to speak to larger audiences, a small table on which to sign books. Now the upper floor appeared to be given over to used books, as indicated by a sign at the bottom of the staircase. Several shelves toward the front boasted "Sale!" A quick glance at the items on sale told me they were several years old, at least. Likely bought by bulk once their popularity had passed.

The keen-eyed Donald instantly dismissed the new hardcovers and mass-produced paperbacks on the ground floor and rushed up the stairs, searching for something by or about Conan Doyle.

Two women were in the shop. Employees, I guessed. I didn't recognize either of them, but that wasn't unexpected. I'd been away for seven years, and staff turnover in the retail trade is high.

One of them was watching Donald, obviously wondering if she should ask if he needed any help. She was tall and thin to the point of scrawny. Her hair was dyed a deep black, parted in the middle with locks falling in two rivers across most of her face, fringe cut in a sharp line at the level of her eyelids. She wore a loose-fitting black dress that showed the network of tattoos on her lower arms. A row of silver rings ran up one ear and her left nostril was pierced. Lace-up platform boots added to her height. Eventually, she followed Donald up the stairs.

The woman behind the counter was in her late forties, dressed in a black blouse under a slightly tattered red cardigan. Her brown hair was in a short, plain cut, and her makeup inexpensive and too heavily applied. She was peering intently at the computer screen in front of her. She lifted her head when we came in and gave us a disinterested glance. Clearly finding us not worth bothering with, she turned her attention back to the screen.

Only one customer was in the store. As we entered, he clattered down the stairs and put a used paperback on the counter. "I'll take this one please." I recognized it instantly. The first Mary Russell and Sherlock Holmes book by Laurie R. King, *The Beekeeper's Apprentice*, with the original cover. The cover was creased, but otherwise the book looked to be in good condition. He passed over a ten-pound note, and the clerk made change before giving the book a little shake and slipping it into a small plastic bag. The shake, I assumed, was to get rid of any residue of bugs that might be inside it. Or any bug that might have taken up residence between the pages. Grant had also noticed, and I felt, as much as saw, him shudder at the very idea.

"Hi," Grant said once the customer had left, gripping his change and the bag containing his book.

The clerk nodded without the slightest bit of interest. Her eyes remained glued to her computer screen.

I often find the excessive friendliness of American shop clerks overwhelming. I can read the signs that say 50 percent off everything, thank you very much. Not everyone in the shop needs to remind me. Likely because I'm English, I'd prefer to be greeted by silence rather than someone cheerily asking how my day has been going so far. Particularly when the expression says the speaker couldn't care less, but the words are a job requirement.

On the other hand, there is something about being almost totally ignored that can be off-putting.

Grant glanced at me.

"We're here to see Mr. Erikson," I said. "Is he available?"

"I don't quite see what I'm looking for here," from upstairs Donald spoke to the younger clerk. "I was hoping for some older books."

"Older? Those there are old."

"First editions and the like."

"Sorry. American, are you? That's nice. I'd like to go to America someday. My aunt's friend lives in Phoenix. She says it's too hot."

"It . . . uh . . . can be," Donald said.

"Mr. Erikson?" I prompted.

The older clerk tore her attention away from her computer. The screen faced away from us, so I couldn't see what she found so interesting without climbing over the counter. Which I had no inclination to do. "Tamara," she called, "is Paul in?"

Tamara's head popped over the upstairs railing. "What?"

"Paul. This . . . lady wants to see Paul. Is he here?"

I also own a bookshop. I like to think my staff know whether I'm on the premises or not. Which reminded me: I needed to check in with Ashleigh as to how things were going in my absence. My main worry about my head salesclerk wasn't that she'd try to steal from me or close early to go to the pub, but that she'd buy another store in my absence. Ashleigh had dreams of owning a bookshop empire. As she wasn't yet financially in a position to be able to pull that off, she was full of suggestions as to how I could have the aforementioned bookshop empire. Starting with opening a second branch of the Sherlock Holmes Bookshop and Emporium and exploring franchising opportunities. Only last week, I'd observed her leafing through a book on the legalities of franchises titled *Franchising for Dummies* while having her break at Mrs. Hudson's. I'd turned and fled, without stopping for my own tea and muffin, before she could call me over to tell me what she'd learned.

"Yeah." Tamara skipped down the stairs, and Donald followed. "I mean, I think so," she said. "The office door's closed, Faye. It was open when I left last night." Her face crunched in thought. "I think it was open anyway. I don't usually pay attention."

"Could you tell him I'm here, please," I said to Faye. "He's expecting me."

"He is?"

Obviously, visitors calling on the boss was not a common occurrence at this establishment. Then again, it was Sunday. Maybe Paul didn't conduct business on Sundays.

It wasn't easy, but I forced out a smile at the woman. "Yes, he is."

Her hand edged toward the phone on the counter. "Paul has a cot set up in the office. He sleeps here sometimes. When he's been working too late to go home. You know how it is?"

"No," I said. "I do not know." If Paul was reduced to spending the night on a cot in the back of a bookshop, he truly had fallen on hard times.

"He doesn't like to be disturbed. If he's sleeping, I mean."

"You're obviously busy here," Grant said. "Why don't we go and check for ourselves? As my friend said, we are expected."

Faye sighed in relief. The decision had been taken from her. "American, are you? If you'd like some books set in the U.K., we have lots."

"I would certainly hope so," I said in my most pompous English accent. "Considering we are in London." I headed for the door at the back, threw it open, and marched into the dark hallway.

Donald and Grant followed.

Muscle memory kicking in, I slapped the wall to my right and the light of a bare bulb hanging from the ceiling came on. The floor was sticky with grime; paint peeling from the walls; damp patches dotting the ceiling. I might have heard the sound of a small animal scurrying for shelter.

"Very Dickensian," Donald said with satisfaction. "Perhaps I should have inquired about books by Dickens rather than Conan Doyle."

"By used," Grant told Donald, "I think this store means Harold Robbins paperbacks. Maybe Jacqueline Susann?"

"Who?" Donald asked.

If the back rooms were still laid out as when I'd been in charge, the manager's office would be at the end of the hallway on the right. The manager had the privilege of a little window overlooking the alley. Staff loo to the immediate left. A small room with a fridge for the staff to keep their lunches in and a table for them to sit at. A door leading to the alley at the end of the corridor. The space above the offices was used for storage of books yet to be unpacked, those to be returned, and all sorts of random junk and things that might be needed someday.

I rapped on the rear right door. "Paul. It's Gemma. I'm here for our meeting, as arranged."

No answer. Even by English standards, this was an old building. The store in it might well be about to crumble into dust, but the walls were thick. No sound came from outside.

I knocked again. "Paul, I'm here now, and I will not be coming back."

I stepped back and threw up my hands. "What a total and complete waste of time."

"Not at all," Donald said. "This is as fascinating as a museum. Look at that brickwork and the intricacy of the plasterwork on the ceiling. When was that laid do you think, Gemma?"

I was about to turn to leave, but I hesitated. I was here now, and I had been invited.

I opened the door and stepped into what had once been my own office.

The buildings surrounding the alley blocked the thin autumn sun, but even if they didn't, it wouldn't matter much. The window in here was no cleaner than the ones overlooking the street. The room smelled of decaying paper, musty carpet, mold in the walls. I hadn't wanted to spend money on nonessential items, so the desk I bought for the store was a DIY one and the bookshelves also. The filing cabinet was a WWII-era junk sale reject. I'd brought a few pictures from home to hang on the walls but had taken them with me the day I left. Nothing had replaced them.

An army cot was set up against the far wall. Sheets in place, a single thin pillow at its head, a red and blue striped blanket neatly folded at the foot. A backpack lay on the cot. A bottle of whiskey was open on the desk beside the computer, an empty glass next to it. A mobile phone rested on the desk.

Paul Erikson was in the office chair, dressed as I'd seen him last night, the jacket tossed over the back of his chair. He did not greet us.

Donald sucked in a breath. Grant's hand shot out and grabbed my arm. "Gemma."

"I see," I said.

Paul was slumped in the seat, his head back, his throat exposed, his eyes closed. His arms dangled at his sides. His throat was red and raw. He did not move.

Chapter Four

I'd loved this man once. I had happily and willingly placed my life in his hands. I tried to remember that. Soon, I'd get angry again, but right now all I felt was sadness. Sadness at what had never been.

I shook Grant's hand off and walked toward Paul. I stretched out my hand and touched the side of his neck. I felt no pulse and the skin was already beginning to cool. "Dead," I said. "For some time."

"Shall I call 911, Gemma?" Donald asked.

"Yes. But it's 999."

"My e-sim doesn't cover phone calls," he said. "How much will it cost?"

"I'll do it," Grant said. "Gemma, are you okay?"

"I will be. Make the call." I looked quickly around the room. No one was hiding beneath the desk, the cot was low to the floor, and there was no place else to conceal anything larger than a rat. A pile of boxes stamped with the names of publishers was stacked against the wall. The drawers of the filing cabinet were closed. The whiskey bottle was about three-quarters empty; the bottom of the glass contained a tiny amount of liquid residue. It appeared as though Paul had been strangled, likely by a piece of rope or a length of cloth. At a quick glance, I could see nothing like that out in the open.

I gave Paul one last look, shook sentiment away, and said, "You two stay here. I'll be right back." I ran into the hallway. In one of my first acts when we bought the store, I'd had a modern lock installed on the door leading to the alley. One glance told me it was unlocked, but just to be sure the lock hadn't jammed in the years since, I pulled the edges of my sleeve over the fingers of my right hand and twisted the knob. It moved, and I edged the door open. I peered into the alley. Even at midday the narrow alley was dark and gloomy, the buildings on either side looming over it, blocking the sun. A seagull was inspecting the trash put out by the business next door. It stared at me through one uncaring eye and then returned to its business. Vehicle traffic moved steadily down the Strand, and pedestrians chattered on Villiers Street, but no one was in the alley. I studied the ground. It had rained heavily yesterday, but the puddles were slowly drying. Some water remained in depressions in the paving stones and in the deeper shadows under the buildings. Several pairs of muddy footprints marked the alley, going in both directions, but they didn't appear to have approached this door. Except for one set of small paw prints. A dog had tried to investigate, but its owner had likely called it to come and walked away. I pulled out my phone and took a photograph of the prints. The police might be able to locate the owner. Did dogs have individual paw prints? I'd never considered that before. I made a mental note to look it up as I checked the alley for CCTV cameras. None that I could see. Didn't mean they weren't there, though. I went back inside. I shut the door behind me, keeping my fingers covered, but I didn't set the lock.

Grant came out of the office. "Anything outside?"

"No one lurking about, no. Nothing else I could see."

"Police are on their way. The dispatcher said a protest is forming around Trafalgar Square so they might have trouble getting through quickly."

"I trust you told them there's no rush."

"I did, and she asked me if I was a doctor. I refrained from commenting on that."

I found the two clerks in the shop. Faye, the older woman, was bent over a map of London, trying to explain to a Japanese couple that you couldn't get there from here. Tamara was chatting to a newly arrived customer.

"Everything okay?" Tamara asked me. "Did you find Paul?"

"No, and yes. I'm sorry, but the store is closing early. Everyone but the employees need to leave. Now."

The Japanese couple looked at me and asked who I was and what was going on. At least I think that's what they said. My Japanese is rusty. I grabbed the map, folded it into a tumbled mess, and shoved it at them. I gestured toward the door. They bowed, I nodded my head in return, and they slipped away.

Which is more than the other customer did. "Hoy! I dinna 'ave what I come for," he said in a Scottish accent I found about as easy to understand as the Japanese.

"Sorry," I said. "Police orders."

He lifted his hands and backed up. "Dinna want no trouble with the coppers."

I followed him to the door and twisted the lock once he'd left. I turned to see Tamara and Faye staring at me wide-eyed and open-mouthed.

"Who do you think you are?" Faye demanded.

I sidestepped the question. "You're closed for the rest of the day. Maybe permanently. No one's to come inside except the police. They're on their way."

"Police? What's going on?"

"If we're closed, I've got places to be and things to do," Tamara said. "Tell Paul to call me if he ever opens again."

"I suspect the police will want to talk to you," I said.

She stared at me. "And why might they want to do that?"

"Paul's . . . dead," I said.

"You can't be serious," Faye said. "What's going on? Who are you people?"

Grant and Donald stood behind me.

"Are you a copper?" Tamara studied my face carefully. Her eyes were so dark they were almost black, rimmed in thick black liner, the lashes sticky with gobs of mascara. But intelligence flared in their depths along with curiosity. I found it interesting that she didn't immediately look to Grant, or even Donald, seeking confirmation. She recognized that I, a woman, was the person making the decisions here.

"No, we're not with the police. Just concerned citizens doing our civic duty."

"Far be it from me to stop you, then."

Faye let out a long moan and dropped into the chair behind the counter. "Dead. Paul. That's not possible."

"Neither of your saw him this morning?" I asked.

Faye just groaned. Tamara said, "I was first in. Like I said, office door was closed, and I didn't check. To be honest, Paul doesn't do a heck of a lot of work around here, so I don't much care if he's in or out."

"How did you get in?"

"Through the door. I didn't climb in the window, you know."

"Which door, and did you use a key or was it unlocked?"

"The street door. I have a key. So does Faye."

"Was the door locked?"

"Yes, it was locked. It's mighty sticky and a right struggle to open."

"It always was," I said.

She grinned suddenly and stabbed a finger in my direction. "Hey. You're Gemma!"

"Yes, I am. The place has . . . declined somewhat since I ran it."

"Yeah. Paul always says things were better when Gemma was here. Can't say I'm surprised you left."

"Grant, watch the door," I said. "Let the police in when they arrive. I'm going to have a quick look around."

"My bag's in the back," Tamara said. "Might as well get some work done while we're waiting. Can I get it?"

"The police will want you to leave everything as it is."

She looked for a moment as though she might argue. If she decided to get her bag despite my warning, even if she decided to take her leave, I would do nothing to stop her. Not that I could do anything in any event. I wasn't going to wrestle her to the ground and order Donald to tie her up.

She shrugged. "I suppose. We've all seen that stuff on telly, right?"

Sounds were drifting down the street now as the protesting crowd increased in Trafalgar Square. I didn't detect the scream of approaching sirens. Grant hadn't asked for an ambulance, but one would have been sent anyway in case we'd made a mistake about the condition of the victim.

"What can I do, Gemma?" Donald was almost bouncing on his toes in excitement.

"Stay here. Ask these women if they noticed anything unusual about Paul's behavior lately."

Donald saluted smartly.

The back door was unlocked and the body growing cold, so I had no worries the killer was hiding in a closet or crouching behind a box of books, ready to leap out at the unwary. As soon as the police arrived, I'd be escorted out of the building. I might even be taken to the station for questioning. I didn't have a great deal of time to poke around.

On first glance, this didn't look like a robbery gone wrong. Nothing appeared to have been disturbed in the office, as there would be if there'd been a fight between Paul and a burglar. He'd been sitting in his chair, behind his desk, not asleep on the cot where he might have been taken by surprise. On the other hand, if he'd been drinking at his desk, he might have passed out before he could collapse onto the cot. When we'd been together Paul hadn't been much of a drinker, and on the rare occasions he did overly indulge, it didn't take much to put him to sleep. That, of course, might have changed in the years since.

The door to the alley was unlocked, but that might not mean anything, not if Paul wasn't in the habit of locking it behind him when he came in or if he'd forgotten this time because he had other things on his mind. Such as the encounter with me.

I wasn't entirely sure why I was bothering to poke around. The police would sort out what had happened to Paul. Or not. Anything that happened in Paul's life over the previous seven years had absolutely nothing to do with me.

Except we'd spoken last night. He'd deliberately sought me out, waited outside my sister's wedding for me. He wanted to talk to me about some book. We'd arranged for me to come here this afternoon.

Did this book, whatever it might be, have anything to do with Paul's death?

I slipped into the office. Maybe I was interested because I'm the curious sort, but I couldn't forget that Paul had once meant a great deal to me. And me to him. He'd betrayed me, and that was all on him. But if I could help him now, I would.

The police were delayed, but they wouldn't be long. Grant had told the 999 operator the victim appeared to have been murdered.

I didn't have time to do a thorough search, but I had a quick look for something that might be a rare book or perhaps an old manuscript. I found nothing. The zipper was open on the backpack. Keeping my fingers covered by the edges of my sleeves, I peered inside the pack. A couple of rumpled T-shirts, a clean tie, a pair of briefs, an electric razor, an open bag containing men's toiletries. No book, no papers. I didn't see the Raymond Chandler he'd been reading at the hotel. I peeked into the topmost box and opened the drawers of the desk and filing cabinet. I dropped to my knees and peered under the cot, with the help of the flashlight on my phone. I saw nothing but dust bunnies and spiderwebs.

I lifted Paul's phone off the desk. To my considerable shock, the picture that appeared when I tapped it was of none other than me. My wedding photograph. How young I looked. How naive and, dare I say, innocent. How ridiculous in that awful dress. I can't imagine what I must have been thinking to have done my hair that way. I shoved the thoughts aside, and I took a deep breath, gathering my courage. I held the screen in front of Paul's face. My image disappeared and the phone opened. All I had time for was a quick glance at his messages. A friend suggesting a meet at the pub. His mum telling him she was home from the doctor's office and it had gone well. A question from Faye asking about a customer's request. I didn't have time to keep looking, and I couldn't take the phone with me. I put it back precisely where I found it and went into the staff room.

I might have stepped back seven years. This room was exactly as I remembered. It was even clean, although the paintwork needed to be refreshed. Two chairs were pulled up to a round table. An electric kettle was on the counter, next to a scattering of mugs, a microwave oven, a sink, and a small fridge. The interior of the fridge was spotless, with a few bottles of water, along with milk and a couple of apples. The trash can contained nothing more than a handful of scrunched up paper towels.

I opened the drawer next to the sink. Two bags were tucked inside. One was a bulging backpack, the other a faux-leather purse. I'm not averse to interfering in people's privacy in situations such as this, so I had no compulsion in opening the women's bags. The purse, presumably Faye's, held the usual collection of things women can't do without. The backpack, to my surprise, was stuffed full of books, none of which were rare or valuable. They were all comparatively new, meaning published in this or late in the previous century. A couple were stamped as property of the library of UCL, for University

College London. One of the books I stock in my own store: *Villains, Victims, and Violets,* edited by Resa Haile and Tamara R. Bower. An iPad was tucked behind the books. I didn't bother to take it out. It would almost certainly be password protected, and I didn't have the time to hack into it.

I finally heard the *whoop whoop* of a siren, struggling to make its way through the traffic. I put everything back into the bags and put the bags where I found them and went out front to present myself to the officers of the Metropolitan Police like the good and loyal subject of the king I am.

Chapter Five

The ambulance arrived first. I gave Donald a slight nod, asking him to show the paramedics to Paul.

In the front of the shop, Faye wept quietly. Tamara simply watched me, showing little emotion. "Have you worked here long?" I asked her.

"Little over a year. It's a part-time gig. I'm still at uni."

She was close to thirty. Old for a university student, I thought, but she might have tried other endeavors first or had a gap year that stretched a good deal longer than a year. She was also a bit old for the goth makeup and clothes, but I read nothing into that. No accounting for taste.

"What are you studying?" Grant asked her.

"English lit."

"This is a good place for you to work then," he said.

"Not that I'd call anything they sell here literature," she replied.

We stopped talking at the sound of more sirens pulling up. Two officers came into the shop dressed in the Metropolitan Police uniform of black trousers, yellow jacket worn over white shirt and stab vest, black-and-white checked band on their hats. I stepped silently into the shadows by the bookshelves.

"The medics are in the back with the deceased." Grant pointed to the open door leading to the private space.

The female officer went where he indicated, while her partner watched us. "You lot have to stay here. The detectives are on their way, and they'll want to talk to you."

"I want to go home," Faye said. "This is all just too much. My nerves aren't good."

Tamara rolled her eyes in my direction. Dismissed, Donald edged back into the main room.

"You can go once the detective's spoken to you," the officer said.

Outside, other officers were cordoning off the street to allow them vehicle access while the bored and the curious gathered to see what was going on.

The medics came into the room, carrying their equipment. "Nothing for us to do here," one of them said.

"Thanks," the cop said.

His partner followed them outside, and she began stringing blue crime scene tape around the store front.

Faye moaned again.

"If we have to wait," Tamara said, "can I get my bag? I have some reading I need to do. It's in the back room. I promise I won't touch anything else."

"No," the cop said.

We didn't have to wait long for the detectives to arrive. She was short and round, olive-skinned and dark-eyed, with chin-length thick black hair. Her partner was ginger-haired, chubby-cheeked, a thousand freckles dotted across his face. His days as a schoolboy must have been a nightmare.

"What have you got?" he asked the uniform as his partner glanced around the store and at us. Donald, Grant, Faye, Tamara. Me.

I saw something cross the detective's face as she struggled to place me. Rather than wait it out, I stepped forward.

"DS Patel, we have met before. I'm Gemma Doyle. Henry Doyle's daughter."

She flipped rapidly through her memory banks and then she had it. "It's DI Patel now, Ms. Doyle." She did not smile at me.

"Congratulations."

"Good afternoon," Donald said. "Donald Morris. We also met on that other occasion. I also extend my congratulations on your promotion. Well deserved, I must say."

She didn't smile at Donald either. She looked at Grant next and shook her head. "I was hoping you'd all gone back to America."

"We did," Donald said. "We have returned. I for one can't stay away for long from your beautiful city."

"What's this?" Faye said. "An old school reunion? Can we get on with it, please?"

"I want to have a look at the scene," DI Patel said. "And then I'll talk to you all in turn. You stay with these ladies and gentlemen," she said to the uniformed officer. "Make sure they don't talk amongst themselves."

"Bit late for that," Tamara said. "We've been chatting happily away all morning."

Patel gave her a look indicating she was not amused. Tamara merely grinned in return. Faye had dragged a tattered tissue out of her skirt pocket and blew her nose lustily. Her eyes were red and wet, her makeup streaked with tears. Of the two store employees, only Faye seemed at all bothered by the death of her boss. It was too early to read much into the women's reactions. Some people are more emotional and demonstrative than others. For some, grief comes later. If Paul was nothing but a largely absent boss, Tamara genuinely might not care what had happened to him.

"You'd better call for help," Patel said to her partner. "We need more people outside. If those protesters head this way, they might take the crime scene tape as an invitation to get in our faces."

He nodded and spoke into his radio.

"Is there a back entrance to this place?" she asked.

"Yes," Tamara said.

"Door's unlocked," Donald said helpfully.

"How do you know that? Aren't you only a customer here, sir?"

"I suppose you could say I'm a customer of sorts. I tagged along after Gemma and Grant. Always love visiting bookstores. As for the door, Gemma checked."

"What else did Gemma do? Never mind that for now. Constable, tell forensics to come in via the alley. We'll try not to create any more of a circus out of this than we have to. Who works here?"

"We do." Tamara pointed to Faye and herself.

"And you three are simply passers-by?" Patel asked me.

"In a way," I said.

"They went into the back. To the office. It was them who called the police," Tamara said. "She, Gemma, said she was here to meet with Paul. She said he was expecting her."

"Constable," Patel said. "Arrange to have these three taken to the station. I'll talk to them later."

* * *

Grant, Donald, and I were stuffed into police cars and driven to the nearest police station, where we were separated. I'd been allowed to keep my phone, so once I was settled in an interview room and told to wait, I texted my parents first and then Ryan and Jayne to say we'd been delayed.

Jayne: *Okay. Have fun!*
Ryan: *Delayed? What does that mean?*

Never had four simple words carried so much suspicion. I didn't know how to reply so I didn't.

We wouldn't be able to keep what had happened from the others for long. DI Patel would no doubt want to haul us back in for further questioning if this case dragged on. But I wasn't going to try to explain the afternoon's unexpected events over text.

I cooled my heels in a not-too-horrible interview room waiting for DI Patel. I'd asked for a cup of tea, and it had been delivered by an untalkative, unsmiling female officer. The tea was simply dreadful, but I drank it anyway, not sure when I'd get the chance to have something better. Grant had been visibly annoyed at being delayed, muttering about not a good look to be late for his first dinner with his new in-laws. Donald had been delighted at, once again, being involved in a Metropolitan Police case.

"You will offer them our, I mean your, full assistance in this matter, of course, Gemma," he said to me as we were bundled out the back door to our waiting escorts, passing people wearing white boiler suits and booties coming in.

"I have the feeling that wouldn't be welcomed," I said.

"Excellent," he said. "You are 'not retained by the police to supply their deficiencies.'"

Donald could always be counted on to have a Holmes quote at the ready for any occasion. In this case, the quote was from "The Adventure of the Blue Carbuncle."

I was stuffed into the back of a police car and driven out of the alley. The sounds of the protest still came from Trafalgar Square, but the intensity seemed to be dying down. The people heading toward the square didn't seem to be the sort who would turn on a police car in a sudden frenzied mob. I saw family groups, babies in slings and toddlers in push chairs, along with nicely dressed middle-aged and older people, women mostly.

"What's the protest about?" I asked the driver.

"Who knows what they're ever about? Some environment thing, I think."

The car had to negotiate the maze of narrow streets and pedestrian-only walkways to reach the Strand.

I got a quick glimpse of someone I vaguely recognized, standing in the crowd at the corner of the Strand and Adam Street, waiting for a light to change. My distant cousin, Lawrence Denhaugh, who'd been at Pippa's wedding with his father, the eighth Earl of Ramshaw. I was about to lift my hand to wave, and then I remembered I was in the back of a police car. If he saw me, he might take it the wrong way. I slunk further down in the seat instead.

I decided to be nothing but completely frank and honest with DI Patel. I had nothing to hide. Paul had died some time before we found him, so we couldn't (reasonably) be considered suspects.

"You maintain you haven't seen Mr. Erikson for seven years," the detective asked me when she finally joined me in the interview room.

"I do."

"And you had no other contact over that time?"

"Our lawyers dealt with the divorce and the dissolution of the business partnership. We had no contact."

"Would it surprise you to know he had a picture of you on the start-up screen of his phone? At a guess I'd say the picture is about seven years old."

I didn't want to confess I'd checked his phone myself, so I put on my shocked face and said, "I would be surprised, yes." That was no lie. I had been surprised. Extremely. "We separated because he was having an affair with another woman. He told me last night that hadn't worked out. Perhaps he had his regrets." I was being open and honest with the inspector, but I saw no need to tell her the finer details of what Paul said to me last night.

"You maintain you don't know what this book is he wanted you to see?"

"I do not. Nor do I know why he wanted me specifically to see it. I don't deal in rare books, and far more people are far more capable of evaluating them than I."

"The shop clerks say they don't know anything about any rare book. But they also say Paul didn't involve them in any business decisions. They were strictly front-of-store sales staff. I have officers searching the premises for something potentially valuable, but considering they don't know what they're looking for . . ."

"Did Faye or Tamara say if something had been bothering Paul lately? Had he had any unusual visitors or unexpected absences from the shop?

"'Mercurial' was the word Tamara O'Riordan used to describe him. I gather she didn't like him much, but I also gather she didn't mind. It was just a student job."

"And Faye?"

"Faye is more—" Patel blinked and pulled back. "I ask the questions here."

"Simply attempting to draw a picture. Are there CCTV cameras watching the back entrance to the shop? I didn't see any, but they might be hidden."

"That's confidential."

"Not a problem. Everyone knows how heavily surveilled London is; anyone up to no good would know to hide their face and probably to smudge their footprints too. I trust your people noticed the dog prints still visible by the back door. I hope no one trod on them. If the dog sniffed at the door because it sensed something happening inside, you want to locate the owner, find out what time they passed. And then—"

DI Patel pushed her chair back and stood up. "Thank you for your time, Ms. Doyle. If you think of anything else that might be relevant, do give me a call. It might be necessary to speak to you and your friends again as the investigation progresses."

I also stood up. I'd been getting bored with this conversation. The best way of getting out of a police interview, I'd discovered some time ago, was to start asking them questions they didn't want to answer.

"Please give your father my regards."

"I'll do that."

I found Grant waiting for me on a cheap plastic chair in the lobby. Donald was speaking to the duty sergeant at the front desk. "I've always thought you English got a step ahead of us in the policing business. Did you know the word 'cop' is derived from constable-on-patrol? 'Bobbie' is a reference to—"

"Yeah, I know, thanks," the sergeant said.

"I'll have to check my reference books to see if Holmes himself had reason to visit this particular station. Do you happen to know—?"

The sergeant threw me a pleading look. "You people can go now. Please."

"Thank you," I said cheerily. "Come along, Donald."

On the way out, we passed a group of protesters being hurried up the steps. "Passive resistance!" a gray-haired woman dressed in a swirling multicolored dress shouted, to the cheers of onlookers.

"It's almost half-five," I said when at last we were standing on the sidewalk. "Total waste of a day. We might as well go straight to your place rather than back to Stanhope Gardens, Grant."

Grant waved down a black cab and we piled in.

"Have you worked it out yet, Gemma?" Donald asked as the busy streets of central London slipped past.

"Worked what out?"

"What happened to Paul, of course. Did the detective inspector inadvertently reveal something allowing you to crack the case wide open?"

Donald's opinion of my detective prowess is sometimes highly exaggerated. In this case, I didn't have a clue. Paul appeared to be on the down-and-out. Sometimes those circumstances led to making unsavory financial arrangements with unsavory people, particularly for a man like Paul who didn't like to put in the hard work necessary to return himself to a sound footing.

Grant pointed at the cabbie, skillfully maneuvering the taxi through the traffic. "Now's not the best time."

Donald nodded sagely and tightened his lips.

Pippa had been living in a small row house in Fulham when she met Grant. As a couple, they needed a home big enough for him to have an office where he could conduct his book-dealing trade, as well as a place to store the items as they as they came and departed. They spent a long time searching and eventually bought a flat in one of one of the best and newest buildings in the East End. On a Sunday, this part of town was relatively free of car traffic, although plenty of people were out enjoying the day, walking dogs, taking children to the park, biking or running. Kayaks and sculls, tour boats, and water taxis slipped soundlessly past on the smooth dark waters of the river.

It was late October. Londoners knew to enjoy good weather when they had it. They might not see the sun again until spring.

The Isle of Dogs is a peninsula, surrounded on three sides by the curves of the river Thames, intersected by watery passageways. When London had been the most important city in the world and its ports the busiest, this had been a network of docks, warehouses, working-class housing, and grimy pubs. When the big ships no longer came here, the area fell into desolation and decay. It was now being reclaimed as a vibrant center of business offices, good hotels, nice restaurants, and luxury flats.

"That's it," Grant pointed out the window as we approached Canary Wharf. "Our place."

"Goodness," I said.

"It's somewhat . . . unusual," Donald said.

A tall circular building on the waterfront, narrowing as it stretched upward into the sky, balconies fitted together like Lego.

The cab pulled up to the main entrance. Donald stumbled as he got out, his mouth agape, staring up at the structure and around at the landscaped gardens, the sculptures, the riverside boardwalk. I might have stared myself. The building was so new, I'd never seen it.

Grant used his fob to open the interior door of the building. "Good afternoon, Mr. Thompson," the uniformed man behind the concierge desk said. "Your guests have begun to arrive."

"Thank you, Reg." Grant couldn't help glancing at me with a decided twinkle in his eyes.

The lobby was beautifully decorated with low, white chairs and sharp-edged wooden tables. The floor of sleek, dark wood was covered with a white and gray carpet. Colorful modern art hung on cream walls. Grant pressed a button for the lift; the doors opened soundlessly and immediately.

I didn't bother to ask how much a flat here cost or how Grant and Pippa could afford it.

"Pippa," Grant said, "wanted a place near the river if we're going to live this far from the center of the city."

"Good idea," Donald said. "The view must be spectacular."

Pippa, I suspected, didn't care about the view. She needed to get to the "office" as fast as possible in case of an emergency, and traveling by water was always faster than through clogged city streets.

The lift stopped at one of the lower floors and the door swooshed soundlessly open. The door at the end of the hallway was unlocked, and Grant held it open for us.

Chapter Six

Guests were gathered in the living room. The conversation stopped midsentence, and they all turned to look at us. Drinks had been served, and a platter of flatbread and cheeses and bowls full of olives and nuts were on the big round glass table in the center of the room. As well as my friends and family, Grant's parents were here.

Pippa was returning to the main room with a bottle of wine in hand. Grant gave her a kiss, and I offered a guilty grin. "Sorry we're late. My fault entirely."

"I have absolutely no doubt about that," my sister said. "I seriously do not want to know why you were, as Grant put it, assisting the police with their inquiries, but I suppose I must."

"You didn't actually phrase it like that, did you?" I said to Grant.

"I might have been trying for levity," he said.

"If you were," Pippa said, "you failed miserably." She lifted the bottle. "Glasses are in the kitchen. Beer in the fridge along with tonic and a bottle of very good gin, courtesy of Dad, on the counter. Help yourselves."

"Gemma, Donald, get you something?" Grant asked.

"A G and T would be delightful," Donald said. We'd only been in England a day and a half, but Donald's Massachusetts accent was beginning to take on a distinctive London tone.

"Gemma?" Grant asked as Ryan came up to me.

"White wine, thanks."

"Everything okay, Gemma?" Ryan asked.

"I'm okay. We're okay."

"Pippa told Henry you were witnesses to a crime."

"Unfortunately, yes. Give me a minute, please, and then I'll join you. I need to wash my hands."

"Second door on the right," Ryan said.

I went into the loo and shut the door. I ran water into the huge bowl of a sink for a long time and used a lot of soap, scrubbing my hands thoroughly beneath the wide-mouthed tap. Like Donald and Grant, I'd been fingerprinted at the station. "For elimination purposes," DI Patel had said. I hadn't minded. I knew, unfortunately, how these things worked. As I washed my hands, I studied myself in the mirror. My usual out-of-control curls were even more out of control than usual. My eyes were tinged red and the delicate skin under my brown eyes was smudged. I'd barely slept in three days, and it showed. I thought over what we'd walked into at the bookstore. Paul. Dead.

Having had some time to think it all over, I still maintained it had not been a burglary gone wrong. No one in their right mind would have thought that store would have anything worth stealing. At first, I'd thought Paul must have known the killer well enough to allow that person to walk up behind him when he was seated in his chair. But on further thought, if he'd been sound asleep—or passed out—the killer might have been able to nip silently around him and slip something over his head and around his throat. The door to the alley was unlocked. Likely no way of telling if it had been unlocked when the killer entered the premises or if they left it that way on their departure.

A light rap on the door, and Pippa said, "Gemma? Are you okay? Mum sent me to check on you."

I opened the door and gave my sister a weak smile. "I'm fine. Just trying to process what happened."

"You look dreadful."

"Thank you so much for pointing that out. It has been a rather hectic few days. I've been meaning to mention something to you. That young woman who sat at our table last night, calling herself Millicent's daughter. She did a good job of pretending to be a bored teenager, but it was too good, if you know what I mean."

Pippa's eyes narrowed and she cocked her head at me. "Whatever *do* you mean?"

"She was far too blasé. Said she was Millicent's daughter, but I didn't meet anyone named Millicent. In particular, she didn't drink her Dom Perignon, although she clearly wanted to, and she was the first one to her feet when that waiter dropped a tray. First after you, that is. You conducted a training exercise? At your own wedding?"

"Where better? I'll pass on your observations to her and tell her to be less obvious next time."

"Glad to be of help. One more thing, that Champagne you served last night must have cost a bundle and there was a lot of it. I doubt Grant could afford it. Can you?"

"Someone I work with gave it to us as a wedding present."

"Someone you work with. Did that person come to the wedding?"

"I admitted to the training exercise. Anything else is none of your business, Gemma."

"I guess not."

"Before we join the others, I got a text from Uncle Arthur earlier, telling me to tell you not to worry. Violet will be fine. Who's Violet again?"

"Our dog. One of our dogs. What does that mean? What happened to her?" I started to worry.

"He didn't say."

"Why didn't he call me?"

"He didn't say. It was a PS to a congratulations on our marriage."

"I'll have to call him. Now I'm worried."

Pippa and Grant's flat was absolutely spectacular. The outer wall was all glass, forming a sweeping curve with four distinct terraces. White wicker furniture with colorful outdoor cushions and iron tables were arranged on the terraces. The view looked straight down to the water and west across the twisting river and the city, flooding the rooms with light even as the sun sank in the distance. Inside, the floors were all dark hardwood, dotted with white and blue rugs. The ultramodern kitchen was open plan, no walls separating it from the dining area and sitting room. The comfortable furniture was in shades of white and navy blue. The walls were painted a gentle cream, the large-scale modern art mostly blue. I thought about my own saltbox house in West London. Buit in 1756, it was positively ancient by North American standards. I decided I liked it better than this place. Our house had been modernized with the times, but much of the old charm still remained.

This flat was gorgeous, but I found it cold and overly efficient. It was, in fact, my sister in concrete.

I didn't detect the scent of dinner cooking and when I took a peek into the immaculate kitchen as I passed, I didn't see any pots and pans on the stove. Nothing bubbled or fried or simmered, and the oven was off. The dining room table was set for dinner. We'd be having take-away, I assumed. Grant could whip up a casual dinner, but he'd been out all afternoon. Pippa was not known as a cook, and clearly she didn't mind her mother-in-law knowing that.

Grant handed me a glass of wine, and I sat on the white leather couch next to Ryan. I couldn't help but think that with two dogs I could never have furniture like this in my house. Which reminded me of Violet. It was after six. Early afternoon in West London. The Emporium would still be open. I sent a quick text to Uncle Arthur: *??????????* . That task attended to, I took the first welcome sip of my wine. Cool and crisp and delicious.

"Are you going to tell us what happened this afternoon?" my father said.

"Best let Gemma do that," Grant replied. "She organized the outing. Donald and I were merely bystanders."

"Do I want to know?" Ryan asked.

"Probably not," Grant said.

"I cannot believe you've done it again, Gemma," Pippa said.

"Sorry," I said. Although I didn't know what I was apologizing for.

"Again?" Grant's mother, Linda, asked. "What do you mean again? Has this happened before? Whatever this is? Henry said something about you being witnesses to a crime."

"We had an encounter with the police when we were here for that convention, Mom," Grant said. "Nothing of significance."

We all smiled at her. Mrs. Thompson didn't look entirely comforted.

I sipped my wine. "Okay. First, this time, we were not witnesses to any crime per se, but we did happen upon the aftermath. When I left the hotel last night a man by the name of Paul Erikson was waiting for me in the lobby."

My father groaned. My mother said, "Good heavens. Please, no." Pippa said, "And so he rears his foolish head one more time." Jayne said, "Isn't that—?"

"Ooookay," Ryan said. "Some of you obviously know that name. I do not. Are you going to fill me in, Gemma?"

"Paul Erikson is my ex-husband."

"You've been married?"

"A youthful indiscretion."

"I can testify to that," Pippa said.

Roger and Linda Thompson exchanged confused looks. Andy was sitting on the couch next to Jayne. He whispered, "Did you know this?"

She gave him a guilty shrug.

"Why did you not tell me?" Ryan asked.

I struggled to answer. I'd put my marriage to Paul behind me and wanted to get on with my new life. I'd been young (although not that young) and foolish (extremely foolish), and I suppose I was embarrassed about how wrong I'd been. I'm the one everyone thinks is so smart, so observant, so clever. "The time never seemed right," I said.

"The time doesn't exactly seem right now." He indicated the circle of curious faces. "But I have to ask what else you haven't told me."

"You two can sort that out later. In private," Mum said.

I was not anxious to get into that conversion, so I gave my mother a grateful smile. She did not smile in return.

"What did Paul want?" Dad asked.

"Money, what else," Mum said.

"No. Not money." I glossed over how he said he still loved me and simply told them he had a book he wanted to show me. "The 'real deal' he called it."

"What did you make of that?" Dad asked.

"I believed he'd come into possession of a potentially valuable item he didn't know what to do with. The shop is now mostly a used bookstore. I assumed he was sold a used book that turned out to be worth a lot more than the original seller knew and Paul wanted an evaluation. It was late, I was tired, and seeing Paul came as a surprise. All I wanted was to get out of there. I agreed to stop by the shop at noon today. I am not a rare book expert, so I asked Grant to come with me."

Pippa glared at her new husband, and he winced.

"I'm not a rare book expert either," Donald added, "but I was hoping it would be something to do with Sir Arthur. We are in London after all, and I must follow—"

"Thank you, Donald," Mum said. "Henry and I admire your depth of knowledge of Conan Doyle and his work."

"You do?" Linda said.

"We went to the shop, as arranged, and found Paul dead," I said. "We called the police and were interviewed as witnesses, that's all."

"Dead," Ryan said. "Do you mean murdered?"

"It would appear so."

"Strangled," Donald added.

"Who's the detective in charge?" Dad asked.

"Jasmine Patel. She was working with Morrison as a DS, and she's now a DI."

"She remembered us." Donald cut himself a generous slice of Stilton. "Gemma, in particular."

I took a piece of flatbread. Lightly grilled, sprinkled with grated parmesan and herbs. Absolutely delicious. Pippa might not be much of a cook, but she knows how to lay out a good charcuterie tray.

DI Sam Morrison had been the detective involved in the case when we'd all previously been in London. He had a long-standing grudge against my father and had been looking for a way to railroad him. Patel, Morrison's junior at the time, had not been happy with the way he conducted the investigation. Morrison had eventually been removed from the case because of that personal conflict and been persuaded to take early retirement.

"What did you three do while you were waiting for the police to arrive, Donald?" Ryan asked.

Donald popped the cheese into his mouth. "We searched the premises, of course. Gemma did, that is. Grant and I guarded the door."

I wouldn't have put it quite like that. My father and Ryan exchanged looks I could only call exasperated.

"I didn't interfere with anything," I said. "But I must admit I had a quick little nose about. I found nothing, nothing at all, worth bringing to police attention. Other than the unlocked back door and the dog prints. If I had, I would have done so."

"Dog prints?" Ryan asked. "The killer brought a dog with him? Any place a dog has been is a gold mine of DNA."

"Prints outside, in the alley. Not inside as though brought by the killer. I thought they might help establish the time of death."

"What about this book?" Mum asked. "Was it there?"

"It was a bookstore," Donald said. "Plenty of books."

"Nothing stood out," I said. "Nothing on the desk, and Paul didn't have a book on his person."

"You know that because you didn't interfere with a crime scene," Dad said.

"Grant, honey," Linda said with an excessive amount of midwestern sweetness. "Might we have a word?"

"Now?"

"Yes. Now."

Grant put his glass down and slowly stood up. He looked as though he was about to be reprimanded for reading under the covers with a flashlight after lights-out. He followed his mother into the kitchen. We all tried not to hear what she was saying, although the tone came through loud and clear.

"He's still her little boy," Roger said. "Always will be. She doesn't like this talk of murder."

"None of us do," Dad said.

Pippa said nothing. She just watched me over the rim of her wine glass, her brown eyes, same shade as mine, sharp and narrow.

"I might have had a quick look around Paul's office," I said. "I didn't search him, though. He was wearing a T-shirt, and his jacket was tossed over the back of the chair. No place to hide a book of any size. I'd expect a rare and potentially valuable volume to be a hardcover at least."

"Not necessarily," Grant said, coming back into the room. He had a chastised expression on his face, and he avoided his wife's eyes. Linda sat down with a huff. She took a piece of flatbread. "Can I cut you some cheese, dear?" she asked Roger.

"No, thanks, hon."

"Anyone?"

We all demurred. Donald speared an olive with a toothpick.

"An extremely old book, something earlier than, say, the eighteenth century, could be very small," Grant said. "Tiny to our eyes."

"A volume like that would never come into Paul's hands," I said. "I was assuming he found something in a box of secondhand books someone decided to get rid of when they downsized."

"The point," Grant said, "is we don't know what he had. Or how it came into his possession."

"True," I admitted.

"Never mind the book for now," Ryan said. "Did the police give any indication you might be a suspect in this?"

Linda Thompson sucked in a breath. Her husband patted her hand.

"No," I said firmly. "She asked for the usual information like phone numbers and the address of where we're staying, in case they have more questions. It was obvious Paul died a good while before we arrived. Likely not long after I encountered him at the hotel, at a guess. He was wearing the same clothes he'd been in when I saw him."

"As I'm sure Ryan and Henry can tell us, ex-spouses are often the most likely suspects," Donald added helpfully, "and for good reason."

"Thank you for those words of support," I said.

"I don't mean you, Gemma. Simply making a general observation."

"I hope you told the detective you had no contact with this guy for several years until last night," Ryan said.

"I did. And because it's true, she won't find otherwise. Before anyone asks, I did not get up in the middle of the night and make my way to a back alley near Trafalgar Square to sneak in the rear door of a secondhand bookshop and murder anyone. For revenge on a cheating man or possession of I don't even know what. Or anything else."

"Is that a possibility?" Linda stared at me, wide-eyed.

"No, Mom," Grant said, "it most definitely is not. Gemma is eliminating that line of inquiry."

"Because it's impossible," Donald said. "I am confident the police of Scotland Yard have learned a thing or two since Holmes's day.

When you've eliminated the impossible, all else that remains must be considered probable."

"Huh?" Roger Thompson said.

"You mean Sherlock Holmes was a real person?" Linda said. "I always thought he was made up."

Pippa's phone buzzed. She pressed a key and stood up. "At last. Dinner has arrived."

"Great," Andy said. "I'm starving."

Pippa and Grant went to the door together. They spoke in low voices. She was, I suspected, asking him if I'd told them the whole story.

"Gemma," Ryan said. "What are you planning to do?"

"Do?" I said sweetly.

"About Paul's death."

I leaned back in my chair and cradled my wine glass. The door opened; Grant accepted a stack of brown bags. Fabulous scents drifted into the flat. Andy leapt to his feet. "I'll help serve. Come on, Jayne."

"What? Oh, you want me to help too? Right. Got it."

Roger and Linda stood up. "I'll wash my hands before dinner," Linda said.

"Donald," Jayne called, "can you bring the wine bottles to the table?"

Soon only Ryan, my parents, and Pippa were watching me.

"Do?" I repeated. "I loved Paul once. And in return he loved me. Or he thought he did, at any rate. It didn't work out, and to be completely honest, I doubt it would have worked even if he hadn't taken up with a shop clerk beneath my very nose. The bloom was off the rose even before that, which was why I didn't make much of an effort to keep the marriage together. We had no children; we went our separate ways. We settled our financial affairs, meaning the co-ownership of the shop, without rancor. I moved to West London. Paul married Sophie."

"I sense a 'but' coming," Pippa said.

"I'd like to do what I can for him. One last time."

"He doesn't deserve it, love," Mum said softly.

"He wasn't a bad man," I said. "Never violent, never abusive. He wanted to make a go of the shop, but he simply wasn't capable of keeping his mind on one thing at a time. He constantly leapt from one great idea to another, never finishing the first." Judging by what I saw last night, that hadn't changed.

"I don't like it," Ryan said.

"Neither do I," Dad said. "Leave it to the police, Gemma."

"How many cases would you guess DI Patel has on her plate at any one time, Dad?"

"More than one," my father admitted.

"And how many do I have?"

"None," Ryan said. "As in zero. I'd like to keep it that way."

"We get your point, love," Mum said. "But this should not be up to you."

I glanced around the flat. Jayne passed steaming serving dishes across the kitchen counter. Andy placed them in the center of the table, while Donald arranged wine glasses. Roger and Linda were standing close together, looking out the floor-to-ceiling windows over the city. Darkness had fallen, and lights stretched to the horizon. Grant had his head buried in the fridge.

"Why don't I ask a few innocent questions?" I said. "See if I come up with anything obvious the police don't have the time or the resources to get. I should call on Paul's mum at the very least. Extend my condolences. She was rather fond of me, although that might have changed. Maybe I can locate this book, and it will turn out to be a find of great historic and literary significance."

"Paul's father's a senior clerk in the chambers next to mine," Mum said. "I should also express my condolences. I believe his parents are long divorced."

"Okay," Ryan said. "No one can deny you have an uncanny way of finding out things the police cannot, Gemma. And I include myself in that statement."

"Nothing uncanny about it," I said. "I simply observe what others do not."

"Not to mention there's no stopping you when your mind is set on something. Guess our fishing trip is off, Henry."

Dad's face fell. He'd booked three nights at a fishing lodge in Derbyshire for himself, Andy, and Ryan.

"No need to do that," I said. "As I said, I'll only be asking questions. It would probably be best for you not to come with me to Grant's mum's place, Ryan. She was not happy when Paul and I split. Not at all. I have Grant and Jayne if I need someone to accompany me. Even Donald."

"Like Jayne's going to be helpful in a fight," Dad said. "Or Donald."

"I don't intend to get in any fights," I said.

"That's good to know," Mum said.

Ryan looked dubious.

"After dinner, I'll put some feelers out to friends I still have in the Met," Dad said. "And to Jasmine Patel herself. I remember her from when she was a rookie constable, and we got on well back then. I'll try to find out what's up with this case. If it looks like it's being handled well, you are not under suspicion, and there's no hint of it being more than a normal killing, whatever normal means, I'm okay with going fishing. Up to you, Ryan."

"I have to admit, I am looking forward to it," Ryan said. "If Gemma agrees to two things."

"What?" I asked.

He counted off on his fingers. "One, you'll check in with me every day. Two, you'll walk away and hand everything you've learned over to the police at the merest hint that whoever killed this guy might be planning to kill again to stop from being found out."

"I agree."

"Three—"

"You said two conditions."

"I've taken the liberty of changing my mind. You have to agree to do research only. Speak to people, but no crafty disguises. Nothing illegal like break and enter."

"Promise," I said.

"I have a condition also," Dad said, "If DI Patel tells you to get lost, you do."

"Okay."

"I and my office must not be involved in any way," Pippa said.

"You won't be."

"That's what you said the last time. My ears are still ringing from the words I heard when I returned to my desk from participating in a police action on the river in front of the Tate Modern . . . as photographed by half the tourists in London."

"I neglected to extend my condolences on the death of your late boss," I said. "I trust you're now reporting to the replacement."

Pippa looked at me. "I have absolutely no idea to whom you are referring, Gemma."

Ryan was interrupted from asking who we were talking about when my phone buzzed to tell me I had a text. Uncle Arthur. "Excuse me," I said. "It's from home. This might be important." I read the message quickly.

You mean the skunk encounter? V chastised. House being cleaned now. Love to all.

Chapter Seven

Once that was settled, dinner was a lovely affair. Andy was excited about the fishing trip and he peppered Dad with questions as to what they might catch and what the conditions would be like. He failed to notice that Ryan was uncharacteristically silent, but Jayne did not.

She lifted her eyebrow as she passed me a bowl heaped high with chicken korma. I gave her a slight nod, indicating we'd talk later.

Donald was beyond delighted to discover that Roger and Linda Thompson were Sherlock newbies. Before they knew what was happening, he'd organized a full day of Holmes activities for them tomorrow. "Anyone else want to join us?" he asked.

"Perish the thought," my mother muttered. Then she added, "Sorry. Court tomorrow. It might be a long day."

"I've been meaning to ask what sort of law you practice, Anne," Roger said. "Corporate? Criminal?"

"All dreadfully dull, I'm afraid," she said as she served herself spinach paneer and passed the bowl to Andy. "Most of the law is exceedingly dull."

My mother was one of the top barristers—trial lawyers—in London. Her career was anything but dull, but she rarely talked about it and never to outsiders.

"I'd enjoy coming to court to watch you in action. Do you wear a wig?"

"I do. And a long black silk robe."

"Very fetching," Dad said. Mum gave him a warm smile.

"Perhaps tomorrow—" Roger began, but Donald interrupted before the other man could start formulating plans. "No time, I'm afraid. We'll be on the hop all day."

"And on Tuesday we're off to Scotland for a week," Linda said. "I'm excited about that."

"Scotland!" Donald exclaimed. "Sir Arthur was Scottish. He went to the University of Edinburgh. There are a good number of sites in that city you can visit. Such as . . ." And he was off and running.

I reached under the table for Ryan's hand. I gave it a hard squeeze. When he turned to look at me, I mouthed, "Love you."

"Love you too," he mouthed back.

When I returned my attention to my dinner, my sister was watching us from across the table. She winked at me.

* * *

As the North American visitors were still largely jet-lagged, and Dad, Ryan, and Andy had an early start the next morning, we didn't linger after dinner.

"I'm reconsidering going on this fishing jaunt," Ryan said to me once we were alone in our room in the house on Stanhope Gardens.

My suitcase had still not made an appearance, and I was wondering if I should take the time for another shopping trip or continue to live in the likely foolish hope that my own things would eventually find their way to me. "Dad will be disappointed if you don't. Andy will be shattered; he's truly excited about the trip. If it makes you feel any better, I don't know that I'm going to accomplish much, if anything. If I have to guess, I'll guess Paul stumbled upon something of considerable value, and whoever killed him killed him to get it. They left with it, and it's either on the black market or out of the country by now. My curiously is aroused, that's all. Not so much about the item in question, but as to why Paul thought I'd be interested in it."

"Have you considered that there was no item or he had something relatively unimportant and was only trying to get your attention?"

"You think that's possible?"

"I think it's more than possible, Gemma. You said the guy was down on his luck, on a downward spiral. If he thought his descent began when you left him, he might have thought getting together with you again would fix everything."

I thought back over what Paul had said to me. I said nothing. Ryan might be right that Paul was conflicted in his attitude toward me, but he had lain in wait for me, saying he wanted to show me this book he'd come across. Both of those things could be true.

"How hard is it to get the scent of skunk out of a house?"

"A year from now, you'll walk through the front door and be reminded."

Chapter Eight

The fishermen were up bright and early, ready to catch the train to Derbyshire. Andy had spent his entire life on Cape Cod; he knew his way around ocean fishing, but rivers were different and he was excited about learning new skills. As a professional chef, he was also looking forward to trying the flavors of fish different from those he normally cooked. The hotel they would be staying at offered to prepare the catch for their guests each night. Ryan had never been all that keen on fishing, but he fished often with his own dad, and he considered the activity to be a male bonding experience.

Not long after my arrival in America, Ryan attempted to propose marriage to me, and I'd made such a hash of it, he fled West London to spend the next several years in Boston. Since getting back together, we'd not talked about making a long-term commitment to each other. But I smiled to myself now, pleased that Ryan wanted to get better acquainted with my dad. To bond, as it were, over something other than policing.

I'd gone fishing once with my own father. That day is a strong contender for the title of the most boring day of my life.

Mum, Jayne, and I waved the hearty sportsmen out the door. Dad was laden with his own equipment, but Ryan and Andy would rent from the hotel.

Mum shut the door as the cab peeled away and said with a happy sigh, "I thought they'd never leave. Breakfast at the boulangerie?"

"Don't you have to be in court?" I asked.

"Not until this afternoon. We've been so busy since you finally arrived, we haven't had a chance to talk, and I do want to hear all about Jayne's wedding plans."

Jayne and Andy's wedding was scheduled for January.

I still hadn't heard from the airline about my bags.

"Breakfast out would be nice," I said, and the three of us went our separate ways to get dressed.

Over lattes and almond croissants in the upper level of the PAUL Bakery on Thurloe Street, while Mum and Jayne chatted happily about weddings good and bad they'd been to over the years, I thought about Paul Erikson. It was highly unlikely I could accomplish anything the police could not, as had been pointed out to me more than once. But, as I myself had pointed out more than once, I could at least have a nose around.

It wasn't only that the police were busy, which they were, but I've found over the years that I can find out things the police cannot. People talk freely to me precisely because I have no authority and they know it. They're not on their guard. Sometimes they tell me things they don't want to "bother" the police with. Things that later turn out to be highly significant. I can blunder "innocently" into places the police cannot because of a pesky thing called the law, which I never mind breaking in a good cause. I've been involved in situations in West London, much to the dismay of Ryan and his partner, Detective Louise Estrada, but at home I'm limited in the time I can devote to it because I have my business to run.

This time, like Sherlock Holmes, I was not encumbered by the triviality of trying to make a living selling books and Sherlockania.

We finished breakfast and went our separate ways. Mum had her briefcase and laptop with her, so she hailed a cab to take her directly to her chambers.

"It'll be just as quick for us to use the tube," I said to Jayne. "At this time of day on a Monday, the traffic above ground can be a horror." We headed to South Kensington underground station where Jayne and I bought Oyster cards.

"What are your plans, Gemma?" Jayne asked as we waited on the platform far underground, while tourists and commuters swirled around us.

"I fear I'm going to have to go clothes shopping."

"I wasn't expecting that. I thought we were investigating."

"That too. We'll go to the bookshop first and check it out. Almost certainly, it will still be sealed off. Unlikely it will ever reopen. That might be an idea. Ashleigh's always telling me I should open a new branch of the Emporium."

"Are you serious?"

"No. One store is about all I can manage these days. I could always hire someone to run it, but hands off isn't my style, and I don't fancy popping back and forth across the pond regularly. Back to the matter at hand. If DI Patel's there, I'll attempt to ask her if she's making any progress. I'd like to have another look at the alley if they haven't sealed it off. They might have missed something."

Jayne smiled at me.

"What?" I said.

"You. You think a team of professional, highly trained forensic investigators will overlook something you can see at a glance."

I didn't understand what was so amusing. "It's happened before."

The announcement to mind the gap echoed around us as the train pulled into the station. The crowd surged forward, sweeping us along with it.

"I hope Andy enjoys the fishing trip," Jayne said after we found seats. "He was excited to be in London, but he's not exactly a big city guy. I got the feeling he was getting a bit uncomfortable yesterday when we went to the Tower of London. The crowds, I mean."

"Did he enjoy it?"

"Oh, yes. Once we were inside, he exclaimed over absolutely everything." She chuckled. "I was at the exit, checking up on the news on my phone, while he was still reading every word on every plaque and marker."

A woman inadvertently shoved the wheel of a baby buggy against my shin. "Sorry," she mumbled. The toddler holding on to the handles of the buggy began to cry. "Sorry," the mother said again. She gave me a tired grimace, and I smiled in reply.

We got off at Embankment station and walked the short distance to the bookshop. The area wasn't quite as busy as it can get in the summer, but it was still packed with tourists taking selfies, browsing the shops, wandering the narrow streets heading for Trafalgar Square and the galleries. "I'd like to have lunch at St. Martin-in-the-Fields again one day," Jayne said. "The crypt is so cool."

"Let's keep that in mind," I said. "If time permits."

"We'll have to go while Andy's away. He'll want to read every word on every gravestone, and we'll never get out of there."

Foot traffic was moving at its normal pace outside Trafalgar Fine Books. Police tape was stretched across the door, but that section of Villers Street was no longer blocked off. A single uniformed cop stood outside the shop, guarding the entrance, looking almost as bored as I would have if I'd gone on the men's fishing expedition. Jayne and I stood on the other side of the street, watching. A few people glanced at the tape and the officer and tried to peer in the windows, but most paid no attention. Londoners can be a single-minded lot.

I could see some movement inside but not well enough to make out who it was or what they were doing.

"In for a penny," I said to Jayne, "in for a pound. Let's see what we can see." We crossed the street.

"Good afternoon," I said to the constable at the front door. "Is DI Patel around?"

He eyed me warily. "Who wants to know?"

"My name is Gemma Doyle, and this is my friend and colleague Jayne Wilson."

"Hi," Jayne wiggled her fingers at him.

Some of the caution shifted as his eyes settled on her lovely face, smooth skin, pink cheeks, shining blonde hair, sparkling blue eyes. He smiled. "Hi," he said, trying not to check out her slim figure in tight jeans and a cowl-necked red jumper beneath a puffy, sleeveless black jacket.

What was I, chopped liver? I was the one who'd asked the question.

I cleared my throat. "DI Patel?"

"Oh, yeah. She's not here."

"You won't mind if we have a quick look inside? I was here yesterday, and I might have left something behind."

"You were here yesterday?" At last, a spark of professional interest in his eyes. "Did the detectives interview you?"

"Yes."

"Then you can ask them if they found your whatever." He gave Jayne one last glance, then returned his attention to the activity on the street.

"Thanks," I said, "Thank you so much. I'll do that."

"You didn't expect them to open the door and bow you in, did you?" Jayne asked me when we were out of earshot.

"No, but I hoped to have a quick peek inside. No luck. Those windows are so dirty, if they had a white elephant in the center of the shop, I wouldn't have seen it. Let's try around the back. Resources are slim in the Met these days so they might not have stretched to watching two doors all the time."

Before we got more than a couple of steps, I caught sight of a familiar figure standing at the end of the street next to a closed wine bar. "Change of plan," I said. "Follow me."

Faye noticed us as we approached. She'd gathered her hair into a sloppy knot at the back of her head and hadn't paid much attention when applying her makeup. Her eyes were still tinged red. She wore a pair of poorly fitting trousers with ragged hems, a white and black woolen coat pilling badly, and trainers tired from too much use. She clutched a tattered tissue in her hand.

"Good morning," I said. "Faye, right? We met yesterday in the . . ." I allowed my voice to crack, "bookshop. When Paul . . ."

"Yes, I remember. What are you doing here?"

"We wanted to pay our respects. My friend Jayne knew Paul and she's finding it difficult to come to grips with what happened."

"Such a shock," Jayne said.

"For us too," Faye said. "I didn't have to come this morning. I know the shop's closed, probably permanently. I was scheduled to work today, so I didn't have anything else to do, and I guess I wanted to make sure I hadn't dreamt the whole thing."

"Do you have time for a cuppa?" I asked. "A coffee, maybe?" I should have suggested a pub, but it was too early for them to be open.

"Sure, that would be nice."

"It's been a few years since I worked around here, so why don't you suggest someplace nice. My treat."

Faye led the way to a popular chain. Like any coffee shop anywhere in the world, the place was full of chatter, the clatter of mugs and dishes, baristas calling out orders, the hiss of the espresso machine. Friends and coworkers talked over their coffee, and several tables were taken by single individuals peering at the screen of their phones with furrowed brows or typing intently on their laptops. Writing the next Great British Novel, most likely. The café was busy, but I spotted a table for four in a back corner. I gave Jayne a nod as we followed Faye through the doors, and she said, "Why don't I get in line while you find seats? What can I get you, Faye?"

"A cappuccino would be nice, thank you. I didn't get breakfast; one of those lovely muffins would be a treat. Any flavor."

"Tea for me," I said.

We settled ourselves at our table. I smiled at Faye. She sniffled, dabbed her eyes with her tissue, and gave me a tight smile in return.

"Sorry, but I didn't get your surname," I said. "Mine's Doyle. Gemma Doyle."

"Forgate."

"Were you fond of Paul?" I asked her.

Her eyes welled up again. "I don't know if you could say fond. I did have a bit of a soft spot for him, though. The poor dear. I did feel sorry for him."

"How so?"

"He couldn't make a go of that shop to save his life." She sucked in a breath. "Bad choice of words. I only mean the business was failing, and he was struggling to turn it around and not having much luck. I thought he should move to another location. The rent can't have been cheap, can it?"

"No, that it isn't."

"But it wasn't my place to say."

"How long did you work there?"

"About a year. I have to say, love, it was an easy gig. We didn't get a lot of customers. Sometimes we were more of a tourist agency, what with the number of Japanese or Americans who came in looking for Buckingham Palace or the National Gallery." She chuckled. "I suggested we charge for giving directions. Paul said it was a good idea, and I had to tell him I was only joking. Sorry, I hope I didn't offend you. You have a lot of American friends." She glanced at Jayne, watching her step as she carefully carried plates and mugs across the room.

"I do, but no problem. We live in a tourist town also, and we know all about hapless tourists. What about Tamara? How long has she worked in the shop?"

"She was there when I came. Maybe about six months before that? She's at uni and all she wants is a non-demanding job and a bit of money coming in."

Jayne put the drinks and Faye's muffin on the table and sat down. Faye picked up her cup and took a sip.

"Any other employees?" I asked.

"I'm full time. Tamara puts in three days a week. There's another couple of girls, but they come and go so often I can hardly keep them straight."

That, I knew, meant a lot of keys would be floating around. When employees leave, they are obviously expected to turn in their key. But sometimes that doesn't happen. They forget, keys get lost. Keys are copied, in case the owner needs a spare. And that spare is never turned in.

"The police found the employee records in Paul's office. I couldn't help but overhear one of them say to the other that the records were a mess. Can't say I was surprised." Faye peeled the paper off her muffin and took a big bite. "When I first started working there, I thought Paul might make a good match for my daughter, Olive, being an independent businessman and all. She's about your age, love, and I'm afraid she's going to be left on the shelf if much more time passes." Faye glanced at Jayne's left hand, proudly displaying her engagement ring. "Congratulations, dear."

"Thank you," Jayne said.

I refrained from asking Faye if, in her opinion, I was about to be left on the shelf.

"I realized soon enough," she continued, "that would be a mistake. For all Paul was a nice-looking man, well educated, good manners, he was trouble."

"In what way, trouble?" I asked. "Do you mean with the police or . . . other people?"

"Oh, no. Nothing like that. Not at first anyway. I just mean trouble as in unable to support a wife and a family. My own son, Greg, now. He's several years younger than Olive and he's doing so well." She beamed proudly. "I never had much money when the kids were young, but my Greg was such a good student, he earned a scholarship for an exclusive school, and then he went on to graduate from Oxford. He's still young but already he's an up-and-coming solicitor with an important City firm. Lovely wife and a new baby. Would you like to see a picture?"

No, I didn't say.

Pictures were produced. Nondescript man in his late twenties, woman about the same age. Fat-cheeked baby. More pictures of the baby, getting steadily fatter as the months progressed. "I don't see them nearly as much as I'd like to, for all they live in London. He's so busy, you know. It's not easy for a young man these days. The hours he puts in at that office. His wife, she's some sort of a bank executive, could bring the baby for a visit now and again if she wanted to." Faye sniffed in disapproval.

Finally, she put her phone away, and I said, "You mentioned Paul might have been in some trouble. Can you tell me more?"

She leaned closer. "He never talked about himself. I'm not one for gossip, you understand."

"I totally understand." And I did. Everyone who reassures me they are not a gossip turns out to be eager to dish the dirt.

"I suspect he was living in that office of his because he didn't have any place else. The last couple of weeks, anyway. He didn't have a lot of clothes and things, but he was sleeping on the cot in there. It's not like he was so busy with the business of the shop, he needed to work long into the night."

"What do you mean, not at first?"

"What?"

"You said he was not in trouble, 'not at first.'"

"Oh, that. Far be it from me to say anything bad about him. I mean, the poor man is dead." She dabbed her eyes with the café-provided paper napkin.

"The police will be trying to trace his movements and his contacts. Unfortunately, there are no secrets in a police investigation."

Her face crunched in thought. She popped the last bit of muffin into her mouth. She'd eaten it in record time and only the dregs of foam remained from her cappuccino.

I sipped at my tea and waited. Jayne sat quietly, watching us both.

"Over the last few weeks," Faye said, "some men came into the store who didn't look like the usual publishing salespeople. If you get my meaning. More than once, too."

I did get her meaning, but I said, "I don't. Sorry."

"They asked for Paul and went into the office. They never stayed long. Big men with East End or northern accents, tough faces."

"Did you hear anything of what they talked about?"

She shook her head. "Not a peep. The walls are thick. Not that I'd try to listen in any event. Not my place, is it?"

"Of course not." I had a mental image of Faye holding a glass to the wall.

"They never raised their voices, though, I can tell you that. Sorry, I can't be of more help, but I only worked there. I didn't usually socialize with Paul." She sniffed in disapproval. "He never so much as took the staff for drinks at Christmas. I don't get the paper and I don't watch the news on the telly, nothing but trouble, but I put the local news on the radio this morning to see if they said anything about Paul."

"Did they?"

"Just a line or two that the coppers are asking anyone who might have seen anything to come forward. No one's going to, are they? No one who might know what's going on."

"Did you ever meet Sophie Long?" I asked casually.

"Can't say as I have. Who's she?"

"Do you know where Tamara lives? What's her last name?"

"O'Riordan, for all her accent's as London as mine. I don't know anything about her. She goes to uni. UCL, I think. She's after a degree in literature or some such useless thing. Don't know any more about her."

"You didn't chat when the store was empty or when you were opening or closing?" Jayne asked.

Faye looked at her. "Why would I do that? I keep myself to myself, and I expect others to do the same." She stood up. "I have to be off. Thanks for the coffee. I hope you enjoy your visit to London."

"Thank you," Jayne said.

Faye left the coffee shop. She turned right on the sidewalk and walked in the opposite direction from Trafalgar Fine Books.

"Did she seem a mite odd to you?" Jayne asked.

"Not odd. But I can't say I liked her very much. Maybe because her son is clearly the apple of her eye, and her daughter is about to be past her best-before date. Never mind that. Faye was definitely interested in what Paul was up to, and I suspect he shut out a lot of her questions. Unlikely for any nefarious purposes, though; she's just nosy and bored at her job. As for her relationship with her fellow employees, if she told Tamara directly to her face that an English degree is a waste of time, I'm not surprised they didn't get along." I chuckled. "I suspect she wasn't so blasé about Paul not entering into a relationship with her spinster daughter as she tried to make out. I use the word spinster deliberately because it's obviously what Faye thinks. Since leaving me for Sophie, Paul might have learned a lesson about mixing business with pleasure. Either that or the idea of having Faye as a mother-in-law sent him running."

"Do you think there's anything significant about these strange men she said have been calling on Paul?"

"I most certainly do. Although I have to say that just because a man is large and has an East End accent doesn't mean he's not a representative of a publishing company or even the equivalent of the street's business association. Might even be an author looking for a book signing opportunity. Plenty of ex-coppers out there writing crime novels these days, as I well know. I will, however, keep these 'strange men' in mind. That Paul was in financial trouble is not in question, and more than a few people have dug themselves very deep holes in an attempt to save themselves."

"You mean the mob? Is there a mob in London?"

"Don't you read British police procedurals, Jayne? The Rebus books by Ian Rankin would be a good place for you to start. I hope Faye described these men to DI Patel."

"You think she might not have?"

"No, I'm sure she did. After plenty of caveats as to how she isn't a gossip and she knows her place, et cetera et cetera."

"What's next?"

"Next? What's the weather forecast for the rest of the week?"

Jayne pulled out her phone and checked quickly. "Rain. Followed by rain, and more rain. Getting colder too."

"I fear what's next is a shopping expedition. I can't keep wearing this outfit, day after day. I'd like to pay a call on Paul's mother. She was my mother-in-law at one time, and I should express my condolences, but today's too early. She'll have been notified about his death and will be in some considerable degree of shock. Paul was her only son, but as I recall, she does have a daughter. I hope the daughter is able to give her some support. Tower Hamlets."

"That's where Mrs. Erikson lives?"

"No. It just popped into my head. It's where Sophie Long lived. Last I heard of her, at any rate, when I had her address on file. That was seven years ago. But it's a place to start."

"The woman Paul left you for? I don't know if that's such a good idea, Gemma. Won't it be distressing for you?"

"Distressing? Not in the least. I owe Sophie a huge debt of gratitude. Better I found out Paul was a philanderer sooner rather than later. It couldn't have worked out better for me. Uncle Arthur opened the Emporium and then he found out that, like Paul, he had no idea of how to run a business. But, unlike Paul, he didn't want to try. I happened to be free to go to West London to help out. And, ta-da, here we are today." I thought of Paul and then I thought of Ryan. Yes, Sophie had done me a considerable favor. "Speaking of Uncle Arthur, I don't suppose you know how to get rid of the smell of a skunk, do you?"

"No, I don't. Why do you ask?"

"Skunks are not native to England. I fear poor Arthur is out of his depth. One thing Arthur does know, however, is how to ask the people who do know such things for help."

"Acting on the assumption that if a skunk had been in my bakery, you'd tell me, I'll worry later why you're asking about skunks. Back to Sophie. You might not have any residual animosity toward her, but if she and Paul are no longer together, do you think she can help?"

"Probably not, but it is an angle to pursue. Otherwise, I have nothing else, other than his mother, and I want to give her some time to process his death before bothering her. I know nothing about Paul's life over the last seven years. From what Faye told us, it's unlikely any of his staff were anything approaching friends with him. Even when we were together, we didn't have friends in common. Come to think of it, Paul didn't have friends. He had drinking buddies and that's about it. We can shop later. I don't know that area of the city very well. Maybe they have nice shops."

Chapter Nine

I've heard it said nothing is ever truly forgotten, we merely sometimes misplace information in the overloaded memory bank that is our brain. Whether that's true or not, I do seem to be able to remember a lot of useless details, long after you'd expect such information to be filed away in unmarked storage boxes, mentally speaking. Out of nowhere, I remembered the Tower Hamlets address Sophie Long had given when she'd been hired at my bookstore.

The last time I'd been in London and wrapped up in a police investigation, I had to travel through the city relying only on my memory, as I didn't want traces of my movements going into any databases, anywhere. This time, as I was not (I hoped) under suspicion, and I had not been warned away from interfering, I freely looked up the location I wanted and the best route to get there.

Jayne and I went to Charing Cross station and took the Baker Street Line to Oxford Circus. From there, we hopped onto a train on the Central Line to Bethnal Green.

"I'm impressed by the London subway system," Jayne said, swaying as she clung to a pole for support in the crowded train. "It's so efficient and easy to use. Apart from all the running up and down stairs, that is. Of course, all I'm doing is following you around. If I had to find my own way, I'd be totally lost."

I stepped back to allow a pack of people off and another pack to get on. "A lifetime of travel and a good map helps."

We emerged into the daylight and I consulted the map on my phone again. "Not far from here. We're not all that far from Pippa and Grant's."

"We could be on the far side of the moon for all I know," Jayne said as we set off walking. "Totally different area, isn't it?"

When we reached the street I was looking for, she said, "Looks like a movie set, or something from the Jeremy Brett Sherlock Holmes show."

"This is the real London, as it was a long time ago." Row houses, a line of two-story brick buildings with white trim stretching from one street to another, opening directly onto the pavement. Most of the houses had lace curtains hanging in front windows. Inside they would be dark and narrow. Two up, two down, unless interior walls had been torn out. A patch of a fenced garden not much bigger than a place to store the rubbish bins out back. In the old days, people would have raised geese or chickens in those yards.

Some of the homes had been spruced up with fresh paint, new windows, a brightly colored front door, good lamps. After all, nothing is cheap in London anymore.

Number 12 wasn't one of the most run-down, but it wasn't the nicest either. Rather in the middle, as befitted, I hoped, a home in which one family has lived for many decades.

"Why didn't we phone ahead?" Jayne asked.

"Two reasons," I said. "One, I don't know the number. Two, I prefer not to give people advance warning I'm about to call on them."

"Do you think we'll find this Sophie at home?"

"No, I do not. This is her mother's house. It was her mother's house seven years ago, and I'm hoping it still is. Sophie told me when I hired her she was between flats. I took that to mean she couldn't afford the rent on anything she fancied. Not an unusual situation, then or now, for a shop clerk in London."

We climbed the step. I rang the bell and then stood back, a pleasant smile on my face. "Look friendly," I said to Jayne.

"Don't I always?" she mumbled.

The lace curtains in the window to the left of the door flicked and moments later I heard footsteps in the hallway. The lock turned, the door cracked open, and a woman peered out. She was in her early sixties, a network of deep lines radiated out from her eyes and the corners of her mouth. Her hair was piled high on the crown of her head, behind a heavy fringe drooping over her eyebrows. The hair was dyed a shocking shade of deep, unnatural brown. She was even shorter than Jayne's five foot two and likely tipped the scales at a hundred pounds if she was soaking wet and carrying a sack of potatoes. She wore a pink blouse with a frilly neckline and black leggings sagging around her knees. The corridor behind her was dark and narrow, and I smelled something not very appealing cooking.

"Hi," I said. "Mrs. Long?"

Her eyes narrowed. "Who's asking?"

"I'm Gemma Doyle. I don't know if you remember that name."

"From the bookshop where my Sophie worked." Obviously, I am not the only one with a good memory. Sophie's mother and I had never met.

"Yes, that's right. I'm in London for a visit with my parents, and I was hoping to catch up with Sophie. Is she still living here?"

Mrs. Long glanced behind me to check out Jayne. "Hi," Jayne said. "Nice day, isn't it?"

"Not so as I'd notice. I don't know what you want, Ms. Doyle, but my Sophie's done and dusted with that shop."

"I am aware of that, yes." Cars drove past on the road, and pedestrians hurried by. A woman approached walking a small dog. Her steps noticeably slowed as she reached the house. "Might we come in? I don't want to take up much of your time."

"Good morning, Ethel," Mrs. Long said to the dogwalker in a loud voice. "Nothing to see here, love."

Ethel and her small dog hurried on.

Mrs. Long turned her attention back to me. "What do you want my Soph for? Can't be because you're such great chums. I know her husband left you for her."

"All water under the bridge now," I said cheerily. "I bear her no ill will."

She snorted. "I would hope not. It's that former husband of hers, of yours, you should be talking to. I knew he was no good right from the beginning. I told her so, but would she listen? Oh, no, not her." Her voice softened, just a bit. "Mustn't forget I was young once too. No telling what gets into a young girl's head, she meets a man like that Paul Erikson. Right charmer he could be. Talked the socks straight off my Soph."

If that was the way Mrs. Long wanted to see it, I was not going to argue. As for being a young girl, Sophie had been twenty-five when she came to work for us, the same age as Paul and me. "Which is why I'd like to speak with her. It's about Paul."

She reared back, suspicion clouding her features once again. "Did he send you here? If she told him once, she told him a hundred times to stay away from her. They're divorced now, and she's not responsible for his problems any longer."

"You haven't heard what happened?"

"What happened?"

I didn't think I needed to worry about breaking the news of Paul's untimely death to this woman gently. "Paul died. Yesterday."

She stared at me for a few long seconds. Behind me, Jayne said, "Are you—?"

Mrs. Long let out a bark of laughter. "Did he now? Can't say I'm sorry to hear it. My girl was lucky enough to get out of that marriage before he took every penny she had and then went on to seduce some other sweet thing. Good riddance to bad rubbish, I say." She stepped back and put her hand on the door frame. "I'll tell Soph the news."

I thrust my foot into the doorway. "Please, I need to talk to her. It's about Paul's financial affairs. With two ex-wives that we know of, things might get complicated. Dividing the estate equitably, I mean. Sophie and I need to get our stories together before his lawyers contact us."

Her eyes gleamed at the word "lawyers." I deliberately used the plural rather than the singular. "Lawyers" sounds as though one has a team at one's back and is in possession of an amount of money that requires a team to manage it. Not that I thought Paul had any lawyers. Plural or singular. Or any sort of an estate to be divided between anyone.

"I can let her know," Mrs. Long said. "Give me your number, and I'll have her call you."

"Great. Thanks." I smiled at her, expecting Mrs. Long to pull out her own phone to take down my number. Instead, she held out her empty hand. I looked at it.

"Here." Jayne rummaged in her bag and handed me the crumpled receipt from the coffee shop along with a pen.

"Oh, right. Pen and paper. Some people still use those." I jotted my number down and handed the receipt to Mrs. Long. She snatched it. "How much do you think he had left? That Paul, when he died? That shop was worth something, right?"

"I have no idea," I said honestly. New unsold books could be returned to the publisher. Provided someone was available to pack up the stock and send them back, and that was not guaranteed. The used ones would likely end up at a dump somewhere. As for the book that was so important Paul had sought me out wanting me to examine it, it might never turn up. Or turn out to be worthless if it did.

"Have a nice day." Jayne and I walked away. I could feel Mrs. Long's eyes on my back.

"She didn't seem too terribly upset at the news of Paul's death," Jayne said. "I suppose that's to be expected, if he didn't treat her daughter well."

I said nothing. Far from the sweet little innocent Mrs. Long believed her daughter to be, it was more that Sophie had set her cap at Paul, and poor, weak, foolish Paul gladly snatched at the bait. I remembered the day she confronted me. The look on her face had not been pleasant when she informed me that if Paul didn't have the nerve to tell me they were "deeply, truly in love, as only two soulmates can be," she would. It was not the look of a young woman in love, but more of smug satisfaction at putting one over on another woman. Sophie hadn't liked me, and from the first day she came to work, I realized I'd made a mistake in hiring her. She was sullen and disrespectful, and when she thought my back was turned, she could be outright rude to the other staff and even the customers. If I hadn't been married to Paul, it was unlikely she would have been at all interested in him.

People tell me I'm observant. In that particular instance, however, my skills and my instincts failed me. Perhaps I hadn't noticed the burgeoning relationship between Paul and Sophie because I considered it part and parcel of her character. Perhaps I trusted him, far more than I should have.

All water under the bridge except that Sophie was one of the only tenuous leads I had to what might have brought about Paul's death.

My phone rang before we reached the tube station. "What do you know?" I said to Jayne, taking a guess as to who the unrecognized number belonged to. "She couldn't even try to pretend to be disinterested for a few minutes."

"Hello?" I said sweetly.

"Is that Gemma Doyle?" asked an East End London accent.

"It is."

"Sophie Erikson here. Sophie Long what was and should be again. You were at my mother's just now?"

"I was. I'd like to speak to you, Sophie. If you're in London, I can come to where you are."

"Mum says Paul's dead, and you want to talk about his inheritance. You think he left me something?"

"I don't want to discuss it on the phone."

"Why would you know?"

"Why would I know he died?"

"He didn't marry anyone after we split so that means I'm the latest wife, right? Why would you know if I'm still in his will? He never spoke to you again. You left England. Ran off to America. That's what he told me anyway."

"When did you see Paul last?"

I could almost hear her thinking. If "latest wife" was supposed to be a dig at me, it went wide of the mark.

"Little over a year, maybe a bit more. We didn't part on good terms. He . . . Never mind that. None of your business."

"Are you going to ask me how he died?"

"Car accident or something, I figured. Wasn't that it?"

"Let's meet, Sophie. Some things need to be discussed face to face."

"Yeah. Okay. I'm at work now. I just got in, so I can't take my break until lunch. I work in a shop on Oxford Street, not far from Oxford Circus." She named a restaurant. "I'll meet you at one. Don't be late. I don't like to wait." She hung up.

"Neither do I," I said to the phone.

"I heard most of that," Jayne said. "She doesn't have a soft voice, does she? It's quarter after ten now. What are we going to do until one? How long will it take us to get to where she is?"

"Not long. Fortunately, we have a way of spending the time until our appointment."

* * *

I shopped.

I'm not usually a keen shopper. I go into stores, see what I like (or not) and buy it (or not). Jayne, on the other hand, loves to shop, and she loves nothing more than to help someone else (i.e., me) shop. It just so happens that Oxford Steet is one of the shopping meccas in London.

Once I located the restaurant where we were due to meet Sophie, I let Jayne lead me around. By ten to one, I had a new raincoat, a pair of trainers, jeans and two cardigans, a leather jacket, one nice dress (which would, the clerk informed me, "take you breezily from that important meeting to the school run to dinner at the hottest new place in town."), shoes to go with the dress, a couple of T-shirts, several pairs of knickers, and even a new bra.

I staggered into the appointed meeting place several hundred pounds poorer and laden with a mountain of shopping bags. Jayne carried more bags. "That was fun," she said. "We should do it again."

"Never," I said. "Table for three please," I said to the hostess. "We're meeting someone."

"You don't suppose this is Sophie's regular lunch place, do you?" Jayne said when we were seated.

"I doubt she's ever done more than glance wistfully through the window. I suggested the meeting, so she'll be expecting me to pay." Standard high-end steakhouse, comfortable chairs, polished wooden tables, big windows, cutlery wrapped in linen napkins secured by napkin rings. No candles on the tables, but I had no doubt those would appear in the evening. Most of the guests wore suits or perfectly coordinated business casual attire. Not a place for shop clerks snatching a quick lunch. "I do not want to linger, so let's make this as quick as we can. Here she is, five minutes early, as expected." I stood up.

Sophie Long approached our table. She stopped a few feet from us and stared openly at me, sizing me up. She did not smile, so I didn't either. I'd last seen her, smug and self-satisfied, seven years ago. She'd been pretty then, in the way that all young women in good health with money to spend on themselves were pretty. The bone structure of her face was still good, her pale skin clear, her eyes large behind glasses with round, red frames. Her sleek brown hair was pulled back into a high ponytail that fell halfway down her back. She'd put on weight in the intervening years but not too much. She wore ironed cream trousers and a fashionably overlarge oatmeal jacket over an emerald-green blouse with huge gold buttons. If she worked in an Oxford Steet clothing shop, she'd have to look the part, and she did.

Her makeup was too heavy, lashes clumped with mascara, excessive amount of face powder, blush applied in visible strokes. Her mouth was a slash of deep red, better suited to a nightclub than a London restaurant at lunchtime. "I'm here now," she declared.

"Thanks for meeting me." I introduced her to Jayne. Sophie barely glanced at my friend before plopping herself down. She picked up the menu. "I don't have long for my break, so I need to order quickly."

The waiter appeared. "A pint of lager," Sophie said. "And the steak pie with mash."

"Jayne," I said. "You should have lunch. I don't know when we'll be stopping again."

"Okay. I'll have the pie too. With a side salad. I don't suppose you have any iced tea?"

"We do, madam," the waiter said.

"Then I'll have one, thank you."

"Just tea for me, please," I said. I didn't bother to say hot tea. In England, that is assumed.

The waiter collected the menus and slipped silently away. He would not be stopping at our table, interrupting the conversation every ten minutes to ask if everything was "okay here?"

Sophie shook out her napkin and leaned back in her chair. She made an attempt to look comfortable, relaxed, not particularly interested. In that, she failed dramatically. Her eyes were wide with curiosity, her neck stiff with tension. She twisted the napkin between her fingers. The polish on her nails matched her lipstick, and it was beginning to peel. "I'm here. So talk. You think Paul left us each something? Why would he remember you?"

"You're divorced from him also," I said.

"I got bored of him right quick, but I stuck it out for a couple of years." She looked so directly at me, I knew she was lying. "I should have listened to me mum and left him long before I did. But I was too nice, you know? Not just him, but I was bored working at that awful bookshop. I don't know why anyone would want to own a bookshop. They're dying, right? Independent bookshops. Can't make a living out of that anymore. Not with ebooks and online shopping and the rest, right?"

"Some stores have found their niche in a difficult environment and are doing very well," I said.

She shrugged, not interested. A tall glass of beer appeared in front of her and she grabbed it. She took a long drink. Jayne sipped at her iced tea, while I poured tea into the fine china cup provided and added a splash of milk.

Before Sophie joined us, I told Jayne to make light, friendly conversation. She threw me a panicked look now, then said, "You work in a women's wear store, your mother told us. I love the color of that blouse. It's so deep and rich. Did you buy it at the place where you work?"

"Yes. We get a discount on the end-of-season stuff. It's a summer blouse, but it's okay with this jacket, don't you think?

"What's the name of your store?" Jayne indicated the mountain of shopping bags piled around our feet. "As you can see, we're here to shop until we drop."

"You're from America, right?" Sophie asked. "We get plenty of Americans in our shop. Some of them buy a lot."

"I love the cut of that jacket," Jayne said. "So big and loose and . . . fun."

"I don't," Sophie said. "I feel like I'm playing dress-up in me mum's clothes. But we have to wear what's in, don't we?"

"We do," Jayne said.

The steak pies arrived, hot and fragrant. Jayne and Sophie picked up their cutlery and dug in. I sipped my tea. I let Sophie enjoy the first few bites and then said, "I don't actually know anything about any inheritance from Paul."

She froze, fork halfway to her mouth. "But you said—"

"I know what I said. It's unlikely Paul had much to leave anyone, other than a mountain of debts and a skipload of used books. When did you say you last saw him?"

She resumed eating. "About a year ago, round about. He moved out of our flat when we split up, and he left some of his stuff behind. When I had to move . . . I mean, when I decided to move back with me mum, to take care of her, like, I told him to pick it up or I'd put it out with the rubbish."

"Did he come to collect it?"

"Yeah. He wanted to go out for a coffee or something, for old times's sake, he said, but I had to get to work, and I told him so."

"What sort of stuff?"

"Some clothes. A suitcase. Not much."

"When did you stop working at the bookshop?"

"When we separated. I wasn't going to stay there, was I, and see him every day? Besides, by then I knew it was a no-hope business. Some days, we didn't sell a single book."

I'd intended to ask Sophie if she had any financial interest in the bookstore, or if she'd helped manage it. I decided not to. The answer was obvious.

"I didn't think he looked too good, tell you the truth. He said the business was going well. I didn't believe him. I was well out of it. Him and that stupid shop."

"You had no further contact with him over the past year?"

She stopped shoveling steak pie and potatoes into her mouth and looked at me. "What's it to you?"

I poured myself another serving of tea. I do like my tea served in a proper pot, not a mug of tepid water with a tea bag on the side like they bring it in America sometimes. Most of the time. "Have you heard from the police?"

"No. Why should I?"

"Paul was murdered."

I stirred my tea while I paid close attention to her reaction. She stared at me and said nothing for a long time. "That can't be right."

"It is. The police are investigating. He was killed in the shop late Saturday night or early Sunday morning. I'm sure they'll be around to interview you shortly."

"Well, I didn't do it, did I, and you can't accuse me." Indecision crossed Sophie's face as she considered standing up and storming out of the restaurant in righteous indignation. But she hadn't finished her beer and pie yet, so she remained where she was. "I was out with Kenneth, that's me boyfriend, Saturday. We went back to his place after the pub closed. So I've got an alibi." She smirked.

I hadn't accused her of killing Paul, and I hadn't asked for her alibi. Not that I consider a boyfriend to be a reliable alibi. I didn't read too much into that. Spouses and ex-spouses are always at the top of any suspect list, and she would have known that.

"What's it to you, anyway?" she asked. "Did you kill him?"

I sipped my tea. "Not me."

"You've got your nice cushy life in America, right? You were well enough rid of the likes of Paul Erikson." Her face twisted and the bitterness came through loud and clear. "If it makes you feel any better, I'm sorry he dumped you for me. I should have known better. He was a right chancer, that one."

"I wanted to meet with you today to ask if you know of any reason someone might have killed Paul. Did he have any enemies? Did he owe money to someone he shouldn't?" I'd hoped Sophie would know something about the book Paul wanted me to see, but I now realized there was no point in even asking. She had no interest in the business; he wouldn't have shown it to her, and they hadn't been in contact lately in any event. It was likely the book, whatever it might be, only recently came into Paul's possession.

"You mean other than me?" Sophie asked.

"Other than you?" At first I thought she was saying she wanted to kill him. "You mean he owed you money?"

"He stuck me with a couple of month's rent when he left. Never mind his share of the grocery money and the like. He always had some excuse about why he couldn't pay, and I finally had enough, and I kicked him out. I told him I wanted me money when I saw him last, but he whined on and on about how business had been slow and he needed some time to get back on his feet. Whatever. I'll give his mum a call. I have her number somewhere. She might know what's happening with his will and the like."

She scraped up the last of her pie and mashed potatoes. "I have to get back to the shop. I'm thinking of quitting, but I haven't decided yet. That manager they've got there is a right dragon. Five minutes late, and she'll be docking me wages. And giving me a talk about the importance of punctuality to boot."

This was a wasted trip. Sophie Long, the second Mrs. Erikson, knew nothing that could help me find Paul's killer. "You can't tell me anything about what Paul's been up to over the last few months?"

Sophie hesitated. She glanced at the pile of shopping bags around us. She lifted Jayne's left hand and checked out the engagement ring. It wasn't big or ostentatious, but it was tasteful and it was nice. The small diamond was genuine.

"I do know one thing," Sophie said, letting go of Jayne.

"What's that?"

"About two months or so ago, I was meeting a bunch of girlfriends for a hen night. I was late leaving work, hurrying down the street, when I saw Paul up ahead. I slowed down, just interested like in what he was up to. He was with a woman. They were coming out of a pub, holding hands and walking close together. They'd been drinking and were laughing and stumbling down the street and giving each other little kisses and all that stuff. I was curious so I followed them."

"And?"

"They didn't go far before they stopped at a door. She used a key and they went in."

"Did you ever try to find her again, to speak with her?"

"I thought about it, but what would be the point? She isn't going to give me the money he owes me. I left. Haven't been back."

"What's the address?"

Sophie grinned at me. "A hundred pounds."

"What?"

"I'll tell you for a hundred pounds."

"The police will want to know this, and they won't pay for it."

"Yeah, but the police aren't here, are they? You are. You and your friend look like you're not short a bob or two. For all that cardigan's a horrible color on you and it looks like it came out of your mother's closet." Which it had, but I didn't see that that detail was at all pertinent at the moment.

"Jayne," I said. "Do you have a hundred pounds cash on you?"

"Gosh, no. I might have about fifty?"

Sophie held out her hand. "That'll do."

Chapter Ten

In exchange for forty-three pounds and seventy pence, Sophie provided us with the location to which she'd followed Paul and the unknown woman. She added a vague description of his companion for free.

She left without bothering to thank me for the lunch, and I paid the hefty bill.

"Did we learn anything, Gemma?" Jayne asked once we were back on the street.

"If this address turns out to be a dead end, we learned nothing close to being worth what it cost us. I'll pay you back for that, thanks. If I'm going to be asked for bribes, I need to start carrying cash."

"Less than fifty pounds isn't much of a bribe."

"No, it isn't. But it was enough in this case."

"Are we going to try to find this woman?"

"Might as well see what our money bought us. It's two o'clock now. If she has an office job, she'll likely be at work, but I want to give it a try, and as we don't have a name, a phone number, or a flat number, there's nothing we can do but pop around and hope she's in. Fortunately, the address Sophie gave us isn't far from here."

"Our luck's holding so far," Jayne said.

"Which is what worries me," I replied.

Once again, we gathered up our shopping bags. I followed the directions on my phone. Down busy Regent Street, turning east before we reached Piccadilly, down narrow streets with narrow pavements, shopfronts on the ground level, flats and offices above. I hoped the place we were going to wasn't a large block of flats. I didn't fancy pushing every entry button and asking for some unknown woman who might know a man by the name of Paul Erikson.

Fortunately, it wasn't.

The area was moderately nice. Flowers spilled from boxes in some of the upper levels, the paint on window and doorframes wasn't peeling, the shop fronts were clean, and the stores looked prosperous. A typical London pub stood on the corner, dark wood, gold print above the door, leaded windows, a couple of small tables arranged outside.

"How many pubs are there in London, do you think?" Jayne asked. "Must be hundreds. Thousands." She pointed to the next corner where sat yet another typical London pub.

"I don't know. I doubt anyone truly knows," I said.

The address we'd been given was in the center of the row. Inside the door, four mailboxes and four buttons indicated the number of flats inside.

I chose Flat One to begin and pressed the button. No answer. Flat Two responded with a deep man's voice. When I said I was looking for Paul Erikson he growled, "Never heard of 'im," and disconnected.

A woman answered the call at Flat Three. "Paul? I have no idea where he is. No reason I should."

"I'd like to speak to you about him. May I come in?"

"Why?" asked the disembodied voice.

"He's been in the news lately. Have you seen the reports?"

"I try not to watch the news. Are you a reporter? I've got no time for reporters, and if he's in some sort of trouble, it's got nothing to do with me."

"My name is Gemma Doyle. I was married to Paul at one time."

"Gemma? The great and mighty, never-to-be-forgotten Saint Gemma herself?"

I glanced at Jayne. She shrugged in response.

"Second floor. On the left," the voice said as the buzzer buzzed and the lock clicked. I pulled open the inner door.

These shopping bags were starting to get mighty heavy. The building didn't have a lift, so we trudged up to the second floor, which would be what Americans call the third floor. A woman matching the description Sophie had given me stood in the open doorway to our left. Late twenties, tall, thin, a mane of flaming red hair. Judging by the number of freckles on her face, the hair was her natural color. She wore black leggings and a loose top and eyed us suspiciously.

"Thanks for seeing us," I said.

"How could I resist?"

"I'm Gemma and this is Jayne. I don't know your name."

"No reason you should. I'm Mimi. Come on in." The main room of the flat was small and nicely but simply decorated. Framed movie posters from the 50s and 60s covered the walls. A brightly colored afghan was tossed over a threadbare couch. A computer and printer sat on a desk under the front window. The curtains were pulled back and the glass sparkled in the daylight. The flat was clean and tidy. Judging by the scent, Mimi had enjoyed reheated leftover pizza for lunch.

Jayne and I dropped our burdens by the door. "Looks like you've had fun," Mimi said.

"No," I said.

"Yes," Jayne said.

"When I heard the buzzer, I was hoping you'd come about the ad."

"Ad?"

"I'm looking for a flatmate. The rent on this place is more than I can handle on my own. My previous flatmate didn't exactly work out."

"Paul Erikson?"

She laughed. "Yeah. Waste of space that one. Why are you looking for him and how did you find me?"

I ignored the questions and asked one of my own. "How do you know my name?"

Mimi dropped onto the couch and curled her legs up under her. She didn't invite us to sit. Jayne crossed the room and looked out the window.

"Paul and I were together for a couple of months. He told me he'd sold his flat and hadn't found another yet, so I let him move in with me. Big mistake that." She grinned, not looking too concerned. "I doubt there was ever any flat to be sold. If there had been, he'd lost it long ago. He was a charmer, I'll give him that. Most of the time, he was a charmer, that is. When he got into his cups, he could get maudlin. All woe-is-me. Gemma this and Gemma that. The best woman he'd ever known and he let her go."

Jayne laughed. I snorted. "Not that I much care what he had to say about me, but he didn't *let* me do anything. I left him, and I haven't regretted it for a moment."

"Then we understand each other, you and me. The thing about that sort of charm, is it wears off mighty fast."

Which was exactly my experience with Paul. Being young and somewhat naive, I hadn't yet realized how quickly a woman could tire of that sort of charm, as Mimi called it. I avoided looking at Jayne. I wasn't the only one who'd chosen badly at one time. Jayne had had a series of boyfriends of whom I'd strongly disapproved. I'd been overjoyed when she finally realized the man for her had adored her all along and that she loved him in return. That man was currently on a fishing trip with my own man and my father. I hoped they were catching plenty of fish.

"I realized what was what, eventually, and gave him the boot soon enough," Mimi said. "One too many instances of him asking me to get the rounds at the pub because someone who owed him money hadn't come across yet. Thus, I need a new flatmate. I don't suppose you're interested."

"No."

"What about you?" she asked Jayne.

"Just visiting," Jayne said.

"What's this news about Paul I didn't hear?"

"I'm sorry to have to tell you this," I said. "He died. Saturday night."

Mimi sucked in a breath. Her eyes filled with tears and she glanced away. "That's tough. We were finished, but I haven't completely forgotten we had some fun together. For the short time it lasted. Before I started noticing I was always the one picking up the bill and he was forgetting to send me his share of the rent money."

"Is that why you broke up?"

"Pretty much. I don't need freeloaders in my life. What happened?"

"It's likely he was murdered." I watched her face carefully and saw nothing but surprise mixed with sadness.

"That's horrible. In a bar brawl or a theft or something?"

"It might have been more personal than that. The police will be contacting everyone on his phone. You should give them a call before they do that."

"I will. Not that I can help or anything. He lived here for something like two months, but he never had friends round. I never met any of his mates." She shook her head. "Poor Paul. All that charm and nothing to show for it."

I let her have a few moments' silence, and then I said, "Did he ever talk to you about books?"

"Books? No. He told me he owned a bookshop. Made it sound like he had a national chain like Waterstones or something. I looked it up online. Just curious, like. One used bookshop. That's the shop he owned with you, right? Before you split. Wisely, if you want my opinion."

"That's right. We did envision having a chain but never mind that now. Did he bring books home from the shop? When he lived here with you?"

"No. I don't read much." She nodded toward the large-screen TV hanging on the wall. "Too much good stuff on telly these days. When I have the time to watch, which isn't often."

"What do you do for a living, if I may ask?"

"I'm a bartender. I work at the pub on the corner, you might have passed it on your way here."

"We did. Nice looking place."

"It's okay. Tourist trap mostly, so I get good tips. Speaking of which . . . I have to get ready. I start work at four today."

"Can I give you my number? In case you remember anything?"

"Sure. It's unlikely I will, though." She pulled out her phone, and we exchanged numbers in the way people do these days. Not scribblings on a scrap of paper. "Like I said, I never met any of Paul's mates, and I never went to his shop so I never met the people he worked with. I never even met his parents, but I gather they live not far away."

"I plan to pay a condolence call on them in the next day or two. If you like, I'll ask them to let you know what the arrangements are."

She nodded. "Thanks. I'd like that."

Jayne stepped away from the window. "Thank you for your time," she said.

I'd reached a dead end. I didn't know how I felt about that. On one hand, I was disappointed. I'd set about to try to find the book Paul wanted me to see, which I believed might lead to his killer. I owed Paul nothing at all, but I did grieve his death, and I wanted to do this one last thing, the one thing I could do for him. I did not care to find myself forced to give up the search.

On the other hand, I most certainly did not want to spend my valuable vacation time trying to follow Paul's trail through the rabbit warrens of the streets of London, as though I were Sherlock Holmes after the source of the goose that swallowed the Blue Carbuncle. Now I could return to the company of my family and friends. I might suggest Jayne and I invite Pippa and my mother to join us for tea one afternoon at a fancy hotel. After that, we could pop into the National Gallery or visit the Victoria and Albert to see some of my favorite pieces.

I was heading for the door, mentally planning a day of being nothing but a tourist in my own city, when Mimi said, "Come to think of it, there is one thing."

I turned around. "Yes?"

"I don't know anything I can tell you, but I can give you something."

"What?"

"When Paul moved out, he left a box here. He said he'd be back for it, but . . ." She shrugged. "I told him I'd give it to him when he paid me the back rent he owes. I never heard from him again."

"What's in it?"

"I had a quick peek. Junk mostly. Some books. Some stuff he brought from work, he said. Nothing I'm interested in. You can have it. This place is small enough. I don't need someone else's stuff cluttering it up."

Chapter Eleven

"This time I suggest we take a cab," I said to Jayne.

"Thank goodness for that."

We stood on the pavement outside Mimi's flat. As well as our shopping bags, we now had possession of a cardboard box. The box wasn't large or terribly heavy, and Mimi had carried it downstairs for us as our arms and hands were full.

"Paul seems to have a lackadaisical approach to his things," Jayne said. "He leaves them scattered all over London. Do you think this is the same box he left at Sophie's?"

"Unlikely. Sophie said clothes and a suitcase."

"Did you believe her, Gemma? About not knowing anything about Paul's life?"

"I did. She seemed honest, not holding anything back." I nudged the box with my foot. "Except for this, which she took her time remembering. I need to do my civic duty and give DI Patel a call. I'm surprised the police haven't yet spoken to the women in Paul's life." I tsked in disapproval.

"Maybe they've found a different trail and are following that one."

"Another reason to call her. If I'm wasting my time because an overly enthusiastic book collector did the deed and has confessed all, I'd like to know."

My phone buzzed with a text from Ryan. I opened WhatsApp to see a picture of a fishing stream. The sky was blue, the woods green with a touch of yellow, the clear water frothing as it bubbled over rocks and boulders. The message accompanying the picture said: *We've arrived. Fabulous hotel. Great river. U still alive?*

I handed Jayne my phone. "Take a picture." I picked up several of the shopping bags, arranged the rest around my feet, and struck a pose. Big smile, right shoulder forward, right leg extended, chin lifted, hair blowing in the breeze. Jayne snapped several shots before giving the phone back to me. I sent one of the pictures to Ryan. *Productive day.*

Ryan: $$$$$$$$$$
Me: *Got that right. Love U.*
Ryan: *Love you too.*

A black cab drove slowly down the street, its light on. I waved, and it pulled up to the curb. "I love London," Jayne said as we struggled to shove the box in, followed by our shopping, and then ourselves. "As easy to find a cab as a pub."

I gave the cabbie the Stanhope Gardens address, and we drove away. I glanced up at the second floor to see if Mimi was watching us, but the curtains didn't move and no one stood at the window.

Before we left Mimi's flat, I'd opened the box to have a quick peek inside, not wanting to bother if it was full of Paul's laundry or schoolbooks he hadn't yet thrown out. Instead, I saw a variety of computer and other electronic device cables, a couple of paperbacks in not-bad condition, a stapler, a box of staples and another of paper clips, a stack of what looked like bills, and a notebook. I hadn't yet opened the notebook. For all I knew, it contained Paul's grocery shopping list, but I wanted to take the time to read it carefully.

We fell out of the cab at Stanhope Gardens. I paid the driver, and we carried all our bags plus the box up the steps. I let us in and called, "We're here. Anyone home?" Not that I expected anyone, other than

Horace, to answer. Dad was on his fishing expedition with Ryan and Andy; Donald was escorting the Thompson parents around Sherlock Holmes's London; Mum was at work.

Horace wagged his stubby tail, and I gave him a good pat. "Why don't you put the kettle on," I said to Jayne, "while I take these bags upstairs. We can meet in the library and see what Father Christmas brought us as an early Christmas gift."

"Will do," she said.

My phone rang, showing an unfamiliar number. "Gemma Doyle," I said.

The message was short and to the point. "I'll be here." I hung up with a sigh.

"Something wrong?" Jayne asked. "Is everyone okay?"

"Nothing wrong. That's the airline. My suitcase will be here in about an hour."

"That's good news. Why do you look so disappointed?"

"I've just spent hundreds of pounds on new clothes I don't need anymore. And, may I remind you, everything we bought was in season so I paid full price."

"Doesn't matter. Your insurance will pay for it, so now you have all those lovely things for free."

"Insurance?"

"Your trip interruption insurance."

"There's such a thing as trip interruption insurance? They pay you to buy new clothes?"

"Don't tell me you're not insured for this trip, Gemma."

I grimaced. "I guess I forgot to look into that."

Jayne shook her head. "I don't know what I expected from the woman who doesn't know Superman's name, but sometimes you do surprise me."

"I know Superman's name. Kent Clark."

"Clark Kent."

"Right. That."

Muttering something about people who are too smart to navigate the practicalities of life, Jayne headed for the kitchen and the kettle. Horace followed her. I wouldn't consider Superman's name, whatever it might be, to be something one needs to know to get through a day, but I didn't call her back to argue. I just carried all my new, and now redundant, clothes up to my room. I could take them back to the shops and ask for a refund, but that would be too much time and bother. I did not feel like retracing our steps through London's shopping districts.

Clothes hung and shoes put away, face and hands washed, I got Paul's box and joined Jayne in the library. Later, I'd look into this trip interruption insurance. Just in case my things didn't make it home with me.

The library at Stanhope Gardens is Dad's room. Meaning it's furnished to his, rather than my mother's, taste. And his taste runs to blue. The carpet was a deep navy, the walls periwinkle, the bookshelves cobalt, the chairs upholstered in blues and whites. A genuine, original John Constable painting of some considerable value hung on the wall opposite the unlit fireplace, gently illuminated by a soft light mounted above. The painting was not blue, but rather a bucolic scene of the green English countryside featuring several cows oblivious to an approaching storm.

Jayne had arranged a proper tea tray with Mum's everyday Royal Doulton china. In true English fashion, she'd added a plate of biscuits. I put the box on the floor next to the couch and took a seat while Jayne poured.

I took a sip of my tea. Excellent. "We'll make a proper Englishwoman out of you yet."

"Need I remind you, Gemma, I own a tearoom?"

"Speaking of which, I should give Ashleigh a call. Find out how it's going."

"I spoke to Mikey last night. She said everything's under control at Mrs. Hudson's."

"Under control can mean a lot of things." My phone buzzed yet again. An incoming text from an unfamiliar number: *Gemma?*

The number had a Massachusetts area code so I replied: *I'm here. Who is this?*

Mrs. R

Mrs. Ramsbatten. My neighbor. Come to think of it, I'd never phoned her and we'd never texted. If we had something to discuss, we did it over tea on her front porch, in her vastly overstuffed front room, or across the garden gate.

The old-fashioned way.

Me: *Everything okay?*

Mrs. Ramsbatten: *Arthur not answering. Wanted to let you know I let the plumbers in. Hope that is all right?*

Mrs. Ramsbatten had a key to our house. When Uncle Arthur was away and I was busy at the shop, she would pop in during the day to care for the dogs.

Me: *Plumbers? Why?*

Mrs. R: *I saw water coming out your back door. Kitchen flooded. Broken pipe, plumbers say. They've cut the water and are working on it.*

I groaned. I didn't bother putting that into a text. As I was leaving for the airport, I noticed a small leak developing under the kitchen sink. I told Uncle Arthur to call a plumber, but he said he'd have a look at it first. No need to be spending money if he could fix it himself. I hadn't had time to argue and left the house. Uncle Arthur was no handyman, but for some reason he liked to try to fix things himself. Usually I was on hand to call the professionals for backup if—when—needed.

Me: *Much damage?*

Mrs. R: *Floor might need to be replaced. I have to say, Gemma, the house smells a great deal like a skunk has been in here. As does Violet.*

Me: *Thanks for the update.*

Mrs. R: *Hope you're having a wonderful time. I've always loved London.*

"Trouble?" Jayne asked.

"Uncle Arthur seems to have neglected to finish a minor bit of home maintenance." I called the store and Ashleigh answered. "Hey, Gemma. What's up?"

"Just checking in. Everything all right?"

"Yeah. We're good. Business has been steady." Her voice dropped. "You know what it's like when Arthur's working here. Every elderly widowed lady within a hundred-mile radius decides she wants to get her Christmas shopping done early. Everyone in their family will be getting books this year. After shopping, they go next door for tea so the tearoom's been busy too."

"Is he there now?"

"He is. His ankle's bothering him, he said, so he's taken a seat in the nook and is telling Mrs. Archibald and Mrs. Fernie about his adventures in the navy. I couldn't help but notice he was getting around just fine before Mrs. Archibald arrived with lemonade and her homemade sugar cookies. Straight from the oven, she says. Do you want to speak to him?"

"Probably better not. Can you tell him his attention is needed at the house. Immediately."

"Does this have anything to do with the kitchen sink?"

"What do you know about that?"

"He said there was a minor plumbing problem, but he fixed it."

"Not entirely." I hung up.

Jayne lifted one eyebrow in question. "Never mind," I said. "Okay, without further ado, let's see what we have in the box."

Jayne helped herself to a piece of shortbread and bit into it. Her eyes almost rolled back in her head. "My goodness, this cookie is good. Do you think your mom would give me the recipe?"

"She'd be happy to. If she knew it. My mother doesn't bake, but she does know the best places to shop."

We crouched on the floor next to the box. I lifted the flaps and we peered in. I suspect everyone has a box full of computer cables somewhere. In case they're needed again. Not that they ever are. I put the notebook to one side and sorted the other things first. The envelopes went into one pile. The paperback books, none of them new, went on another pile. The books were all modern thrillers, heavily dogeared. I checked the copyright pages, flipped through them and shook them in case something had been concealed between the pages, but found nothing. Something niggled at the back of my mind, but before I could grab it, Jayne said, "Any value in those books?"

"No. They're all mass market, and none of them are signed. Likely they're Paul's own reading material. As I recall, he was heavily into American spy stuff."

"No accounting for taste." Jayne sniffed in disapproval, and I chuckled.

The envelopes all bore the logos and addresses of banks, utility companies, credit card companies. I didn't need to open them to know they were bills, but I did anyway. Paul owed a lot of companies a lot of money.

Poor Paul. A substantial number of the envelopes hadn't been opened, although they were dated months ago.

"He was in serious financial straits," Jayne said.

I left the notebook until last. I sat on the couch and Jayne crowded next to me. The pages contained Paul's nearly illegible scribble. Names and telephone numbers, mostly men's names but a handful of women's. Many had dates next to them. The earliest date, the first entry in the book, was about two years ago. "At first guess," I said, "this is a list of potential customers."

"Don't you say you never guess?"

"Shorthand for an educated assumption in the absence of provable fact I will act upon until provable facts present themselves. Paul was selling used books. It is not unknown for rare first editions or books signed by important authors to be dropped off at a used bookstore along with all the other junk accumulated over the years. It would be logical for Paul to keep a list of people interested in buying such things if he came across them. Such as this one, Jean Hamilton, and this phone number. Next to the name Paul wrote ACD. That can only mean one thing."

"Sir Arthur Conan Doyle."

"It must. Here's a name with JA and a lot of plus signs. At another educated assumption that means Jane Austen and her contemporaries or similar authors."

"A first edition Jane Austen isn't going to show up at the bottom of a bunch of moldy books out of Grandma's attic."

"You'd be surprised, Jayne. It can happen. Not often, but it does."

Some of the names were crossed out. By which I guessed (that word again) the client was no longer interested in whatever Paul might come across.

I flipped a few pages. I had nowhere to go with this. A list of names and telephone numbers. I couldn't start making calls and asking whoever answered, "Did you kill Paul Erikson for possession of a rare and valuable book?" All I could do was hand the notebook and the box to DI Patel. Which reminded me that I intended to call her, but I still hadn't.

I turned a page. A familiar name leapt out at me. *John Saint-Jean*. "There's a name we know." I tapped the page with my forefinger.

"Isn't he the guy we met the last time we were here? The one who found your grandparents' long-lost painting?"

We both looked at the picture hanging in pride of place on the library wall. The Constable landscape.

"The very one," I said.

Jayne indicated the initials next to the name on the page. "What's IF mean, do you think? *If* something shows up, he wants to know? If what?"

I quickly sorted through my mental database of authors' initials. "Ian Fleming, quite likely. That would suit Sir John. James Bond. 007. MI6. British spy stuff and all that. Considering we have Sir John's acquaintance, as Jane Austen would say, I suggest we pay him a call."

"Must we? I'm beat and still feeling jet-lagged."

"I wasn't going to suggest we go now. He might not be in. If you don't mind, I'd prefer to take Grant in any event. Grant met him on that other occasion, and Grant's better placed to talk about books than you are. No offence intended."

"None taken. Speaking of Grant, he's trying to make a name for himself here in London as a book dealer. Shouldn't he have known Paul?"

"It's possible their paths never crossed. Grant deals in the major collectable stuff, and Paul handled," I pointed at the stack of paperbacks, some of them showing signs of damp, "stuff that sells by the pound. Weight, not money. But maybe I should involve Grant more. I can ask him to put out feelers in an attempt to find out if there was any indication as to what Paul might have come across. The book he wanted me to see."

"Grant's on his honeymoon, Gemma."

"Technically not. Pippa's at work. They're going to try for an actual vacationing honeymoon in the next couple of weeks."

I turned my attention back to the notebook. On the last page, one other name leapt out at me. "Here's another person I know. Alistair Denhaugh."

"Who's that?"

"The eighth Earl of Ramshaw. A cousin of my mother. You met him, along with his wife and son, at the wedding."

"Yes, I did. And I was highly annoyed at you because you never told me your mother's a genuine member of the aristocracy."

"Because she's not. Her second cousin once removed is. Or first cousin twice removed; I sometimes forget. If everyone who was distantly related to someone with a title was nobility, that would consist of almost the entire population of the British Isles. I'm not entirely sure why they were invited to the wedding; I don't remember having much contact with them when I was growing up. Which is beside the point because I now have another name to call upon. The game, my dear Jayne, is once again—"

"Afoot. Yes, I know. There aren't any initials next to that name. Do you suppose that means he'll buy anything, or that Paul recorded the name for another reason?"

"No way of telling. Not yet. Before I do anything else, I fear I need to check in with DI Patel."

"Why is that a bad thing?"

"It is my experience that the police don't like civilian interference. I will argue that I haven't interfered. I only wanted to express my condolences to the women with whom Paul has previously been involved. If they tell me things," I nodded at the box, "or give me things they don't have room for, that's not my fault." I pulled out my phone. "But first—"

"First?"

"She'll take this box and its contents as evidence. I want a record of the pages of the notebook for my own use." I began taking pictures of each page while Jayne collected the tea things.

"Should we have worn gloves checking through this stuff?" Jayne asked me as she lifted the laden tray. Between us, we'd finished off the shortbread.

"I considered it but decided not to. If I have to use the sentimental excuse for my possession of the last of my late ex-husband's possessions, having taken care not to leave evidence of my presence might look a touch suspicious."

"I'll clean up in the kitchen, and then I want to give Andy a call. See how he's getting on."

Once I finished photographing the notebook, I called the number on the card DI Patel had given me. She answered almost immediately.

"Good afternoon," I said cheerfully. "Gemma Doyle here."

"I was about to pay you a visit, Ms. Doyle. I'm not entirely thrilled to find that I'm following in your footsteps."

"You are? I mean, good to know you were able to contact Paul's . . . female friends."

"Both of whom told me you'd spoken to them already. You had lunch with Sophie Erikson and then dropped in on Mimi Reid."

"Which is why I'm calling. To pass on information I learned from them."

"You took a box from Reid's flat."

"For sentimental reasons only."

"You expect me to believe that? Where are you now?"

"My parents' home in Stanhope Gardens."

"I'm sending a car around to get this box."

Just then the doorbell rang. For a moment I thought the Metropolitan Police might have begun using *Star Trek*-style transporters to avoid the notorious London traffic.

From the kitchen Jayne called, "I'll get it." I heard the click of Horace's nails on the hallway tiles as he hurried to beat her to the door.

"I'll have the car pick you up too," Patel said. "I want to know what else you've been up to today."

I heard the front door open and Jayne say thank you. Horace barked. A suitcase rattled into the house, and the door was closed. My possessions had arrived.

"I've been up to nothing," I said. "My marriage to Paul ended, but we held no ill will toward each other. Sophie was also married to Paul at one time, and I wanted to express my condolences to her. She told me about Paul's latest girlfriend, Mimi Reid, so I did the same with her."

"Sophie tells me Paul left you for her, and you were extremely bitter about that."

"Sophie might say a lot of things. Doesn't mean they're true. I was glad to be rid of him. Both romantically and financially. I've been living in America for the past seven years. I have a new, and far better, relationship there and a successful business. Two successful businesses."

"You own a Sherlock Holmes themed bookshop."

"That is correct."

"Do you fancy yourself some sort of Sherlock Holmes imitation?"

"Most certainly not."

"Do you still have any involvement in the Trafalgar Square shop? Own any shares or anything like that?"

"None. Paul bought me out completely, for a fair price. I didn't even know the shop was still in business until this week. I thought he'd sold it. That he hadn't should tell you how little I cared."

"Yet you were in that very shop yesterday at noon."

"I explained how that came about."

"I'd like to hear it again."

"I'm sure you're very busy, DI Patel. The first forty-eight hours of a case are the most critical. Or so my father, the ex-DCS, tells me. I have the box, and I'm happy to hand it over."

"You have no choice in the matter."

"Always glad of the opportunity to be of assistance. If I'm not here when your officer arrives, my friend Jayne will give it to them. Oh, one more thing. Naturally Jayne and I had a casual look through the contents of the box, so you might find our fingerprints on some of the items. You have my prints on file because of the previous case. Jayne's can be found at the West London PD. She was printed once after a serious incident at her place of business. That's Jayne with a Y, Wilson, as in . . . Wilson."

"Ms. Doyle, I must insist—"

"I hear a key in the lock. That will be my mother, Anne Doyle, the prominent Inns of Court barrister arriving home. She is a silk, by the way. Give me a call if you need anything else." I hung up.

I hadn't been lying when I said I'd heard my mother, as she was now calling, "Horace, do get down. No, Henry isn't here. You'll have to put up with me in the interim." Horace was actually my father's dog. My mother was allergic, so we'd never had pets when I was a child. After retiring, my father not-very-casually suggested he'd love a canine companion for his "long lonely days alone at home," and Mum gave in, provided the dog was hypoallergenic and stayed off the beds and the furniture.

I also hadn't been lying that Mum was a barrister—a trial lawyer—and a silk. That's a fancy word for a senior lawyer. Those so honored get to wear a nicer robe in court than their unhonored fellows.

Mum and Jayne came into the library. "I see your suitcase showed up," Mum said.

"Do you buy baggage insurance when you fly?" I asked. "In case it gets lost or is late arriving?"

"Always. No sensible person would travel without insurance these days."

"Can I get you a cup of tea, Anne?" Jayne asked, smothering a snicker.

Mum dropped into a chair. "How lovely to be served in my own home. It's after four, so a glass of wine would be nice. It's just us girls tonight. What would you like to do for dinner?"

"We can go out," I said. "Someplace casual."

"Sounds good," Mum said.

"Haven't you two forgotten someone?" Jayne said.

"Who?"

"Donald. Have you heard from Donald? He might be back soon."

"Oh, yes. Donald." I sent our friend a quick text: *We're at the house. Going out for dinner later. You?*

"Can I get you some wine too, Gemma?" Jayne said.

"That would be great. Thanks. How did your court case go?" I asked my mother.

She beamed. "Exceptionally well. I was arguing for the defense. I scarcely had to say a word. The prime witness for the prosecution admitted that he was owed a considerable amount of money by the accused and he might not have actually seen the accused in the area where the assault took place. But if he hadn't seen the accused with his own eyes, that didn't mean the accused wasn't there."

"Gosh." Jayne passed the drinks around. "Does that happen often?"

"That the chief witness completely contradicts his or her testimony on the stand? Sometimes they get nervous at the sworn testimony concept, but the opposing barrister usually does a better job of ensuring their witness knows what they're talking about before wasting court time." She laughed to herself and lifted her glass. "Cheers."

The doorbell rang once more. "That might be the police here for the box," I said. "Can you take it to them, Jayne. If they ask for me, I'm not here."

"You want me to lie to the police?"

"Something along the lines of temporarily unavailable. Which, considering I don't want to have to abandon this glass of wine, is true."

"Good thing I'm not giving sworn testimony," Jayne muttered as she got to her feet and gathered up the box.

My mother raised one expressive eyebrow at me. "Productive day, dear?"

"Productive enough I don't want to have to go over it in detail down at the police station. I made a few discreet inquiries as to the recent activities of Paul Erikson. I didn't learn anything significant, and nothing the police can't find out for themselves if they ask the right questions."

Jayne returned. She handed me a piece of paper, dropped onto the couch, and picked up her wine glass. "That's a receipt for the box. He did not ask for you."

"Do you have any contacts at UCL, Mum?"

"I keep in touch with Margaret Slaughter, who's still a professor there. You might remember them, from next door but one."

"Sadly, yes. They had a horrible boy. A bully through and through. He hated me, and the feeling was returned. What was his name? Geoffrey. Which of His Majesty's prisons is he currently doing time in?"

"He's currently serving in His Majesty's Royal Navy. First officer on a nuclear submarine."

"We're all doomed," I said.

"Margaret and her husband moved once the children left home. She teaches in the department of English literature at UCL."

"Does she now? How terribly convenient."

"I doubt she teaches Sherlock Holmes. Margaret would consider that to be far too low-brow."

"I need the contact information of a student. Do you think she'd provide it for me?"

"I do not. What student and why?"

"Tamara O'Riordan who worked at the bookshop. I believe she's a student at UCL, and most likely taking English literature, judging by the contents of her backpack."

"How do you know what was in her backpack?" asked the prominent trial lawyer.

"Don't ask. Her contact info will obviously be in Paul's employment records, which are kept in his office, to which I do not have access. I could always break in, but I'd prefer not to as the place remains under police surveillance."

"It's the twenty-first century, Gemma," Jayne said. "She's bound to be on social media."

"I have checked that, yes. She has a presence on Facebook and a couple of other sites, but she hasn't used them much lately, and she keeps her accounts set to private. Many people would be eager to tell everyone about the drama around the police arriving at their work, but nothing from Tamara. At least, nothing I can see. I've sent her a couple of messages asking her to get in touch, but many people don't see direct messages from people not in their contact list. I'll keep working on that, but I don't have a lot of time. I could try to hack into the shop's computer in search of her phone number. It's entirely possible, likely even, Paul hasn't changed any of the passwords since I set them up."

"Was he computer literate?" Jayne asked.

"Not particularly. Not at all, come to think of it. Thus the password not changing issue."

"In that case, he would have hired a company or individual to update and maintain the store's accounts and web page. Technology has changed a lot over the last seven years. No matter how illiterate he might have been, no publishers or book distributers will agree to do business on paper and mailing stuff back and forth these days. They'd insist on it all being online and secure. Same for his tax accountants and bookkeepers, I'd imagine."

"That's true," I said. "As we know from our own businesses. Meaning, I could still hack in, but it would take me some time and I might leave a trail, inadvertently of course, for the police techs to follow. If they were so inclined. Margaret Slaughter, Mum?"

"I'll give her a call and ask. I suspect she'll only agree to pass on your phone number to this woman, and she can then ring you if she wants."

"That'll work," I said.

My phone pinged to tell me I had a text.

> Donald: *Brilliant day! On my way to house now. So much to talk about! Linda and Roger gone to Grant and Pippa.*

"Donald will be joining us for dinner," I said.

Mum stood up. "Horace needs a walk. That is never my responsibility, so take care of that, please, Gemma. I'll call Margaret now, and after that I have about an hour's work to put in. Then I'll be ready for dinner. You two decide where you'd like to go. Anything is fine, but I am in the mood for Italian. Choose someplace we can walk to. I'd like to stretch my legs later." She left the room, taking her wine glass with her.

"She is so much like you, Gemma," Jayne said. "Or, I suppose I should say, you are so much like your mom."

"In what way?"

"Dinner choice is entirely up to us, as long as it's Italian and in a mile radius of this house."

Nothing I could say in response to that, so I didn't. "Feel like a walk?"

"No. I'm going to lie down for an hour. If I fall asleep, wake me up when it's time to go out. Have fun."

Horace leapt to his feet the moment he heard the magic word "walk." He looked at me with a hopeful expression I recognized from my own dogs. "Okay," I said. "Let's go."

He ran out of the library at top speed.

I followed at less than top speed.

At five thirty on a Monday, the mews of South Kensington were busy with people returning from work or school. Rather than stroll down the pavements, I took Horace to the enclosed private garden on the opposite side of the street from the house and unlocked the gate. The sounds of a crowded city fell away almost instantly. The flower beds had been turned over in preparation for winter. Most of the big old trees were still in leaf, although a few of the branches were turning and a scattering of dull yellow leaves dusted the ground. An elderly gentleman walking an equally elderly black lab was heading our way. "Horace," he (the man, not the dog) exclaimed. The dog lifted his ears and his tail twitched in recognition.

"Good evening," I said.

"If that is Horace with you, young lady, you must be visiting Anne and Henry. I know they have visitors from America here for their daughter's wedding. As you are obviously English and not American, and you look very much like Anne, particularly the hair, I will assume you are one of the daughters. As you are not Pippa, whom I have met on more than one occasion, you must be Gemma." His eyes twinkled.

"Nicely deduced," I said.

They walked on and so did we.

We didn't get far before my phone rang, showing an unfamiliar number. "Gemma Doyle here."

"Hi, Gemma. It's Tamara. You wanted to talk to me."

"Thanks for calling me back so promptly."

The ubiquitous nature of mobile phones these days presents some problems to the consulting detective. Not that I am a consulting detective, nor do I want to be. Mobile numbers are not recorded in a publicly available database as landlines are. People can see who's calling and decide not to answer. Because of the amount of spam calls and the availability of voicemail, a great many people never answer a number they don't recognize.

On the other hand, now that people carry their phones with them everywhere, they are always contactable. Anyplace and anytime.

"I took first year's Introduction to the Romantics course from Professor Slaughter. That was ten years ago, but I still live in fear of incurring her displeasure," Tamara said.

"I understand. Reminds me of a certain headmistress at my old school."

"I assume you're calling about the bookshop. Far as I know, it's still closed. Are you thinking of taking it over when it can open again?"

"Me? Goodness, no. I rather doubt it will ever reopen."

"That's what I was expecting, but I can't say I'm not disappointed. I need the job, but what can you do? It was just a job. For me, anyway."

I watched Horace sniff at the base of a park bench. Judging by the amount of attention he was paying to it, he'd found something of enormous interest there. "I'd like to talk to you about recent goings-on at the bookshop. Do you have time this evening?"

"Absolutely and totally not. I have a seminar to give tomorrow, and I am way behind in my prep. The police have called on me a couple of times and completely threw my schedule, not to mention my attention span, off."

"Seminar to give? Are you a graduate student?"

"I'm a PhD candidate."

"In English literature?"

"Yup. My dissertation is on subversive feminist influences by male authors in Victorian literature."

"There were subversive feminist influences by male authors in Victorian literature?"

"Believe it or not, yes. Sadly overlooked until recently, but not entirely sadly as it's given me a fresh field of research. I could talk to you about that forever, but now is not the time."

"What about tomorrow? Would you have time to meet with me tomorrow? Not to discuss subversive feminist literature, but Paul Erikson."

She lowered her voice and a tinge of apprehension crept in. "Why are you asking? You've been divorced from him for a long time, right?"

"Have the police said anything to you about cause of death?"

"I know they're regarding it as suspicious."

"That would appear to be the case. As for why . . . I can't always explain, Tamara, but I sometimes find that I can be of help to the police in these matters."

"What are you, some sort of Sherlock Holmes?" She laughed heartily.

"If you're ever interested in feminist influences on Sherlock Holmes," I said, "I can recommend a few good books."

"I considered doing my thesis specifically on him at one time, but that's a very crowded field."

"So it is. Did you have anything to tell the police?"

"Not really. Look, I'm sorry, but I have to go. I do have a lot of work to get done tonight."

"How about tomorrow? I can meet you anywhere. Any time."

She was silent for a few seconds. "Okay. My seminar's at ten. If I'm not finished my prep tonight, I'll kill myself. Just kidding. We can do breakfast. I get off the tube at Warren Street station and there's a place I like near there. Say eight o'clock. I'm out of a job, remember, so you're buying. I don't suppose you know who's going to pay me for last week?"

"See you tomorrow." I hung up.

"Most satisfactory," I said to Horace. If anything underhanded had been going on at Trafalgar Fine Books, the people most likely to know about it were the staff. Shop clerks spend a good part of their day just watching. Watching people browse, waiting until customers indicate they need assistance. Watching people who might have an eye to selecting something and leaving without bothering about the minor matter of payment. Watching the boss and their fellow employees for gossip-worthy tidbits.

Some employees, as I well know from years of owning a shop, don't pay much attention to anyone or anything, unless the customer coughs in their face for attention. Faye, for example, had been filling in her time while searching for a suitable husband for her "spinster" daughter. Tamara, younger, probably smarter, would have been on the lookout for something to occupy her mind while she spent what could be a long, boring day.

Horace and I arrived back at the house as a black cab was pulling up, and Donald leapt out. He wore a Harris tweed jacket over a brown vest and was carrying his sturdy black umbrella. He had a self-satisfied glow indicating he'd had a marvelous time. I sincerely hoped Linda and Roger Thompson had similarly enjoyed their tour of Holmes's London. Donald's enthusiasm can get the better of the unwary at times.

"Good timing," I said. "Did you have a nice day?"

"It never ceases to amaze me," he said in his newfound London accent, "how, despite believing I know everything there is to know about the Great Detective and his creator, I can always learn more."

"I hope Linda and Roger enjoyed themselves."

"Oh, yes. They did. I believe I quite tuckered them out. I suggested dinner at the Sherlock Holmes Pub, but they wanted to get back. Jet lag, you know. It effects some people adversely." He bounded up the stairs. "The most exciting thing has happened."

"What might that be?" I asked as I let us into the house. I undid Horace's leash and he wandered off in search of water and attention.

"I have an invitation to lunch tomorrow with none other than members of the Sherlock Holmes Society of London. We're going to the Langham Hotel, an important place in Sir Arthur's literary life. Grant arranged it. He has their acquaintance—"

"As Jane Austen might say."

"Exactly! He has their acquaintance through his book dealing. He purchased some first editions of the Canon in excellent condition and is looking for buyers. I would dearly love to have possession of even one of them, but . . ." His voice trailed away.

"But," I said, "you can be satisfied knowing they are loved and enjoyed and cared for."

"Exactly!" he said again.

"Is Grant joining you for this lunch?"

"I don't believe so."

My mother descended the stairs. She'd changed out of her court suit into cream trousers and a navy blouse with a thin white belt. "All finished for the day. I rang Margaret and gave her your message, dear."

"Thanks. Tamara called me already."

"That was fast. She must have been keen to talk to you."

"People can rarely resist when they're caught up even peripherally in a police investigation."

"Did you and Jayne decide on someplace nice to go for dinner?"

"We thought Italian, and as it's a nice evening, we can walk."

"What a good idea," Mum said. "Donald, I hope you'll join us."

"Thank you. I'd love to. Are you scheduled to be in court tomorrow, Anne? I'd like to sit in and observe, if I may."

"My case wrapped up sooner than expected, so no. Tell me, Donald, when you were practicing—"

I ran upstairs and tapped lightly on the door of Jayne and Andy's room. "Wha . . ." said a muffled voice.

"Dinner time. You don't have to get up, if you don't want to."

"Gosh no. I don't want to be left behind. Wait for me. Be right there."

While I waited by the front door for the others, I called Grant. "If I can tear you away from your marital bliss, I'd like your company tomorrow."

"In terms of marital bliss, I'm free. My wife—such a nice word—has an important meeting all day tomorrow. Something about the uncertain situation that has arisen in the South China Sea and the necessity of briefing the minister. I suspect that doesn't involve going to church, does it?"

"It does not. Grant?"

"Yes?"

"I don't think you're supposed to tell anyone what Pippa lets slip." Never before, in all her life, had Pippa likely let anything slip. Marriage was making her soft. I smiled at the thought.

"Not even you?"

"Not even me. Did your parents enjoy their day?"

"I don't know. They walked through the door like a couple of zombies and went straight to their room, saying they didn't want dinner. My mother might have mumbled something along the lines of if she never heard the word 'Holmes' again, it would be too soon. What's on tomorrow?"

"I need your book collector knowledge. This time I'm going to phone ahead to ensure our subject is available. Any time you are not?"

"At your service, madam."

"I have someplace to be in the morning, so I'll try to set this meeting up for noon. I'll let you know when it's confirmed."

Chapter Twelve

Jayne, Donald, and I joined the commuting hordes the following morning. Over dinner last night, I'd told Jayne she didn't need to come with me, and she should take advantage of the opportunity for a lie-in. She'd shaken her head firmly. "Ryan told me I'm to look after you."

I rolled my eyes. "Are you going to be my close protection officer? I don't know if you're quite up to the part, Jayne."

"Jayne might not be," Donald interrupted as he twirled long strands of pasta onto his fork, "therefore I will assume the role. You may remember whom it was who brought down the miscreant when we were last in this fair city." He glanced lovingly at the umbrella he'd been carrying all day, even though the expected rain had vanished from the weather forecast.

"He's got you there." Jayne speared a scallop.

"I don't know if I care for this talk about bodyguards and fighting with criminals," my mother said. "I found it difficult enough when your father was on active duty, particularly in the early days."

"I'm asking questions," I said. "Nothing more. In pleasant surroundings of higher learning."

My mother hadn't looked entirely mollified but she turned the conversation to other topics.

* * *

"I need you two to sit at another table," I said to Jayne and Donald the next morning as we approached the café Tamara suggested for our meeting.

"Why?" Jayne said.

"So it won't look like three against one." I had to admit my companions didn't look at all imposing. Jayne, all bouncy and blonde; Donald, balding and nearsighted, wearing Harris tweed and swirling his brolly like Patrick Macnee in *The Avengers*. I had no doubt Tamara could hold her own, conversationally speaking, against us, but I didn't want her to feel as though she were being interrogated.

Fortunately, this meeting wasn't going to amount to another attack on my credit card. We were meeting in a typical London workers' café. Pleasant, clean surroundings, long line waiting for takeaway drinks. Plain wooden tables and chairs. Men in construction vests and heavy boots, others in business suits. The welcome scents of hot grease and strong tea.

Donald rubbed his hands together in glee. "Exactly like Speedy's Café," he said, referring to a location from the Benedict Cumberbatch show *Sherlock*. "Don't know if I mentioned we went there yesterday as part of the tour."

"More than once," I said. "You two take a table, and I'll sit there, by the window."

We separated. I took a seat at a table for two, facing the door. I drummed my fingers on the table top.

"What can I get you, love?" the waitress asked me. She was in her late fifties, and at five to eight in the morning, she looked as though she'd already put in a long, hard day.

"Tea for now, please. I'm waiting for a friend."

She left and next called on Jayne and Donald. Donald asked a lot of questions as the waitress shifted her tired feet. He eventually settled on a bacon buttie and tea. Jayne asked for poached eggs, toast, and coffee.

I stared out the window, watching the passing traffic. I'd called Ryan last night when we got back from dinner, and we talked for a long time. I'd been pleased at the pleasure in his voice as he described his day. I told him, truthfully, that all I'd been doing, aside from unnecessary shopping, was talking to people who'd known Paul. I had come to no conclusions, and the police had not issued a warrant for my arrest for interfering in their investigation. Not yet anyway.

It was too early in West London to call Ashleigh or Uncle Arthur for an update on the dogs and the shop. As for the plumbing situation, I preferred not to know.

I was starting to get restless by eight fifteen, worried this was going to be a wasted trip, when I saw Tamara O'Riordan hurrying down the street. She looked harried. Hair uncombed, shirt half untucked, the laces of one black boot trailing behind her. She came into the café, saw me, and dropped into the chair opposite with a sharp exhale. "Sorry I'm late. My mum called as I was leaving, and I unadvisedly answered. She can be hard to get off the phone."

"Did you get your seminar prep finished?"

"Yeah. Finally. Those silly students don't know what's going to hit them. They seem to get younger every year."

The waitress appeared. Tamara ordered tea and the full English, and I asked for one poached egg and toast.

"How's your dissertation going?" I've been told on more than one occasion (thank you, Jayne) that I can sometimes be too direct, so I attempted to open the conversation on a friendly, informal note. Across the room, Donald was almost falling out of his chair as he tried to listen in. Unfortunately for him, the table between us had been taken by four men wearing construction overalls, safety vests, and steel-toed boots, all of whom talked a great deal and in booming voices. Every time the door opened, a wave of sound washed in from the busy street.

"It's up. It's down," Tamara said. "Some days are better than others. I'm thirty-five and my parents are constantly on my case about when I'm going to get a proper job and get married and have kids and all the rest. Such was the topic of our conversation this morning. Bad enough I'm working on a PhD, but Mum wonders why I can't study something more useful than Victorian literature."

I smiled at her. "I quite understand." My father had been a senior police officer. My mother's a barrister. My sister . . . I don't quite know what my sister does except that she seems to run the British government single-handedly. When I announced that, rather than climbing the ladder in the civil service job my sister found for me, I was planning to marry Paul and we were opening a bookshop, the parental disapproval had been obvious. Perhaps not expressed as forthrightly as by Tamara's mother, but it had been there, nonetheless.

"Enough of my problems. You want to ask me about Paul and the shop. Shoot." She leaned back to allow the waitress to put our plates in front of us.

"You said you worked at the bookshop for—"

"Don't look now," Tamara said, "but that man over there. The guy in the silly jacket with the umbrella. He's paying a lot of attention to us."

I didn't need to "not look" to know who she was talking about. Donald and Jayne had finished their breakfasts and were trying to delay their departure by asking for more tea and coffee.

"MI5," I said.

Tamara's eyes opened wide. "You're kidding. The woman with him looks like she might have popped in for breakfast after dropping the kids at school, but he stands out as much as if he were wearing a clown suit and carrying a bunch of balloons."

"I am kidding," I said. "They're my American friends. Trying to look unobtrusive while you and I chat."

"Weird." She dug eagerly into her black pudding. "I recognize the guy now. He was with you on Sunday. What do you want to know?"

"I can't truly say. I'm fishing, if you want to put it like that. You worked at the shop. I suspect business wasn't all that brisk."

"That's an understatement. I don't know how Paul managed to pay the rent."

Judging by the increasingly strident note of the bills I'd found stuffed into a cardboard box, he hadn't paid the rent for a long time. "You're smart, you're observant." I added a drop of jam to my toast and took a nibble.

"Flattery will get you everywhere. Feel free to lay it on."

"You likely bore easily, which leads me to conclude you spent much of the working day watching everything that went on in the shop."

"I managed to get a lot of work done in my head, which I can remember and transmit to print when I get to a computer, so I didn't spend as much time listening at office doors as you might expect. Occasionally a book would come in along with a pile of the regular used junk, one I'd been looking for or I realized I could use. But yeah, I did some watching and listening."

"And?"

"And, I started there about eighteen months ago. At first, it was a regular bookshop struggling to stay alive. Paul was always coming up with bright ideas as to how to make the shop a success, but I soon learned to ignore him. Either the idea was impractical, or he didn't have the commitment to see it through."

"You're aware Paul and I divorced because he began seeing a shop clerk. Did he have any entanglements while you worked there?"

"No. He didn't try anything on me. Not his type maybe." She laughed. "Or he knew that would be a waste of time. When Faye first started there, she dropped not very subtle suggestions about her unmarried daughter. She eventually got the hint and said no more. I never met her daughter, but I felt sorry for her. As far as Faye's concerned, the sun orbits around her son and grandchild and the daughter's pretty much an afterthought. If that. She never stops talking about the fancy school her son went to and his degree from Oxford. Anyway, Paul didn't talk about his private life. Not at all. I didn't know if he was seeing anyone or not. As for the other staff at the store. I can't say for sure, but I can say for sure I never noticed anything between them."

She dragged a piece of toast through a smear of the runny yoke, all that remained of her two fried eggs.

"You said *at first* it was a regular bookshop. Does that mean that later things happened?"

She popped the last of her toast into her mouth, put down her fork, and looked at me. "I only worked there, right? Three days a week, and not once did I ever give the place another thought once I'd walked out the door. But I'll admit I've been thinking about it, considering what happened to Paul. Recently, a couple of times over the last few weeks, two men came in and asked for Paul. They didn't look like the sort to be in search of a good book, if you take my meaning."

Faye had told me much the same. About tough faces and East End accents.

"Not," Tamara said, "that I ever want to judge anyone by the way they look. But these blokes didn't even glance at the books. They barely glanced at me either, and I don't think I'm a total dog. If Paul wasn't in, they came back. If he was in, they went into his office, without asking if he could see them, and shut the door. I heard nothing like screams or threats being made. They came out, politely said goodbye, and left."

"The same men every time?"

"Yes. Two of them. Big blokes, short hair, thick necks. Not shabbily dressed, but you got the feeling they weren't . . . people you wanted to cross."

"You have no idea why they were interested in Paul?"

"I totally have an idea. He owed money to people he shouldn't have borrowed from. In my limited spare time, I read police novels. Don't you?"

"That would seem the most obvious conclusion. Did you tell the police this?"

"I did. They sat me down to help them make one of those sketches like I've seen on telly. They do it on a computer these days, but it's still fun. I don't think my description was worth much. They wore caps and loose jackets and didn't have anything out of the ordinary to help identify them like eye patches or scars on their faces."

I'd noticed several CCTV cameras in the vicinity of the shop, but I hadn't seen anything pointed directly at the door so as to observe who entered the bookshop and when. The police would have gone through the available footage looking for these men. Difficult to match thousands of images with a vague description such as provided by Tamara. If they were professionals, they would know how to avoid the cameras, such as wearing caps pulled low and loose jackets with high collars.

"Saturday night, Paul told me he'd come into possession of a rare book he wanted me to see. Do you have any idea what it might have been?"

Tamara shook her head. "Not a clue. We didn't deal in rare books. We got fifty or seventy-five quid now and again for something someone wanted to add to their collection, but nothing of any real value. Not that I knew of anyway, and there's no reason I should if he was dealing in that stuff without going through the front of the shop. Your friend is tapping his watch. I think he's trying to tell you he wants to go."

I avoided looking at Donald. Some undercover agent he'd make.

Tamara pushed back her chair. "I have to go. Thanks for the breakfast. If you hear anything about funeral arrangements, can you let me know? I didn't know Paul all that well on a personal level, but he was nice enough to me."

"I will. Thanks for meeting me."

She left. I poured myself a fresh cup of tea, added a splash of milk, and stirred. Did I believe Tamara? It's possible she killed Paul and stole the rare book, but I didn't think so. It's possible she killed him for other reasons and the book simply couldn't be found, but again, I didn't think so. She was a university student, struggling to get her PhD before she reached retirement age. As I've learned, almost anyone can be a killer, if the stakes are high enough, but in this case, unless she was an actress of considerable skill, I didn't think she held any strong feelings toward her late employer, certainly nothing to bring her to murder. She did, however, work with books and she studied literature so she was in a position to know what might be of value if it accidentally crossed her path. She was short of money, but judging by the way she dressed and the bag she carried, she wasn't destitute. Just a normal, thirtysomething PhD candidate picking up odd jobs to get by. I'd done a quick internet search on her last night, and nothing raised any alarm bells for me. Lived in London most of her life. Bachelor of Arts from University College London, master's from Northumbria, back to UCL for her PhD. O'Riordan is not an uncommon name in London, and without the names of her parents, I couldn't do much to trace her family connections. Maybe they were heavily into organized crime.

Unlikely, but if that was the case, the police would find the link.

Leaving me to concentrate on more personal angles.

I stood up. "Are we done here?" I called to Jayne and Donald. They gathered their things and scrambled to their feet.

"Learn anything?" Jayne asked as we left the café.

"I learned a negative, which is sometimes almost as valuable as a positive."

"Huh?"

"Tamara herself had little to nothing to do with Paul. Either his life or his death. I did learn one thing that was not entirely surprising but still of interest. He may have borrowed from people who wanted their money back."

"As in criminal gangs?" Donald asked.

"As in. If he came into possession of a rare or otherwise valuable book, he might have borrowed against it in expectation of paying the money back after making a good sale. If, for some reason, that sale didn't happen . . ."

"He was up the creek without a paddle," Jayne said.

"Precisely."

We stood at the entrance to the tube station as a river of people flowed around us.

"I'm meeting Grant at quarter to eleven," I said. "Donald, you have your lunch with the Sherlock group. Do you know the way?"

He tapped his jacket pocket. "I have detailed directions right here and the address is in the map on my phone, should the directions fail. Which, considering they were given to me by devoted Sherlockians, in his very city, I do not expect they will."

"Jayne, do you have anything planned for the rest of the day?"

I'd phoned Sir John Saint-Jean last night and arranged a time for Grant and me to call on him this morning. I didn't want to show up with an entourage. Not that Sir John was likely to be intimidated by Jayne. Unlikely he was ever intimidated by anyone.

"If you don't mind, Gemma, if you'll be with Grant, and if it's okay, I'd like to see some of the things I missed the other time we were here. Like the Victoria and Albert or the London Museum. Your mom told me she's in her chambers today. That means the office, right?"

I nodded.

"She's in all day, so she suggested that if I was free in the afternoon I give her a call and we'd meet for tea. If you need me though . . ." her voice trailed off.

"You go and enjoy yourself. You are supposed to be on vacation. Grant can assume the role of my bodyguard."

Jayne tried not to look too pleased. I felt a pang of guilt. My friends, Jayne most of all, were so loyal to me, and on more than one occasion, I'd dragged them unwittingly into situations that verged on the dangerous. I gave her a spontaneous hug. Donald joined in. A most un-English display.

I pulled away and the three of us entered the tube station together before going our separate ways.

Chapter Thirteen

My train was packed, every seat taken, so I held on to the pole, and as we bumped and swayed and I tried to keep my footing during the turns, I recalled what I knew about Sir John Saint-Jean.

The title was inherited along with an estate and a substantial amount of family money. He hadn't let that stand in the way of doing what he wanted in life, and he'd joined the Royal Army to become part of SAS, the elite strike unit, where he served with considerable distinction. The first time I met him, I'd taken him for a gang enforcer: short but powerfully built, with a bullet-shaped head, no hair, a tattoo of an eagle reaching up out of his shirt collar, claws stretching across his neck. I am rarely wrong in my first impressions, but on that occasion, I had been seriously off. To be fair (to me) he'd deliberately given me that impression, putting on a tough working-class accent and a "don't you dare mess with me, mate" demeanor.

He lived in an extremely handsome house in St. John's Wood, complete with a butler who seemed to be able to move through walls, a substantial book collection, and excellent art, mostly the old masters. He knew Pippa on a professional basis, although neither of them would tell me what that basis was.

I left the train at Marble Arch station and found Grant waiting for me by the street entrance as arranged. He slipped his phone into his pocket when he saw me making my way through the crowds toward him.

"Did your parents catch their train to Scotland?" I asked Grant after we'd exchanged greetings.

He laughed. "They did. I suspect they were glad to be out of London before Donald could arrange another outing. Mom said she put in over twenty thousand steps, according to her phone, and she does not ever want to do that again. Dad said he had no idea people care so much, and know so much, about a fictional character."

"Donald means well," I said, "but he sometimes doesn't understand that not everyone shares his enthusiasm. How's Pippa this morning?"

"Worried. Something big is happening at work, and it's got her usual calm composure showing some cracks."

"Must be serious," I said. "I'm sure she'll sort it all out."

As we walked through the leafy streets past white row houses with black pillars and iron railings, I explained the purpose of the visit. "I found Sir John's name in Paul's client book. I was surprised, as I would have thought Sir John collected things out of the remit of a rundown shop like Paul's."

"Collectors collect many and varied things, Gemma. As you should know. We both know people who have thousands of dollars' worth of *Strand* magazines or copies of *Beaton's Christmas Annual* because they contain Holmes stories, but who also grab *I am Sherlocked* coffee mugs and *World of Sherlock* jigsaw puzzles off the tables in your store."

"Keeps me in business. Have you ever done business, book business, with Paul?"

"I was warned off."

I stopped and stared at him. "What does that mean? Warned off by who and why?"

"Pippa told me the man used to be married to you. That he cheated on you with at least one other woman, and after you left him, he was running the business you established, with little or no help from him, into the ground. She thought it best our paths didn't cross."

"You were okay with that?" We resumed walking.

"Plenty of book dealers in London. Which keeps me in business. I'll confess it wasn't a hardship. Your Paul was strictly bottom shelf."

"He wasn't my Paul, but I hear what you're saying."

"I'm working hard to establish contacts among collectors and other dealers. It can be hard sometimes, a new guy, and a foreigner to boot, breaking into a crowded market, but I'm making progress. If Paul had come across something special, something of great value, I haven't heard about it. And I like to hope I would have."

"Here we are," I said. Culross Street. Very posh, very expensive, close to Hyde Park.

We approached the house at the corner of the row. Noticeably there were CCTV cameras at each end of the street, pointing away from the house we were interested in. Not a coincidence. Sir John did not like to be observed, and he knew the sort of people who could take care of that sort of thing for him.

We climbed the three steps. I didn't bother to knock. They knew we were here. Sir John might not like to be observed, but he observed everything happening around him very carefully indeed.

The door swung silently open.

"Ms. Doyle. Mr. Thompson. Always a pleasure." The butler, David, was tall, skeletally thin, with sunken cheeks, a high forehead, close-cropped gray hair, and a neat gray mustache. He wore a black suit, immaculate white shirt, and shoes polished to such a shine I could check my makeup in them. He dipped his head in an almost imperceptible bow.

"Nice to see you too, David," I said. "I hope we find you well."

"Very well, thank you, Ms. Doyle."

We stepped into the house.

"My congratulations on your marriage, Mr. Thompson." David's accent still caried faint traces of the Scottish Highlands.

"Thank you," Grant said.

"Sir John is expecting you. He's in the library."

"Where else?" I asked.

A face muscle might have actually twitched, but in the dim light of the hallway it was hard to tell. "Please, follow me."

We followed David past framed portraits of Saint-Jeans past and present, including one of Sir John's niece dressed in hospital scrubs with a stethoscope around her neck.

David opened a door at the end of the hallway and announced, "Ms. Gemma Doyle and Mr. Grant Thompson." We entered the room and the door shut soundlessly behind us.

Our host was standing at a window, looking into the back garden. He turned to us with a smile, the curtains fell closed, and he crossed the room rapidly, hand outstretched. He wore many-times washed brown corduroy trousers, a beige cardigan missing a button and sporting several holes, and much-loved bedroom slippers.

Unlike its owner, the library might have come straight from Baskerville Hall. Heavy gold and red curtains and matching carpet, a fireplace, now empty as the day was warm for the time of year, fine art on the walls, rows of bookshelves. Chairs upholstered in red and gold damask, solid wooden desk.

"Never would have believed it if I hadn't heard it from totally reliable sources," Sir John said in his deep voice, the vowels like cut glass. His tone was warm and friendly, his eyes twinkled with welcome and good humor. "Phillipa Doyle got married." He slapped Grant on the back with such force my friend stumbled.

"And Gemma, as lovely as always."

"Are you a fan of *Downton Abbey*?" I asked. "Fond memories of *Upstairs, Downstairs* maybe?"

Sir John laughed heartily. "You mean David? We can both play roles, as required. He enjoys impressing American visitors. Although you're not so American anymore, are you, Grant? In London for the long haul?"

"I intend to be, yes."

"Please, sit, and tell me how I can be of service."

The door opened, and David came in with a tea tray. Fine china cups and saucers in a delicate pattern of pink and light green with gold trim, matching teapot, plate of chocolate-covered biscuits that looked to be homemade. He laid the tray on the table and slipped soundlessly away. "I took the liberty of assuming it was too early for whiskey," Sir John said, "but if you'd prefer—"

"Tea will be fine," Grant said. Sir John hadn't asked me. He knew I didn't care for whiskey.

Our host fussed with the tea things. "Milk? Sugar?"

"Milk," I said. "Please."

"Both," Grant said.

Tea served, biscuits passed around, Sir John took a seat. "I'm sure you want to get directly to the point. You didn't specifically say why you wanted to meet with me today, Gemma, so let me guess. Your former husband, one Paul Erikson, proprietor of Trafalgar Fine Books, barely clinging to life as it was, has been murdered. And you, my dear Gemma, impatient of police routine, are out to get justice for him." He studied my face carefully. "Because you hold a remnant of feelings for the man, in sentimental memories of better times, or simply because you, along with Grant here, were the ones who found him? I do believe you are still with the American policeman, are you not? His name escapes me."

I doubted anything escaped Sir John Saint-Jean. "I saw Paul on Saturday evening in the lobby of the hotel hosting Grant and Pippa's wedding. He told me he had a book he wanted to show me. That it was, and I quote, 'the real deal.' We arranged for me to come to the shop the following morning to see this book. Which I, along with

Grant, did. Whereupon we found him dead and no book to be found."

"Why are you calling on me? If you need information not publicly available, Pippa would be a better source."

"I am under strict instructions not to involve Pippa or her office in this."

"She might have said something along those lines to me as well." Grant put his teacup down and went to examine the books. He let out an occasional gasp as he ran his finger across the spines.

"Paul himself directed me to you," I said.

An eyebrow twitched. "How so?"

"I found your name in a notebook he kept of either current or potential clients. Next to your name and phone number, he had written the initials IF. Which I assume, although I insist I never assume or even guess, means Ian Fleming."

"Well done, Gemma. I have lately taken an interest in Ian Fleming. Did you know he was an intelligence agent during the Second War?"

"Everyone knows that," Grant said.

"Not everyone, but yes, it's part of his biography. Fleming—an actor playing him, at any rate—has a part in the movie *Operation Mincemeat*. Excellent production. If you haven't seen it, I suggest you do so. To continue, I want to amass a collection of Fleming. Biographies, mostly. Important historical records in which he's mentioned. And, of course, his works of fiction."

"James Bond."

"To that effect, I have put my name and news of my interest out to book collectors and the like. I wouldn't normally bother with anyone on the level of Paul Erikson, but considering Bond is as famous these days as he ever was, that the name of both the character and the author is instantly recognizable, and people are still reading the original books, I considered it possible, likely even, someone might drop off a box of books containing a first edition among all the other jumble of worthless pulp fiction at a used bookstore." He sipped his tea.

"Such as Trafalgar Fine Books."

"Yes."

"Did you get a bite?"

"I didn't go to the shop personally. I rang Paul about six months ago. He took my name and number and said he'd keep an eye out. I never heard from him again. You don't suppose this book he wanted you to see is a Fleming?"

"I don't know why he'd show something like that to me. I sell Conan Doyle and his contemporaries as well as current fiction featuring the Great Detective or set in his time, which we call gaslight. James Bond has never put his fictional foot into my shop."

"I might be able to locate some items of the sort you're looking for," Grant said.

"Let me know if you do," Sir John said. "I'm prepared to pay whatever's required."

"What do you know about Alistair Denhaugh?" I asked.

"Your mother's cousin. The Earl of Ramshaw. We are not friends, but I know of him. Why do you ask?"

"His name was also in Paul's book. Do you know what he collects?"

"I didn't know he was a collector. I've never been to his home. On the occasions our paths crossed, it was strictly work. Alistair was important in diplomatic circles in his day, our ambassador to China for a number of years, as well as a few other posts in the Far East. He's officially retired now."

"Officially?"

He grinned at me. "The pertinent word. I've heard he still maintains his contacts and can be persuaded to use them if required."

"What does that mean?" Grant asked.

"He knows people who know people," I said. "And he can be called upon to introduce people to people they need to know."

"Precisely," Sir John said. "Case in point: his name was mentioned in the *Times* recently as being invited to participate in talks around that Australian freighter business."

"Is that the South China Sea problem I heard about?" Grant asked.

"That's where the ship was seized, yes. It's hoped the situation will not escalate. As these initially minor things can sometimes do."

I brought the subject back to the matter at hand. "I doubt that, or anything do to with Alistair's contacts or past job record, has anything to do with his name being in Paul's book. Paul definitely did not know that sort of people. There were no initials next to Alistair's name, as with most of the others, including yours."

"Alistair might have varied tastes. Some amateur collectors will collect anything they hope is worth showing off to their less-knowledgeable friends."

Grant laughed. "Keeps me in business."

I asked Sir John if he knew of anyone Paul might have owed money to, other than his bank and credit card companies, and he said he did not. "The London underworld is not my area of interest, Gemma. I have to confess I don't have many contacts in the Met either. Sorry I haven't been able to be of help."

I stood up. "A negative can be as valuable as a positive."

"Except," he said, also standing, "if you only accumulate negatives, you'll get nowhere. When do you return to America?"

"We're supposed to go on Sunday. I intend to be on that plane. I've left our businesses and our home in the not-at-all-capable hands of my great-uncle."

"First-rate master and commander, Arthur Doyle," Sir John said. "Hopeless businessman."

I turned around to find the library door was already open, David standing stiffly next to it. I wondered if he and Sir John communicated telepathically. Nothing would have surprised me.

"The police called a few moments ago, sir. I told them you were temporarily indisposed, and they request you return the call at your earliest convenience. Something to do with a gentleman by the name of Paul Erikson."

Sir John looked at me.

"I gave them his notebook," I said.

"Once again, you're two steps ahead of the authorities."

Chapter Fourteen

"What's next, Gemma?" Grant asked.

We were standing on the street corner. I could almost feel the CCTV camera recording my every twitch. "Do you think I'm wasting my time with this?"

"Your time to waste."

"Okay, do you think I'm wasting everyone else's time with this?"

"Your friends are here to support you. Always. Do *you* think you're wasting your time?"

"Let's walk for a bit," I said. "I need to think things through. I'm getting nowhere. The book Paul wanted me to see is preying on my mind. If not for this mysterious book, I'd assume he made enemies somewhere, and those enemies killed him, and it would be completely beyond my skills to find them. A matter for the police only. But there *is* the book. What is it? And why did he think I'd be interested in it?"

"A Conan Doyle? Would that be worth killing for?" Grant asked.

"Don't forget the magazine containing the first-ever mention of Sherlock Holmes, which passed through my hands at the time you and I met. What was the potential value of that? Three quarters of a million dollars. Maybe more now."

"Worth killing for," Grant said. "For some people, anyway. What's next, then?"

"Sir John said I'm two steps ahead of the police. That's only because they have a heck of a lot more people to talk to, never mind hours, days of CCTV tape to pore through, bank records to examine, forensic results to pick through, and all the rest of that time-consuming, budget-straining stuff. I've spoken to as many of Paul's former lovers as I could find. Which is almost certainly not all of them. I spoke to the shop staff I've met, which is again not all of them. I called on Sir John only because I recognized his name in Paul's notebook, but I don't have the time to visit everyone, and most of them are unlikely to invite me to tea, at any rate. More likely to hang up on me. Do you think my sister would like a souvenir of London?"

"No."

"Buy Pippa one anyway. This shop should do. It's conveniently empty of customers at the moment so you can have a good browse. I have to phone someone. It's going to be a difficult conversation, and I'd prefer not to have a lot of noise in the background."

"Who do you need to call?"

"Paul's mother. Not in search of evidence, but a condolence call."

I'd earlier looked Mrs. Erikson up in the directory. She was still living at the address she'd been at when Paul and I had been married, and she still had a landline with the number I remembered.

While Grant spoke to the salesclerk in his American accent and pretended to be interested in mugs with visages of the king and queen on them, I stepped into a dark, quiet corner of the tiny, overcrowded shop and made the call.

A familiar voice rattled off the number, as many older English people still do as a way of answering. The voice sounded older than I remembered, choked with fresh sorrow.

"Mrs. Erikson. Alice. It's Gemma here. Gemma Doyle."

"Gemma. Oh, my dear, it is so wonderful to hear from you. Are you in London?"

"I am. I heard about Paul. I am so sorry."

"My poor lost Paul." Her voice broke. "Gone far too soon. I've missed you, dear. Are you still living in America? Paul told me you'd moved there."

"I am. I came to London for my sister's wedding."

"I hope you'll have time to pop round for a visit."

"Yes, I'd like that."

"Mum?" a voice asked. "Who is it?"

"My daughter Kate is here. You remember Kate, I'm sure?" Mrs. Erikson asked me.

"I do." Paul's sister lived in Bristol. I'd only met her on a few occasions, and when I had, I found her outgoing and friendly.

"It's Gemma calling," Mrs. Erikson said. "Isn't that nice? Hold on a minute."

I watched Grant taking his time to choose between an official coronation mug or one of the new king relaxing at home with the new queen. As much as anyone can relax in a business suit and tie or in a dress with heels and pearls. Grant's gaze wandered on to commemorative cups of Charles's first wedding. I wondered how many of those were still hanging around.

"Gemma? Kate here. It's nice of you to call."

"I wanted to extend my condolences. How's Alice doing?"

"Not well. But to be honest, she hasn't seen much of Paul over the last years. Nor have I. Not often since you left, come to think of it. Mum was not at all happy when he took up with that horrid Sophie."

"Water under the bridge. When would be a good time for me to drop by for a visit?"

"We're about to go out. We have to shop for," Kate's voice dropped to a whisper, "funeral clothes. It's not going to be a fun outing, and Mum will find it hard. The police are still holding the body, and they're not telling Mum much of anything. My father tells me the same. We're having a gathering here on Thursday. Sort of a wake, I guess. You'd be welcome."

"I'll try to make it."

"Two o'clock or any time after. It will be nice to see you, Gemma."

"Until then." I put my phone away.

Grant picked up the box nearest him and took it to the sales counter. He'd settled on an official coronation set. He pulled out his wallet, not looking at all happy at completing the transaction.

Before I put my phone away, I called up the pictures I'd taken of Paul's notebook and found the number next to Alistair Denhaugh's name. I dialed and a mechanical voice told me the number was no longer in service.

Interesting, but until I found out why Paul had Alistair's phone number, I wouldn't read too much into it being wrong. Alistair might have given him a made-up number, or Paul might have written the number down incorrectly.

I next called my mother and she answered immediately. "This is a surprise. A pleasant one, I hope."

"I want to visit your cousin Alistair Denhaugh. I don't know where he lives."

"Why?"

"Families don't get together often enough these days, do they?"

"I see them as often as I like. Which is at weddings and funerals. I was surprised when Pippa told me they were coming to her wedding. Apparently she has recently been meeting with him on some business matters so she extended the invitation. They were staying at the townhouse in London, but Genevieve told me on Saturday they were going up to Yorkshire the following day. Why?"

"Do you have a number for either of them?"

"I do."

"Mum!"

"I'm meeting Jayne at three at the Wolseley on Piccadilly for tea. Popular place with the tourists, but they do an excellent tea, so I knew it would please Jayne. You're welcome to join us. The table is under my name."

"Once I've spoken to Alistair or Genevieve and arranged to call on them, I'll try to make it."

We were at an impasse. Mum gave in first and rattled off a phone number. "That's Alistair's personal number. I was once given Genevieve's and I managed to lose it. Most unfortunate. I'll have my PA adjust the reservation to three people, shall I?"

"Can I bring Grant?"

"Certainly." She hung up.

"Did I hear my name?" Grant now carried a small brown paper bag.

"We're going to tea later. Command performance. Unless . . . Let me make a call." Trains between London and various cities in Yorkshire run several times a day. If my distant cousin could see me, I'd dump my mother and send Grant in my place. She would be unlikely to mind.

Such was not the case. Alistair's voicemail picked up and all I could do was leave a message. I'm not averse to dropping in on people unexpectedly in the hope of finding them at home and off-guard, but I didn't want to travel all the way to Yorkshire, having paid the exorbitant fare for a last-minute ticket, to find them unable to receive me.

"We have two hours to kill," I said to Grant. "Want to visit the Portrait Gallery?"

"I'd love to."

* * *

I have to admit, it was nice to have an afternoon "off duty." While Grant and I had a quick tour of the National Portrait Gallery, studying the faces of the great and the good, and the great but not at all good, of Britain past and present, I wondered how to approach Alistair Denhaugh, if ever he returned my call. We could talk on the phone, but I prefer to meet people face to face whenever I can. Should I come right out and tell him why I was interested in speaking to him? If he did know something about any illicit activities Paul might have been up to in the book-buying business, he wouldn't tell me over the phone. He might not tell me in person either, but I could get clues from facial expressions and body language.

I could say I wanted to pay a family-friendly visit as we hadn't spoken much at the wedding. Which would have made him instantly suspicious as we hadn't spoken much at the wedding because neither of us wanted to. The only other time I'd met the eighth earl and his wife had been at my christening.

All of which would have to wait until, even if, he returned my call. At the appointed time Grant and I made the short walk to Piccadilly to meet Jayne and Mum for tea.

The Wolseley is located in, of all things, a former car dealership. Black marble pillars, white and black checkered marble floor, golden walls, heavy chandeliers, wait staff in white shirts, black vests, and white aprons. Ironed white tablecloths, silver place settings. Despite it being a Tuesday in October, the place was full. Most of the clientele had gone to some trouble to dress well. Men were wearing suits and ties or shirts with collars and jackets; women, dresses or tailored slacks. A noticeable number of people were jumping up and down taking pictures of their friends posing with the silver teapots, white china, and three-tiered stands of the traditional afternoon tea offering.

"I asked Pippa to join us," Mum said as she accepted a peck on the cheek from Grant. "But she couldn't spare the time. I've taken the liberty of ordering for us all. As I recall, Gemma, you're fond of Lapsang Souchong?"

"That I am," I said.

"I'm used to Pippa being busy," Grant said. "Par for the course. But something extra seems to be up right now. I'm surprised she could take the time to make it to our wedding."

"The advantage," Mum said, "of inviting a large number of guests and paying a substantial down payment. Hard to back out the night before, claiming pressure of work."

Grant chuckled.

Our waiter began rearranging the cutlery on the table to accommodate the individual teapots and the accompanying containers of milk and sugar. A silver strainer was perched on the rim of each cup. "Shall I pour, madam?" he asked Mum.

"No, thank you," she said.

"Any idea what's going on that has Pippa's interest?" I asked Mum as I poured my tea through the strainer, the scent deep and rich and smoky.

"I can always guess. So could you if you read the papers."

"I'm beginning to think Pippa isn't really a secretary in the Department of Transport, or whatever it's called." Jayne said. "This tea is absolutely amazing. I wonder if I can order a supply for the tearoom."

Our food arrived on two stands. It all looked marvelous, and we dug in. I happily slathered jam and clotted cream on my currant scone. The scone was almost as good as the ones Jayne makes. Almost but not quite, and I told her so.

She studied everything before picking up a slice of cake and chewed thoughtfully. "This cake's a little bit dry. I'd add a splash of cream to the batter or maybe another egg. Otherwise, it's good. My customers would probably like icing on the top, rather than the powdered sugar. And drop the jam filling. I don't like jam in cake. I'd replace it with pastry cream."

"In other words," Grant said with a smile, "it's a perfect Victoria sponge but not to your taste."

"A matter of cultural and culinary differences," she said with a laugh.

My phone buzzed, and I checked the display. None other than my cousin Alistair. "Excuse me," I said. "I'd like to take this."

"I hope you're able to have an actual vacation this time," Mum said to Jayne as I slipped away. "Not be constantly following Gemma around on her wild-goose chases."

"I can do both," Jayne said. "Donald and I toured Tate Britain this morning, before he went to meet his Sherlock friends, and now I'm here having tea."

"Alistair Denhaugh, returning your call," said the man at the other end of the phone.

"Thank you. A matter has come up I'd like to speak to you about. I can come up to Yorkshire later this afternoon and—"

"Is everyone all right? Your mother?"

"Sorry. Yes. This isn't a family matter."

"What is it about then?"

"Do you collect rare books?" I asked.

"You own a bookshop, Anne tells me. Not only that, but Pippa's new husband is a dealer in such items. Do you or he have something you think I might be interested in?"

"I'd rather not talk about it on the phone."

"Is your sister sending you?"

"Pippa? No, this has nothing to do with her."

There was a long pause. "I'm engaged this evening and most of tomorrow, but I have some time in the late morning. An LNER train leaves King's Cross at seven, arriving in Halifax at ten. You'll have to change at Leeds for Halifax. A taxi will bring you to the house. Garfield Hall. Until tomorrow."

He hung up. Notably the eighth earl had not given me an address like *123 First Road, turn left at the second intersection past the church.* He assumed any taxi driver would know where to find Garfield Hall.

"Andy called me last night," Jayne was telling my mother when I returned to the table. "He's enjoying the trip so much. He was hesitant to take the time away from the restaurant to come here, but he's glad he did. Although he's having a heck of a lot of trouble getting up in time for the morning fishing outing. And then he's wide awake when everyone else at the hotel is off to bed." She chuckled. "He's still suffering seriously from the time change and jet lag."

I sat down and fluffed my napkin. Unlike Jayne, I do like a nice Victoria sponge, and I helped myself to the last slice of cake. "England, Britain, is so much more than London. How about we venture into the countryside tomorrow morning? Catch a train bright and early. Yorkshire is particularly nice at this time of year."

My mother turned her head sideways and peered at me from over the rim of her glasses. "Gemma?"

I smiled at her.

"That would be great," Jayne said. "Can we go to Highclere Castle? That's where *Downton Abbey* was filmed, and I'd love to see it."

"I have in mind someplace almost as impressive, and we'll get the private tour there. Grant, care to join us?"

"I would if I could, but I have something I can't get out of. I've spent a lot of time trying to arrange a meeting with a prospective buyer and she finally agreed on tomorrow."

"Take your Donald," Mum said. "Not exactly bodyguard material, but he's better than—" She didn't say Jayne.

"Why do we need a bodyguard?" Jayne asked.

* * *

We separated in front of the restaurant. Mum was heading back to work to finish up for the day; Grant going home to finalize the details for his meeting tomorrow. "Hopefully," he said, "I can drag my wife away from work to join me for a special celebratory dinner tonight."

"What are you celebrating?" Jayne asked.

"It's our third wedding anniversary. Third day, that is."

"Isn't that sweet?" Jayne said as we watched him head for the tube station, a decided bounce in his step. "I never knew Grant had it in him to be such a romantic."

"It's sweet all right," I said. "Sickeningly sweet."

"You are such a cynic, Gemma. Never mind, What's on the menu for the rest of the day?"

"It's five o'clock now. I need to do some research to prepare for our trip tomorrow."

"You mean like the sights in Yorkshire you want us to see? I can do that."

"Not exactly. As you may have guessed, Jayne, I have an ulterior motive." I turned to face her. "I shouldn't have presumed you'd want to come with me."

She put her hand lightly on my arm. "Always, Gemma, always. And I sort of guessed, I will admit, this has something to do with the death of Paul."

"Be warned. Our train leaves at seven, so we'll have to be up early."

"I'll manage. Are you getting anywhere?"

"As has been pointed out to me, all the negative evidence I'm finding is leading me only to negatives."

"Whatever that means. As for today, I'm fine on my own for a while. I'd like to see Piccadilly Circus and maybe take a walk down Whitehall, cross the river, and walk along the riverfront. Just take everything in."

"Let's do that together," I said. "The London Eye might be fun, and we can visit a couple of pubs along the way. Mum won't mind if we miss dinner, but Donald probably will. I'll call him and ask if he wants to meet up with us."

"If I can fit in dinner after that tea."

Chapter Fifteen

I took my iPad into the library and sent Ryan a text asking if he wanted to talk. Despite him telling me to check in every day, I got the do-not-disturb notification. I chuckled to myself and decided not to override the notice. It was all of ten o'clock. If Ryan had gone to bed that early, he must have had a very exciting fishing day indeed.

I'd enjoyed my evening with Jayne enormously. Just two girlfriends on vacation. Who knew how much fun that could be? We visited all the tourist sites we had time for, most of which I'd never seen, enjoyed a fancy cocktail at a luxury hotel, and then met Donald at a seventeenth-century pub overlooking the river, near Shakespeare's Globe Theatre. An after-dinner stop at another pub and we were home by nine-thirty. Mum was watching something on the telly, slippers on, feet up, cup of tea at hand. Jayne went to make herself a cuppa (as she was now calling it), and Donald excused himself to go to his room and read before turning in. He'd had a marvelous time meeting the members of the Sherlock society and talked about it all through dinner. He was excited about tomorrow's expedition and wanted to find out what places in Yorkshire might have inspired some of the locations in the Canon.

I called up the front pages of the major English papers. Only because I was curious, I wondered what crisis Pippa might be involved in. The South China Sea, Grant had said. I didn't have to search hard. The major story over the last few days concerned an Australian freighter boarded by the Chinese navy in disputed waters, which had everyone in the area tearing their hair out. I read the articles, not because I'm particularly interested in the goings on in the South China Sea but so I could impress my elder (and smarter and thinner and prettier) sister with my depth of knowledge. We were due to have dinner with her and Grant the night before catching our flight home.

The seizing of the freighter was only the latest in a series of disputes. International tensions were running high in that area and getting higher. Enormous amounts of shipping passed through those seas; China claimed much of it; no one else agreed.

Knowledge obtained, I turned my attention to the eighth Earl of Ramshaw and his family. His ancestors had been given the title and the accompanying estates by King George III back in 1767. Like many, if not most, of the grand estates, these days Garfield Hall was open to anyone who could pay to see it. Have to make a buck somehow. The maintenance alone, never mind heating and electricity bills, on these old piles must be enormous. Educated at Eton and Oxford, Alistair had served in the Foreign Office for many years before retiring five years ago. His wife, Genevieve, the current Countess of Ramshaw, was a moderately successful author of contemporary romance novels. She wrote giant tomes with lurid covers under the pseudonym of Francesca Midmarch. Not the sort of thing I stock at the Sherlock Holmes Bookshop and Emporium. And definitely not the sort of thing serious collectors would be caught dead dealing in. Although, judging by her sales, it was possible the money earned by the Countess of Ramshaw (aka Francesca Midmarch) was what allowed the family to hold on to the estate.

They had two children. Lawrence, whom I'd met at Pippa's wedding, heir to the title and the estate, and a daughter, Zoe. Lawrence was twenty-six, Zoe twenty-nine. Lawrence had attended Oxford, following in his father's footsteps, but dropped out before finishing.

These days he'd didn't seem to do much of anything that I could find. Zoe worked for a public relations firm in Halifax.

Lawrence took up a lot of space in the gossip columns, whereas his sister kept her head down. He was, in short, a party boy. Attendee at parties and grand openings thrown by the rich and famous. I found plenty of pictures of him on Mediterranean yachts or escorting a pretty young wannabe actress or socialite to a premiere. He was a very good-looking young man. With a beautiful woman on his arm, he made a great photo for the gossip rags. Which, I suspected, might be part of the reason he was invited to those sort of parties. That lifestyle costs money. A lot of it. More than made by an unemployed Oxford dropout even if he had a best-selling romance author mother. Particularly if his parents had a manor house and an estate to maintain.

Daughter Zoe was married to a bank executive. They had two children and lived in Yorkshire. She and her husband went to the odd charity function in London or Halifax, but the sort of thing that got space only in the local papers. Hospital and hospice fundraisers. School and church fetes.

Alistair and Genevieve didn't engage in the sort of activities I'd expect of a retired landowner. Likely because she was still writing an impressive two books a year and touring with her books, and he was only "officially" retired. I found a couple of references to him being called out of retirement by the Foreign Office when needed to consult on events in Southeast Asia.

I didn't come across anything about his book collection. There were plenty of pictures of Garfield Hall on the internet, but only of the grounds and the public rooms. If he did have an extensive library of valuable books, it might not be on display for the great unwashed to paw through.

I consider myself to be among the great unwashed, but I am my mother's daughter, and hopefully the earl would treat me as a friendly relative. I might even be allowed a peek at his book collection.

I leaned back in my chair and stretched my shoulders. The house was quiet, everyone gone to bed. Horace snoozed on the carpet at my feet. No sounds came from outside.

I yawned and closed my iPad. I don't like to go into any situation unarmed, and I'd learned enough for now. I didn't, for a minute, believe Alistair, the eighth Earl of Ramshaw, had murdered a used bookseller. But his name had been in Paul's notebook and that was a lead. No matter how flimsy it might be.

* * *

"Platform twelve and three quarters." Donald read the direction sign. "Is that a real thing?"

"No, it is not a real thing," Jayne said. "It's a Harry Potter reference."

"Harry who?"

"The boy wizard. You've never heard of Harry Potter? You're almost as hopeless as Gemma sometimes, Donald."

"I know who Harry Potter is," I said. "I also know all to be found at platform twelve and three quarters is a photo opportunity."

We were at King's Cross station. Our train was on time and so were we. Jayne managed to dissuade Donald from checking out the famous nonexistent platform by telling him we were late.

Last-minute train tickets for three had cost me a heck of a lot. I tried not to grumble as we made our way down the crowded aisle to our seats as passengers struggled with children, luggage, and directions.

Donald's face was a picture of sheer disappointment. Today, he'd dressed in his Ulster cape and a deerstalker hat, in imitation of his hero. He carried his ever-present black umbrella. "I was expecting a private carriage, Gemma. Of the sort that whisked Holmes and Watson through the 'smiling and beautiful countryside' to the Copper Beeches."

"Train travel has changed in the last century, Donald," I said.

"Excuse me," Jayne said as she bumped a pair of knees protruding into the aisle. The large man spreading himself across two seats and beyond was about to give her a sharp retort, but then he caught sight of her long blonde hair and pretty face and mumbled, "All okay, love."

We found our assigned seats and squeezed in. Jayne and I were together, with Donald in the row ahead. No point in talking about our mission, not with all these people around, so I pulled out my phone and checked the news for updates on the South China Sea situation. Vietnam had now become involved, as they claimed China had no rights to the area where the Australian ship had been traveling.

Next to me, Jayne took out a book. She was reading *The Isolated Séance*, by Jeri Westerson, a recent book featuring the adventures of a couple of the Baker Street Irregulars.

"Haven't you finished that yet?" I asked. "You got it to read on the plane."

"I slept on the plane."

"I will never understand how anyone can do that."

"We've been so busy during the day, I'm asleep as soon as I lie down." She opened the book.

I half stood to peer over the seat in front of me to see what Donald was reading. *The Worlds of Sherlock Holmes*, by Andrew Lycett, a recent book analyzing the times of the Great Detective and his creator. Right up Donald's alley.

I had not brought a book, so I stared out the window as the outskirts of London retreated and the "smiling and beautiful countryside" came into view. It might not have been smiling, but it was beautiful, and I enjoyed sitting quietly, letting my mind focus on the problem at hand as we sped past old farmyards and lush green fields.

"Have you heard from Mikey?" I asked Jayne, referring to the woman she'd hired to do most of the baking for the tearoom in her absence.

"I told you yesterday," Jayne said, "everything's going well. Why do you keep asking?"

"No reason."

"You think the place is going to fall down around Ashleigh and Arthur if you're not there to keep it standing. Relax, Gemma. If the building burned down, you can be sure Maureen would have let me know."

"Maureen has your number?" Maureen MacGregor owned the shop across the street from us at 221 Baker Street. She and I were not exactly friends. Jayne, on the other hand, got on with everyone.

"In case of emergency. Will you please let me read. I'm at an exciting part."

I went back to staring out the window.

* * *

We changed trains at Leeds for Halifax and after a short trip disembarked at our destination. The day was sunny but cool, a strong wind blowing off the rolling green hills. I hailed a taxi waiting outside the station.

"Garfield Hall," I said to the cabbie. "Do you know where that is?"

"Regular stop, love," he said.

"Is it far?" Jayne asked.

"Not far. From America, are you? Welcome to Yorkshire. First time here?"

"Yes, it is," Jayne said.

"We're staying in London," Donald said. "This is our first venture out of the city."

For the rest of the drive the cabbie entertained Jayne and Donald with an exhaustive list of the delights to be found in Yorkshire, beginning with, "My sister owns the best pub in Halifax. Mention I sent you and she'll take care of you."

We soon left the city behind and drove up and down steep, narrow, twisting roads lined with hedges or houses with doors opening directly onto the narrow pavement. "Are people allowed to park every which way?" Jayne asked, and the cabbie laughed. "Gotta put the car somewhere, love. Not a lot of space on some of these streets."

"It is beautiful," Jayne said. "Look at all those sheep."

"Do you like lamb, love?" the cabbie asked as he took a sharp corner without slowing to check if anyone was coming from the opposite direction. Fortunately, no one was.

"Oh, yes."

"My sister's pub does a brilliant lamb stew every night of the week."

Donald pointed out the green hills, dotted with sheep, and the network of dark, low drystone walls crisscrossing them, while I mentally reviewed what I hoped to learn at our destination.

My research told me that Garfield Hall, like most of the grand old houses, closed for the tourist season at the end of October, but it wasn't that date yet and so our taxi joined a scattering of cars and tour vans driving through the ornate gates. The driveway was about half a mile long, surrounded by perfectly maintained lawns and expansive gardens, nicely maintained woods rolling into the distance.

"Oh, wow!" Jayne said when the huge house came into view. "Look at that."

"Far as I can go," the cabbie said. "Ticket booth's ahead to your right."

I paid and we piled out of the cab.

"I hope you gave the driver a nice tip, Gemma," Donald said. "He was very friendly."

Jayne's mouth hung open as she took in her surroundings. "Imagine living here."

Garfield Hall wasn't one of the largest, most historical, or most famous stately homes in Yorkshire, but it was impressive nonetheless. Work began in 1770, under the first earl, and it took more than fifty years to complete to the satisfaction of the second earl. Made of soft golden stone and brick, two stories tall in the center, wings flaring out to the east and west, the main entrance accessed by a wide, sweeping staircase. Doors and upper windows guarded by classically draped stone angels, rows of tall windows in arched recesses. More sculptures dotting the roofline.

"Imagine cleaning the place," I said. "Or paying the heating bill. Like most of the great houses built in centuries past, the estate is now reduced to a tourist attraction. Only because Lady Ramshaw earns a respectable living as a writer of popular fiction is she not selling tickets or leading tours herself."

"Where do we go, Gemma?" Donald asked. "We don't have to buy a ticket, do we?"

"I hope not," I said. "Let's follow the path to the doors and tell them we're expected."

If I wanted us to look like members of the family, as though we belonged here, that impression was doomed to failure. Jayne's eyes were as wide as her mouth, and she oohed and aahed over every perfect pot of flowers, admired the tall, beveled windows and the rows of Greek columns, pointed out the roofline, the turrets in the corners, and the patina of great age in the stone walls to Donald. Donald strode along, his Ulster flapping, his black umbrella swinging, looking not like the lord of the manor or a visiting consulting detective, as he no doubt intended, but more like a movie extra late for the day's call. He also couldn't help commenting on the perfection of the grass and the craftsmanship of the house.

We joined the small queue at a side entrance. Ahead of us, a woman dug through her cavernous handbag mumbling, "I know I have the tickets, George," in a broad South Carolina accent. Next to her, George rolled his eyes and said, "I told you to let me handle it, Lou."

"Last time I let you handle it, you lost them and we had to pay again. Sorry," she said to me. "Please go ahead. They're in here somewhere."

"Gemma Doyle," I said to the smiling young lady in a black trouser suit and white blouse guarding the door. The family crest of red and white bands was sewn on her right breast pocket. "We're here to see Lord and Lady Ramshaw."

"You may inform them of our arrival. I am Ms. Doyle's personal security advisor. D. Morris, of West London, Massachusetts," Donald intoned.

"Yeah, okay," she said. "You're expected. Go on in. Go around the red rope to your immediate left, past the private sign, and take the staircase. I'll tell Genevieve you're here, and she'll meet you at the top of the stairs."

"Did you hear that, George," Lou whispered. "Those people have been granted an audience. I wonder who they are, that she has a bodyguard."

As though the Earl of Ramshaw was the pope or something and we were supplicants.

We did as instructed. The staircase was a good thirty steps, and Donald was trying hard not to huff and puff when we reached the top. If this was the private stairs and hallway, I could only imagine what the public areas must be like. The stairs were made of black marble, the banister of thick oak, no doubt from trees felled to plant the lawns. Paintings of family members long gone hung in gilt frames on the walls, a huge chandelier was suspended above the landing, and light flooded in from the wide arched window at the top of the staircase.

Genevieve, the Countess of Ramshaw, stood at the top of the stairs next to a huge table of swirling brown and cream marble with gilded legs. Two-foot-high candlesticks of ornate silver rested on the table on either side of a marble bust of a young woman, bodice cut low, hair tightly curled around her head.

Genevieve extended both of her hands toward me, and I took them in mine. "Welcome to Garfield Hall. This is an unexpected pleasure, Gemma. And you brought friends. How nice."

I introduced her to Donald and Jayne. Jayne politely said, in a considerable understatement, "You have a beautiful home." Donald started to sort of bow, but then thought better of it and stammered out greetings.

"Alistair is in the drawing room. Have you been to Garfield Hall before, Gemma?"

"No, I haven't."

"Dreadful old pile," she said, "but my husband and I are fond of it. The upper portion of the east wing, where we are now, is where we live during the tourist season. Next month we'll be able to stretch out a bit and use some portions of the rest of the house for Christmas entertaining and the like. It's not always easy, living in a home open to the public, never mind the comings and goings of volunteers and staff needed to run it. But it keeps the heat on. I was hoping to get a chance to talk books with you at the wedding, but such never happened."

"Books?" Donald said. "Are you a collector also, m'lady?"

She laughed. "Genevieve, please. I am an author. As I'm sure Gemma knows."

His eyes lit up with interest. "I apologize if I didn't recognize the name immediately." I could almost see his mind whirling through the list of authors he did know, desperately searching.

"Unlikely you would," she said. "I write under a pseudonym, and my books are probably not to your taste." She studied his attire, the Ulster cape, the unnecessary umbrella, the obviously fake accent, and smiled again.

She opened a small side door, and we went into what was the family sitting room. Alistair was relaxing on a plush red couch, reading something on his iPad. He closed the device, put it to one side, and got to his feet with a smile of greeting. "Gemma. Welcome. How was the train journey?"

"Easy and comfortable," I said. I introduced him to Jayne and Donald. Once again, Donald did a quick half bow and said, "An honor to make your acquaintance, m'lord."

"Alistair, please."

"Tea, everyone?" Genevieve asked. "The journey from London can be not only tiring but boring. Unless you Americans would prefer coffee."

"Tea for me," Jayne said. "Please."

"Excellent choice," Donald said.

"I'll get it," Genevieve said. She slipped out of the room, and her husband invited us to take a seat.

"I know you're busy," I said as we found places on the ornate but not very comfortable chairs. "I thank you for seeing me at such short notice."

"I regret not keeping in better touch with your mother all these years. I traveled extensively for most of my career, foreign postings and the like, and when we were at home we had the house," he waved in hands in the air, taking in close to three hundred years of responsibility and tradition, "to worry about."

Genevieve must have had the tea things ready, as she was soon back, carrying a tray. Jayne leapt to her feet to help her, and Genevieve gave her a warm smile of thanks. Seven cups and saucers were on the tray, and I wondered who else would be joining us.

Donald, it wasn't hard to tell, was simply in his element. He was seated in a drawing room of a stately manor house initially built in 1770. He was sipping tea out of Royal Doulton teacups and nibbling on chocolate biscuits. That the biscuits were stamped with the name of a commercial vendor, the tea was overly stewed, and his saucer had a chip out of the side, was irrelevant.

That Alistair Denhaugh, the eighth Earl of Ramshaw, wore faded trousers and his socks had holes in the heels, and that Lady Ramshaw was in jeans and a T-shirt proclaiming the glories of her favorite football (i.e., soccer) team was also irrelevant.

"You told me you have appointments today," I said, once tea had been served and formalities finished. "I'll get straight to the point of our visit. Do you recognize the name Paul Erikson?"

"I do," Alistair said, "but only because that name has been in the news in the last few days. The man was found dead in his bookshop in London, and the police are treating the death as suspicious. I haven't kept up with your mother's side of the family as much as I should have since the death of her parents, but I do remember her telling me some years ago you and your new husband bought a bookstore specializing in crime novels, if memory serves. I was sorry to miss your wedding. I believe we were in Malaysia at that time, is that right, darling?"

"Around that time, yes."

The rest of our little tea party came into the room. The couple's son, Lawrence, Viscount Ballenhelm, along with a woman I recognized from last night's online research as Zoe Denhaugh. Lady Zoe, as she would be more formally known. Alistair introduced us all, omitting his children's titles.

"Hey." Lawrence dropped into a chair and lounged back, stretching his legs out. A lock of blond hair fell over his forehead, and he was fashionably unshaven. He was dressed in beige trousers and a brown linen shirt, seriously wrinkled. I wasn't entirely sure if he was totally bored at meeting us or if that was just a pretense he put on. Likely he didn't even know. I had to admit, he was extremely handsome with high sharp cheekbones, full lips, and startlingly blue eyes under thick black lashes.

Zoe, on the other hand, gave us a broad smile and walked toward me, hand outstretched. I leapt to my feet. She was dressed as though heading to a business meeting, in a slim-fitting navy trouser suit, hems just short of her ankles, white shirt with top button undone, discreet gold jewelry, and black pumps with two-inch heels. Strawberry blonde hair was tied loosely at the back of her head. "A long-lost distant relative. Always so exciting."

We shook hands. Her manicure was perfect, the nails a soft pink. I said, "Not exactly. I haven't been lost."

"Lost to us, I fear. My parents are dreadful at keeping up family ties. I hope you don't mind me intruding on your little get-together. I dropped in to talk to Mum about the publicity campaign for next year's book. You have a bookshop in America, she tells me. Perhaps we could arrange an event there."

"You'd be very welcome," I said. "I have to warn you that contemporary romance is not in our mandate, but we'd be delighted to make an exception."

"Great. How about it, Mum? Fancy a trip to America?"

"That might work," Genevieve said. Her accent could cut glass, as could her daughter's.

Lawrence pushed himself out of his chair, took his cup of tea to the window, and looked out. "They get more slovenly every day," he drawled. "That woman missed the rubbish bin by yards and is pretending not to notice. Mind if I open the window and give her what's for, Mum?"

"Yes, I do mind," Genevieve said in a voice indicating they'd had this conversation many, many times before.

"Don't know why you put up with it. We can manage fine without—"

"Gemma and her friends have come a long way to speak to me," Alistair interrupted. "Gemma, please, you have questions for me about this man who died? I'll help if I'm able, but I don't know why you think I can."

Lawrence turned from the window. Zoe sat up straighter in her chair.

"Paul Erikson," I said. "And yes, he was my former husband. He owned a bookshop near Trafalgar Square. At one time the shop dealt exclusively in new releases, but over the past few years, it branched out into used books. Popular fiction, generally. Most used books sell for a pound or two at that sort of store, but occasionally something of interest might pass through their hands."

"You've found some of Mum's old books and think we're interested in having them?" Zoe said. "Heavens, no. We scarcely have enough room in the cellar for all the publishers' copies we can't get rid of."

"That's not it," I said. "Because of my relationship with the deceased, and other factors, I'm assisting the police in this matter." Jayne's head swiveled toward me as I stretched the truth a tiny bit. I wouldn't call it a lie. I was assisting the police. That they hadn't asked for my assistance was irrelevant. "Have they been in touch with you?"

"No, but no reason they should," Alistair said. "I didn't know the man."

"Your name and a phone number were in his client list."

"What?" Genevieve said.

"I tried calling the number, but it's out of service."

"We had the landline to our private number disconnected recently," Genevieve said. "No need for it any longer. No need to keep paying for it."

"The cops came around Monday morning," Lawrence said. "You weren't here. I told them that and they left."

"You didn't tell me?" Alistair said.

"Guess I forgot. My bad." Lawrence didn't look terribly concerned.

"My name is not unknown in certain circles." Alistair put his teacup on the table. "Likely a casual acquaintance of mine gave that information to your friend and didn't know we can no longer be reached at that number. I'm sorry you've wasted your trip."

"If your name was given to Paul, it would be because you have potential as a client. Are you searching for anything in particular? In the way of a book, I mean?"

Zoe laughed. "This family is hardly in the position to be collecting rare books. If we had that sort of money, we'd be better to fix the plumbing."

I kept my focus on Alistair. He shifted slightly and gave his daughter a stiff smile. "Good investments never come amiss, Zoe. Yes,

I remember now. I once mentioned something to a Foreign Office acquaintance. Forget his name. Must be getting old." He laughed. No one joined in. "I'd heard books make excellent investments. Have to find something to invest in these days, what with the stock market doing what it's doing."

"You have stock?" Zoe said.

"No," Genevieve said.

"We're not entirely destitute," the Earl of Ramshaw said.

"Could have fooled me," his son and heir said.

Jayne and Donald simply looked confused.

"Which is why," Lawrence said, "I keep telling you we need to get out of the tourist business and put this dump to its real value, which is—"

"Not again," Zoe said. "As I keep telling you, every stately home in England wants to be the new Downton Abbey. It's not going to happen. We're not that special."

"As I keep telling you," Lawrence snapped, "we know who's going to be in charge one day and then we'll see."

"If you and your crazy schemes do anything to damage the reputation of this family and disgrace our forebearers, I'll . . ." Zoe sputtered to a halt before she could tell us what she'd do.

"Lawrence, I'd rather you don't discuss your father's eventual death in front of guests," Genevieve said.

"And I'd rather you don't sound as though you're looking forward to that eventuality," Alistair said.

"Nothing wrong with planning, haven't you told me that many times?" Lawrence asked.

"I am only sixty-five," Alistair said. "Plenty of life in the old dog yet."

Jayne shifted uncomfortably in her chair. This conversation was getting entirely too personal for her. As for me, I didn't mind in the least. The more personal it got, the more likely something interesting would slip out.

"I've changed my mind. I'm going to London today. Don't know when I'll be back." Lawrence put down his teacup and headed for the door. Before he could make a dramatic exit, he finally remembered some of his manners and turned to us. "Nice meeting you. Thanks for coming. Have a look around the house before you leave. We'll have to ask you to pay, though. Can't be offering freebies to distant relatives who crawl out of the woodwork. Seventeen pounds. Each."

Not so mannerly after all.

The door slammed shut behind him and an awkward silence ensued.

"More tea, Jayne?" Genevieve said brightly.

"Thank you. Yes, please. It is excellent." It wasn't excellent, more like mediocre as though bought in a box of two hundred bags from the local Tesco, but Genevieve appreciated Jayne's attempt to be polite.

"It's awful," Zoe said. "My great-grandmother had her tea delivered directly from Twinings. Isn't that right, Mum? They prepared a mixture of leaves to her exact specifications."

"The good old days," Genevieve said, "for those who had money, anyway."

"Which could be us again, if only Lawrence manages to grow up before he's in charge."

"Enough!" Alistair said. "I'm tired of hearing about it."

Zoe crossed the room and gave her father a light, affectionate kiss on the top of his head. "Sorry, Dad. He deliberately tries to rile me up, and I fall headfirst into it every time. I have to be off. Can I offer you a ride to the train station, Gemma?"

"We still have some time before we have to leave," I said. "Nice to meet you."

"And you. I will be in touch about Mum's book. I hope we'll get a chance to meet again, Jayne. Donald." She left.

"That," Genevieve said, "was incredibly embarrassing. Those two are not toddlers, but they haven't learned not to air the family laundry in front of anyone who happens to wander into hearing range. I apologize."

"No need," I said. "I'm aware of the stresses on aristocratic families these days and that these estates can often be more a curse than a blessing."

"So true," Alistair said. "I feel the responsibility to the past. To my family. To our proud history. Much to do and little time to do it. Garfield Hall is one of the very few old houses that never suffered a fire; almost all of the materials and fixings and the like are original. Genevieve, darling, the tea has gone cold, and I would like another cup, as would Jayne. Do you mind?"

She hesitated and then stood with a smile. "Not at all."

She left the room without closing the door behind her.

Alistair shifted in his chair and stared in the direction of the windows.

Donald said, "The weight of history is—" I lifted one hand, and he stopped.

"Paul Erikson's client list," I said quietly.

"Yes. I'll confess, now my wife has left the room, that I'm not surprised to be on it. As you might have gathered, my family is reasonably comfortable from my job in the Foreign Office and my pension, as well as my wife's writing. We enjoy a comfortable, upper middle-class income. The estate is nothing but a burden, but one I'm willing to bear for the sake of my family legacy. I should not be investing our money in collectables such as books. But," his face twisted, "I have been sorely tempted. My grandfather's great library was sold many years ago by my own father. Something had to be done about the black mold in the walls and the holes in the roof and to install modern tourist facilities." He rubbed his forehead and looked very tired all of a sudden. "I'd prefer my wife not know I've been dipping my toes into the waters, so to speak. Perhaps I have some foolish dream of rebuilding the library as it once was."

Donald couldn't hold himself back any longer. "That would be an excellent idea. A great library would make your home stand out. Collectors would flock to see it. As you might know, Sir Arthur Conan Doyle has strong connections to Yorkshire. He did a short medical placement in Sheffield, which I believe is not too far from here, and he married his first wife, Louisa Hawkins, in a church in Masongill. Did you know, as a matter of extreme interest, that the vicar was named Sherlock? In addition—"

Alistair blinked. I said, "Perhaps you can send an email with your suggestions, Donald."

"Excellent idea, Gemma. Emphasizing the Conan Doyle angle, as well as a library specializing in his works, would be a wonderful promotional opportunity. I myself have many contacts and—"

"I don't know much about Conan Doyle," Alistair said.

"We'll leave those details with you for now, Donald," I said. "We don't want to take up too much of Alistair's time." Donald whipped a small notebook and pen out of his coat pocket. He wet his index finger with the tip of his tongue, touched it to the nib of the pen, and began making notes.

"Before Genevieve gets back," I said, "did Paul contact you about a particular book you might be interested in, Alistair?" The woman was no fool. I suspected she was standing just outside the door, listening.

"No, he did not. As you mentioned, he didn't have a current number for me."

"Did you hear of a book he recently came into possession of, which he was trying to sell?"

"I did not. I still do some consulting work for the Foreign Office, and I've been caught up in . . . business, the last while. My foolish idea of rebuilding the library was, truth be told, a whim, Gemma. One I will be unlikely to pursue any further." Smiling, he nodded toward Donald. "Despite your friend's enthusiasm."

We heard the clatter of china and silver in the hallway, and Alistair said brightly, "What other sights do you plan to see while you're here? If you haven't been to York, it is well worth the visit."

Genevieve came in with the tea tray. She pointedly avoided catching my eye as she bustled about with the teapot. "All out of biscuits. So sorry. I'll have to make a run to the shops later. What time is your conference call, love?"

That was quite likely the broadest hint I'd ever heard that he should make his escape. Alistair checked his watch. "It is getting on. I still have some work to do to prepare." He stood up. "Thank you for coming, Gemma. I hope it won't be so long until next time. Please, don't hurry. Visit with Genevieve a while. You can tell her all about selling books in America. Nice meeting you, Jayne, Donald. I hope you don't have to hurry off. Regardless of what my son says, please tell Melissa at the door you're to be my guests if you want to tour the house and gardens."

He left the room. The door shut quietly behind him.

Genevieve smiled brightly at us. "This house is, of course, not my own, as I simply married into the family. But I love it as though my own history were wrapped up in its walls. Like my husband, I will do a great deal to protect it."

"I'm sure you will," I said.

Chapter Sixteen

"Why don't I give you the tour?" Genevieve said. "I lead them myself sometimes, when we're particularly busy or we're understaffed."

I was about to say I wanted to get back to London, but Jayne squealed in delight. "That would be so fabulous. Yes. I mean, is that okay, Gemma? We're not in a hurry, are we?"

"Sure," I said. "We have time before we have to catch our train."

If you've seen one English country estate dating from the eighteenth century, you've seen them all. And I have. But I patiently followed Genevieve around as she showed off her home to Donald and Jayne. The ancestral portraits in the great hall looked to be modern reproductions, and the suit of armor guarding the doors to the morning room likely came from a theatrical costuming department. Some of the furniture, the dining room chairs in particular, appeared to have been given a few knocks with a hammer and had a patina of age recently applied. But the ancient wood and the great blocks of stone of the house itself, along with the beveled windows on the ground floor, were original. As was the enormous tapestry, faded and tattered with age, in the dining room, and the twisting spiral staircase in the oldest part of the house, leading up to the turret room at the top, which Jayne particularly delighted in.

This late in the season, the gardens were not at their best, but they were still beautiful in the soft light of the autumn sunshine. Visitors took selfies or posed for family pictures in front of the statuary or the fountains, and laughing children chased each other across the immaculate lawn or down the carefully raked gravel paths.

"I could live for this view," Jayne said, as we stood at the end of the garden walk and gazed over the verdant green hills and the sheep-dotted meadows of Yorkshire.

"As I do," Genevieve said. "This garden is the greatest joy of my life. Other than my grandchildren, of course. But even then, it's close."

Genevieve and Alistair, I now understood, hadn't come to Pippa's wedding in old or unfashionable clothes because such was all they could afford, but rather that she, very sensibly, had more important things to spend their money on than appearances.

We watched a young man digging up weeds in the rose garden and tossing them into a wheelbarrow. "Do you employ a large garden staff?" Jayne asked.

"Nowhere near the numbers Alistair's ancestors would have had. We have a professional horticulturist on staff year-round and employ young people in the spring and summer to do the cutting, deadheading, and weeding. Over the fall and winter, just Simon there." She waved, and the gardener straightened up with a smile. The wind caught a lock of his blond hair as he waved back. "Fortunately for our pocketbook, the local gardening society helps a great deal. When I'm not writing or on tour, I enjoy getting my hands stuck into the dirt. We have a tearoom on the grounds, if you'd like to take some refreshment."

"No, thank you," I said. "We've got just enough time to catch our train."

Genevieve called a taxi for us. I protested I could do that myself, but she insisted she had a special driver she always used who would give me a good rate.

The cab was waiting for us at the entrance, and we said our goodbyes to Genevieve.

As we drove away, I could see her standing by the gate, watching us. She waved.

"I'd say that was a wasted trip," Jayne said, "except we got to see that fabulous house. And that garden, oh, my goodness. I can understand why they try so hard to keep it in the family."

"Was it a wasted trip, Gemma?" Donald asked. "Or another one of the negatives you enjoy proving? Did you believe Alistair when he said—ouch. What was that for?"

I gave Donald a second sharp poke in the ribs and tilted my head in the direction of the cabbie in the front. His eyes were on the road, his hands in the proper ten to two position on the steering wheel. He didn't appear to be paying any attention to us, but cabbies were always listening, and this was not the place to talk.

I had learned a great deal. And some of it was positive.

We alighted at the station, and I handed over the money for the fare. The driver accepted it with a mumbled, "Ta," but didn't offer me any change and drove away without waiting to see if anyone getting off the rapidly approaching train would need a ride. Genevieve had instructed him to take us to the station, and he hadn't said a word on the drive.

This time we had three seats facing each other over a fold-down table on the train. The fourth seat was unoccupied.

"Zoe looks to be older than Lawrence," Jayne said to me once we were moving. "By the way they were talking, he's going to inherit, not her."

"Such is the ancient English tradition of primogeniture," I said. "Zoe will not inherit the title on her father's death. As for the estate, things can get extremely murky depending on the time of and the conditions of the granting of the initial title. I'll assume Alistair won't want it to be divided between his children. In some cases these days a daughter can inherit the property. Otherwise, if something happened to Lawrence, Alistair would be searching the family tree for a distant heir. Haven't you seen or read *Pride and Prejudice*?"

"Happens in *Downton Abbey* too, but I thought they changed that rule recently."

"Entail of property is no more. I believe that was done away with in the 1920s, but titles still pass down the male line. The rules of royal succession changed a couple of years ago, yes, so daughters come in the same order as sons. But that didn't affect the aristocratic families."

"You'd think they'd have learned a thing or two since Jane Austen's day," Jayne said. "As in the example we've just seen. Seems to me Zoe's a lot more levelheaded than her brother, but she expects he's going to own it some day, not her."

"Rather rude to talk about that in the presence of their parents," Donald said.

"It seems so to us, yes, but that's about all these families can think about. As in *Pride and Prejudice*, when they were desperate to find husbands for their daughters before they were kicked to the curb on their father's death."

"What do we do now, Gemma?" Donald asked. "As regards the case, I mean?"

"Let me think." I closed my eyes and rested my head against the back of my seat.

"Jayne, did you notice how—?" Donald said.

"Please don't talk amongst yourselves," I said. "We are in public."

"Sorry," Donald said.

"No talking," Jayne said.

"In that case, I'll continue drawing up my suggestions for a Conan Doyle tour of Yorkshire. Do they have Wi-Fi on this train, do you know?"

* * *

As the train pulled into King's Cross, I studied the crowd of people on the platform and said, "We have plenty of time. Would you like to walk part of the way?"

"Great idea," Jayne said. "I'll never get enough of walking in this city."

We emerged from the station at Euston Road. Donald set off at a brisk pace, arms pumping, umbrella swinging, but Jayne and I walked slowly, enjoying the day, enjoying being in London. We stopped regularly to look in shop windows, and Donald eventually fell back to join us.

"I'd enjoy a gelato, how about you?" I said to my companions after about twenty minutes of casual strolling.

"Good idea," Donald said. "The sandwich I had on the train was less than satisfactory."

We went into a brightly decorated gelato shop. Jayne asked for a single scoop of lime, and Donald had the double chocolate. I ordered strawberry. While the young clerk scooped our treats and Donald fumbled in his pockets for the correct bills with which to pay, I stood at the window, looking out onto the street.

"Gemma?"

I turned to see Jayne holding a bright pink concoction out to me. I took it and smiled my thanks. "Enough walking. Let's get the tube at Regent's Park."

"Okay," Jayne said.

I set off down the road at a considerable pace.

"Why are we suddenly in such a hurry?" Jayne panted.

"No reason," I said.

It was nearing rush hour, and commuters were pouring into the tube station. I tossed my uneaten, dripping cone into a trash container and nipped behind an advertising banner. "Here," I said to Jayne and Donald. "Quickly."

They did not move quickly. Instead they peered around the sign at me. "You okay, Gemma?"

I said nothing and watched people hurrying for their trains. No one paid any attention to us. I should say no one appeared to be paying any attention to us. A tall young woman in a loose raincoat swiped her Oyster card and passed through the turnstiles. I watched her disappear down the escalator that led to the northbound Bakerloo Line toward Harrow and Wealdstone. Not southbound to catch a train to Gloucester Road station in Kensington.

"Yeah," I said at last. "I'm okay. Let's go."

Chapter Seventeen

"We were followed from Garfield Hall to London," I said. "And likely to here. I said nothing to Jayne and Donald."

"Can you be sure?" my father asked.

"Sure? No. Do I suspect so, yes."

"Then you were," he said. "Should we be having this conversation over the phone?"

"Probably not, but you're not here and I am not there, and I need your advice."

"Tell me."

"Genevieve Denhaugh called us a taxi, despite my saying I could do it. The cab was genuine, but the driver was not. There are cab drivers who don't engage in chitchat, but not usually with two friendly Americans in the back who might leave a large tip if you're friendly in return. He didn't wait for another fare from the station even though a train was pulling in at that moment. He dropped us and left. Almost certainly someone was waiting for us when we got off the train at King's Cross. I saw a man buying a newspaper at a kiosk, and then I spotted the same man a couple of blocks later, behind us. When I stopped to look in a shop window, he hesitated. He did eventually pass us, turn the next corner, and disappear, but a woman took his place. She was behind us before we went into the gelato shop and picked us up again when we reached the entrance to the tube station. She went down the escalator for the train going north, not the southbound as we did to get to the Piccadilly line to Kensington. The tube was crowded, and I was unable to spot anyone else, but I suspect they didn't give up."

"A coordinated effort then," Dad said. "Almost impossible to detect if several people are working a tail together and in communication with each other."

I sat on my bed, the door closed, talking to my father in a low voice. When we arrived at the house in Stanhope Gardens, Donald went straight to his computer, saying he was going to contact his new English Sherlockian friends to ask them more about the relationship of the Great Detective and his creator to Yorkshire. On the train, he'd said something to Jayne along the lines of offering himself as a consultant to Lord and Lady Ramshaw on "Sherlock's Yorkshire." I suggested Jayne call my mother and ask if she had dinner plans, and if not, to make some.

"The question is," I said into the phone, "why would Genevieve and Alistair want us—want me, I should say—followed? And why to London? I was coming here. Anyone who cares knows I'm staying at your house."

"At a guess, they wanted to be sure you went directly to Stanhope Gardens. Call your sister, Gemma."

"Pippa? She'll say she can't possibly know what I'm talking about."

"Let her say it. She needs to know about this, and she can decide if it's significant. We're due to check out of the hotel in the morning. Would you like us to come back tonight?"

"No. I'll call Pippa. I'll keep you posted. How's the fishing?"

"Good. Our catch is on the menu again tonight. Ryan and Andy are having a great time, and I'm enjoying getting to know them both better."

"Glad to hear it. Perhaps don't mention this phone call to Ryan."

"Is that wise, Gemma?"

"Probably not."

"Do you want some advice from an old man?"

"No."

"You're going to get it anyway. Ryan's a good man. He's obviously worried about you. It was hard for him to leave you in London, knowing you're interfering in a police matter. But he did leave because he knows you need your space. Your mother and my marriage worked, still works, because we know when to be protective of the other and when not to be. And, more importantly, when to let the other be protective. Do you understand what I'm saying, love?"

"I do, Dad. I do."

"Up to you if you want to keep DI Patel in the loop, but again, my advice is that you should."

"See you tomorrow, Dad."

I made another phone call, and not to the police detective. If I told her I'd been followed from Yorkshire and through the crowded streets of London, by persons unknown and unidentified, she'd dismiss me as deluded. I went downstairs. Jayne was in the library, curled up with her book. "I told your mom I'd like to cook for us tonight, so she gave me the address of the nearest good grocery store. I've been waiting for you. Want to come?"

"Sorry, I have to go out. I might not be back in time for dinner. You go ahead."

"Go where?"

"I need to talk to Pippa."

"Want me to come? Your mom will understand if there's no dinner. I suppose we can always ask Donald to make it." She laughed lightly at the idea. "Maybe not."

"I need to go alone this time. Something we can't talk about on the phone."

Jayne gave me The Look. The one that means she knows I'm up to something. "If you're sure?"

"I am. Thanks. I'll text and let you know when I'm on my way back."

* * *

At this time of day, it's usually faster to cross London underground than by road. I grabbed my coat, took a scarf and a hat off Mum's shelf and stuffed them into my tote bag. I'd travel openly to Isle of Dogs. If, for some reason, I had to come back incognito, the hat and scarf wouldn't do much, but they might do something to help keep me unrecognizable in the images gathered by the CCTV cameras.

I walked quickly to the tube station and rode the long, long escalator down. A train was coming as I reached the platform, and I jumped on. Several people got on at the same time as me. The car was full, people clinging to the poles or the back of seats, crowding the doorway. A pack of boys in school uniform, laughing and elbowing each other. Men in business suits and women in yoga gear, mats under their arms. Women in business suits and men in running gear, gripping water bottles. Red-eyed tourists with huge, wheeled suitcases. Two women laden with shopping bags. At least half the people, likely more, were on their phones.

Any one of them might have been there specifically because I was. Other than the schoolboys.

I didn't bother to pretend disinterest. They would have known I knew they were following me by the way I behaved on the street earlier. If I was being followed. I might be suspicious for no reason. Then again, just because you're paranoid doesn't mean they aren't out to get you. Although no one, as far as I knew, was out to *get* me.

Had someone been watching me, watching us, all along? It was possible a tail had been following us for days. I could see no reason anyone would exert a coordinated effort, hugely expensive in terms of time and resources, to find out what I was doing about the murder of Paul Erikson. Had I attracted attention when I called on Alistair Denhaugh earlier today? Impossible to say. I'd only been alerted to the possibility by the behavior of the cabbie who'd driven us to the Halifax station. The one summoned by Genevieve. Had Alistair given his wife a secret signal, one I'd missed as I was heading for the door?

If so, I could only conclude that something of far more importance than the murder of a London bookshop owner was going on here. Had I stumbled across something I shouldn't?

I'd phoned Pippa after my conversation with Dad and told her I needed to talk to her. In person. Now. No excuses.

"I've no reason to make an excuse, Gemma. I'd be delighted to see you. Grant wants to surprise me with something special for tonight. Isn't that darling? I'm home now. I took the liberty of slipping out of the office early. I can finish up what I'm working on at home."

"On my way," I'd said.

I took the Circle Line from Gloucester Road station to Paddington, ran up and down long escalators and through halls full of people to the Elizabeth Line, and got off at Canary Wharf. A heavy bank of clouds had moved in; the wind had picked up, blowing cold off the river. I didn't put on my hat and scarf. I'd wait to see if I needed them.

Pippa told the concierge I was expected, and she met me at the door to her flat. She was dressed for work in a suit that must have cost in the thousand-pound range. A deep crimson wool skirt and gold-buttoned jacket worn over a black silk shell. The jacket was cut so fashionably overlarge, it showed her thin frame to perfection. She was in stocking feet, and her smile of greeting was surprisingly warm. "Come in. Grant's ensconced in his study so we can talk freely."

Her laptop was open on the dining room table, a towering stack of papers next to it.

"Please, have a seat." She gestured toward the sofa. "Can I get you anything? Tea, a glass of wine. It is after six."

"No, thanks." I walked into the flat but didn't sit down. I turned and faced my sister. She wandered over to the laptop and closed the lid. "Something has you concerned. What?"

"I went to see Alistair Denhaugh today. At Garfield Hall."

Something moved behind her intense brown eyes. "I did not know that."

"That surprises me. I believe we were followed when we left his house."

"You believe you were, or you were?"

"The former. It was professionally done. Might be my mind looking for trouble where there is none. But I don't think so. I told Dad, and he told me to tell you. So I am. Telling you, that is."

Pippa dropped into a chair and indicated for me to do the same.

I sat opposite her.

"First, who do you mean by 'we'? Jayne, I assume."

"Her and Donald."

"Why did you go all the way to Halifax to see Alistair? I doubt it was for a continuation of the family reunion."

"It was not. I found his name in Paul Erikson's client list."

One perfectly sculpted eyebrow half rose. "Is that so? The same book containing John Saint-Jean's name? Sir John has been in touch with me about that."

"Yes."

"Sir John is a collector. He has a nice library. Nothing extraordinary, but works of some importance and value. I wasn't surprised to hear a used bookseller had his name, and neither was he. It was more that he wanted to inform me of your interest. I didn't know Alistair collected. No reason I should, I suppose."

"He doesn't. And that's what has sparked my interest. Rather like the curious instance of the dog in the nighttime, the curious instance of a non-book collector having a listing in a bookseller's client list. He tried to fob me off with some story about wanting to rebuild the family library, but his children and his wife were there, and they didn't play along. Alistair can't afford to collect at that level. He can't afford to collect at any level other than via regular high street bookshops. When his wife left the room because he dismissed her on the pretext of needing fresh tea, he tried spinning his story, telling me his wife didn't approve of his collecting, so he hadn't told her about it. It's my impression Lady Ramshaw controls the spending in that family. If he dropped a few thousand pounds on books, she'd have something to say about it. Alistair's name was the only one in Paul's notebook that didn't have a mark beside it indicating what the buyer was interested in. Sir John's, for example, said 'IF,' for Ian Fleming. He confirmed that."

"I can see Sir John being interested in Fleming, yes."

"No one collects nothing in particular."

"Alistair might. If he doesn't know a great deal about books and only wants to build a grand library with whatever he can get his hands on. But I do take your point. Such is unlikely. You're also correct that the family is barely hanging on to Garfield Hall, and Genevieve runs the estate as best she can. Alistair spent much of his working years overseas in Foreign Office postings. Genevieve spent winters with him and the rest of the year at the house, trying to keep the place going. She's done a remarkable job. Her writing income has been invaluable to them. Goodness knows what's going to happen to Garfield Hall when Alistair and Genevieve are no longer around. Nothing good, I'm sure."

My sister studied my face for a long time. In the corner a lamp switched itself on. Night was rapidly falling and lights coming on all over the city. Pippa stood up and crossed the room. She pulled the curtains closed.

"Alistair's name was in Paul Erikson's client book," I said. "But he's not in the market for books. His name is the last entry in that notebook. I wonder why. I suspect you'd like to know too, Pippa. Genevieve Denhaugh called someone who was not a taxi driver, but pretended to be one, to take us to the train station. When we disembarked from the train, people were waiting for us. Not one person, clumsily trying not to be seen as they trundled along behind us, but a coordinated effort involving several individuals. Three at the minimum. By the way, I don't know if I was followed here. I didn't spot anyone, but I'm not a professional at that sort of thing."

"You possibly were, although it might not have been necessary. My address is not unknown. I'll make sure it doesn't happen again."

"You do that, Pippa."

"I know you have some notion that you're an amateur private detective back in America, but I'm going to advise you to tread very, very carefully here, Gemma. Things are happening that are none of your concern."

"Whatever you and Alistair are up to is none of my concern. But the murder of Paul Erikson is. Alistair is involved in that whether you and he want him to be or not. Let me remind you, if you need reminding, who it was who got Dad cleared of that murder accusation."

"I haven't forgotten." She sighed.

I waited.

"Alistair is highly placed and highly regarded in the Foreign Office. He served as our ambassador or high commissioner to several countries in the Far East and the Pacific Rim. Served with considerable distinction, I might add. He's highly regarded, not only by us and our allies but also by some of our adversaries. If I can call them that."

"The South China Sea situation. The seized Australian freighter. Is it something more than a freighter?"

"No, it is not. But it is Australian, and Australian citizens are among the crew. As are some British. The situation is delicate, and Alistair is heavily involved in discussions. Other countries are interfering, each with their own priorities. This sort of thing does happen on occasion, unfortunately, and they're eventually sorted out and everyone keeps face. But in this instance, there is a considerable complication, of great significance to the United Kingdom, which I am not free to discuss with you."

"Which is why you're involved."

"Which I am not free to discuss with you. Alistair's personal contacts are important in this situation. As I said, he's highly respected by all sides and has an impeccable reputation. I can say the same for his wife. They have, however, one flaw."

"The son, Lawrence."

She nodded. "Viscount Ballenhelm himself. The word layabout and wastrel come to mind."

"That's two words."

"So it is. I can think of more. Happens sometimes, in the great families. The daughter, Zoe, is exactly as she appears. A hardworking mother and successful businesswoman. Lawrence is also exactly as he appears. As I said, a disappointment to his parents."

"Okay, but what's the specific deal right now? I read about him in the gossip papers. He goes to all the best parties. Knows all the other failsons."

"He's having an affair with a minor royal. That has not yet been picked up by the lesser quality papers. We'd prefer it never is."

"What of it? This isn't Sherlock Holmes's time where the king of Bohemia's marriage can be derailed because he once had a picture taken standing next to an opera singer, both of whom were fully dressed. No one's going to be scandalized. Unless she's underage. Is she?"

"The opposite. She's considerably older than him. Her children are his age. She's married."

"Again, a tempest in a teacup. Older women will be cheering her, the minor royal, on. And all the lads will be slapping him on the back. As for the royal family themselves, they have enough troubles these days with the major royals, never mind the lesser ones. They might be grateful if the spotlight is turned away from them for a while."

"All of which is true. But it does put Alistair in a position to be compromised."

"I don't see it. But then I'm not the eighth earl of anything and I don't move in the highest levels of government. Or the royal family. You think it's possible Alistair could be blackmailed over his son's indiscretions? I mean, you know about it. Does he?"

"I don't believe so. Not specifically, but he and Genevieve are concerned about the boy."

"The boy is twenty-six."

"He acts like he's sixteen."

"Point taken. I met the little charmer today. He's anxious for his father to kick the bucket, as the Americans say, so he can take over the title and run the estate the way he wants to."

"Yes, into the ground. But that is not my concern."

"Now, we circle around back to Paul Erikson. You think it's possible Paul was blackmailing Alistair over something to do with Lawrence? Why would he do that, and how would he get himself into the position to do so? Paul didn't exactly move in the same circles as Lawrence and his minor royal."

"Social circles are not as strict as they once were."

"No, but moneyed ones are. Paul was so broke he was living in the back of his shop."

"I don't know, Gemma. I don't even know if Paul had anything on Alistair or his son. Maybe he jotted the name down in his little book for some totally innocent reason." Pippa stood up. "Now, I have a dinner date with my husband, to which you are not invited."

I remained seated. "How do you want me to proceed?"

"I do not. Drop this, Gemma. Completely. Walk away and forget about whatever happened to Paul. You and your friends are going home on Sunday. Enjoy London. Take Jayne to all the places she so desperately wants to see. If you like, I can get you into the private rooms at Hampton Court Palace."

"Oh, goody. A bribe."

"Precisely. Think how happy that will make Jayne. Arrange a special dinner date with your delectable detective. I can recommend some nice places, well off the tourist trail. What's happening is now far beyond you, Gemma."

I considered arguing, just because that's the way a younger sister treats a bossy older sister. But I decided to quit while I was still able to. Pippa was connected enough to have me arrested and held in the dungeons under the Tower until further notice. I stood up. "Hampton Court Palace it is. Can you make it Friday? Paul's mother has invited me around tomorrow, and I would like to see her. Is that okay?"

"Perfectly okay. I'm not telling you not to care that someone you once loved has died, Gemma. I'm advising you to leave the investigating to the people who do that for a living."

I walked to the door. "Bye, Grant," I called.

"Can I come out now?" he called back.

Chapter Eighteen

The fishermen were due to return Thursday afternoon. Paul's sister had suggested I come to their mother's house sometime after two, but I decided not to wait and take Ryan with me. That might be a bit awkward. Mrs. Erikson had not been happy when Paul and I split up. I suspected she liked me more than she liked her son.

"You don't have to come," I said to Jayne as I studied the contents of my closet wondering what to wear. I had not brought suitable mourning clothes on this vacation.

She sat on the bed and watched me. "I'd like to. Truly. I didn't know him, obviously, but I do know you. You weren't together anymore, but this is still going to be difficult for you. Although you'll pretend it isn't. Besides, it's not as though there's anything else to do in one of the greatest cities in the world, is there? Donald's skipping off to play with his new friends, and I do not want to spend an afternoon listening to whatever Sherlock Holmes people talk about when they get together."

"Sherlock Holmes. They talk about Sherlock Holmes. If they take a break from talking about Holmes, they talk about Arthur Conan Doyle. This should do." I selected a pair of dark jeans to wear with a white shirt and a navy blue cotton jacket.

"Should I worry about dressing properly?"

"I don't think it's necessary. You're coming as my friend, not as a mourner."

"Meet you downstairs in fifteen minutes."

* * *

I'd been to this house many times before, when I was with Paul. It was in Hounslow, to the west of the city on the way to Heathrow Airport, on a street of matching red brick duplexes with red roofs and chimneys and postage stamp–sized front gardens. Cars lined the street, and many of the houses had converted those front gardens into parking areas. Most of the houses were clean and well maintained: fresh paint on the doors and window frames, hedges nearly trimmed, flowers in window boxes or tubs on the front step.

The day was chilly, but the sun had come out after an overnight rain. The front door stood open, a group of sixtysomething men chatted and smoked in the small garden. One of them cracked a joke, and his friends roared with laughter. Someone slapped him on the back. I could see women gathered by the front window; the sound of voices and laughter came from inside. This was a somber occasion, but whenever people got together, eventually they laugh. And that is a good thing.

"You okay, Gemma?" Jayne said to me. "Being here must be bringing back a lot of memories, and some of them not very good ones."

"The memories are good. It was Paul I fell out with, not his family." I breathed in the cool air, tinged with smoke, car exhaust, and industrial fumes. "Paul and I did have some good times, and I'm here to remember those, not the less pleasant memories that came later."

Jayne opened the small gate, and we walked through. The men nodded politely to us, not showing a lot of interest. "Go on in, love," one of them called to me. "No need to knock. No one will hear anyway, not once that bunch get to yammering."

His companions laughed heartily. I assumed "that bunch" meant their wives.

Jayne and I walked into the house.

Several women turned to face us and gave us polite smiles. Most of the people here were Paul's mother's age, not Paul's and mine. Fair enough, as it was the middle of the day and this was the street on which he'd grown up. Paul's parents divorced when he and his sister were very young, and the children and their mother stayed in the house.

"Help you, love?" a smiling woman with overly dyed blonde hair and far too much red lipstick asked. The overpowering scent of cigarette smoke, both fresh and stale, wafted around her.

"I'm Gemma and this is Jayne. We're friends of Mrs. Erikson."

"Friends! Is that what you call it now?" Before I knew what was happening, I was enveloped in a warm, crushing hug. Powerful hands slapped my back. Wet lips rained kisses onto my cheeks.

Paul's mother finally released me and stood back, gripping my arms in her hands. "Let me look at you. My, but you look marvelous. Doesn't she look marvelous, girls? This is Gemma, the one Paul let get away."

A circle of women, and a couple of men, had gathered round. They stared openly at me. I gave them a weak smile, feeling quite uncomfortable at the attention.

Jayne thrust out her hand. "I'm Jayne. Jayne Wilson. Gemma's friend and business partner. You must be Mrs. Erikson. I'm sorry for your loss."

"None of that Mrs. Erikson nonsense, love. I'm Alice." Paul's mother wrapped Jayne in almost as affectionate an embrace as she had me. "Any friend of Gemma's is a friend of mine. Come all the way from America, have you? Everyone, this is Jayne. All the way from America."

English people are stereotypically unemotional. All that stiff upper lip stuff. Paul's mother did not suit the image, and she never had. My parents had loved Pippa and me deeply and unreservedly, but such feelings were never something expressed openly in our house. I'd found Paul's mother overwhelming. I'd never quite decided if I liked it or not.

"Now, come in and meet everyone." Alice dragged me into the small, overdecorated sitting room.

Behind me, I heard someone say to Jayne, "Our Gerry, my sister's boy, moved to Denver. Gerald Morgen, do you know him?"

"I don't recall," Jayne said. "I've been to Denver, though. Once."

"America's a big place, Joanie. They don't all know each other," another woman said. "Where exactly do you live, love?"

Everyone resumed their conversations, and Alice and I were alone in a sea of people. She looked older than when I'd last seen her, but as that had been seven years ago, it was to be expected. She'd put on some weight, but not too much, and had her hair cut very short, which suited her now it was almost completely gray. Her warm blue eyes studied my face. "I'm glad you've come, my dear."

"I'm glad I have too. I'm sorry I've not been in touch."

"Not to worry, love. You had reason to want nothing more to do with my Paul." She sniffled and wiped at her eyes with a well-used tissue.

"Anything that happened between him and me had nothing to do with you."

She forced out a smile. "Can you believe how many have come? I haven't said a word to some of these people in years. But folk pop round when they're needed, don't they?" She gave me a wink and jerked her head toward the couch where an enormous woman occupied pride of place, a plate piled high with food balanced on her lap. She lowered her voice. "Then again, I haven't said a word to some of them in years because I don't want to."

"Alice, I can't find any more of those crackers," someone called.

"Top shelf on the right, behind the jars. Never mind, I'll do it. You make yourself comfortable, Gemma. Plenty of food laid out the kitchen, tea in the pot, and drinks in the refrigerator. People have been kind."

She slipped away. All this fuss, I knew, was only covering her pain. Everyone would leave. The dishes would be done, the floor swept, the leftovers packed away. Leaving her alone in her grief.

"Hey, Gemma. Thanks for coming." Paul's sister, Kate, stood in front of me.

"I wanted to. For your mother's sake, if nothing else." I glanced around the crowded room. Jayne had been cornered, people peppering her with questions about where she lived and how she liked London. Jayne was comfortable with strangers, comfortable making small talk, so I knew I didn't need to worry about her. Someone pressed a glass of beer into her hand, and she said thank you.

"Have you heard anything more from the police?" I asked Kate, keeping my voice down.

"Nothing new. They can't say when they'll be releasing the body. If they hang on to it, it'll be hard on Mum. My dad stopped by last night. They sat together for a long time, not saying much, and then they went for a walk. It was nice to see them together. He's taken time off work, and he's mainly the one dealing with the police and trying to wrap up the business of Paul's shop. What have you been up to over these years, Gemma?"

I told her, and then I asked about her life. Two children now, twins, a girl and a boy. They were home in Bristol with their father but would be coming to London soon. They adored their nana, and Alice was looking forward to seeing them. "Excuse me. I should circulate, see if Mum needs anything." Kate turned to go and then swung back to me. "You might want to keep an eye on your friend over there." I looked to see Jayne chatting with a younger man. Her back was against the wall and her smile stiff. "That's Ian from next door. Slimy as ever. He and Paul were thick as thieves all the time they were growing up. Anything Ian said, Paul did. If Paul thought it was okay to cheat on you with a shop clerk, you can be sure he got the idea from Ian. Not your problem. I'll rescue your friend."

Kate crossed the room. "Hi, welcome. I'm Kate, Paul's sister. You're Gemma's friend, right? I want to hear all about the tearoom Gemma tells me you own. Must be so fascinating. Let's go into the kitchen and chat." She tucked Jayne's arm into hers.

Ian threw Kate a dirty look, cocked his head at Jayne and winked, shrugged, and headed for the door to join the men outside. Jayne's smile at Kate said thank you.

"Never you mind my Ian," a woman said to me. "Always had an eye for a pretty girl. Never did know when his attentions were not welcome."

She was in her midsixties, almost as round as she was short, with plump pink cheeks, sparkling blue eyes, and a mass of gray curls. Mrs. Claus, come to life in the South of England. She held a glass of beer, half finished. "I'm Betsy, Ian's mum. From next door. Used to be from next door, that is. I've lived on this street since my wedding day, more than forty years now. Raised four children here. Ian was my late one. Came as a surprise to Freddy and me, I can tell you." She laughed heartily. "Still can't quite believe I've moved away. The new people haven't made any changes yet, although it's only been a week."

"Pleased to meet you," I said. "I'm Gemma."

"Oh, yes, I know. Used to see you with Paul sometimes when he brought you around to visit his mum. Poor Paul. That's life, isn't it? Change. Always change. My own Freddy died last year. His heart, bless him. Always had problems with his heart. Even when he was a young lad. The smoking never helped, but would he listen, no. I said—"

"Sorry, but I think my friend's calling me."

"No, she's not. She's talking to Kate. Lovely girl, Kate. Your friend's a very pretty girl. I see she's wearing an engagement ring. Too bad. My Ian's free."

"How nice. I'm also in a relationship," I added before she could get any ideas of fixing us up.

"Paul and my Ian were ever so close when they were lads. Inseparable, really. They didn't have much to do with each other once they grew up and moved into their own flats, went their own ways in life, but the last few months they started seeing each other again. Isn't that nice?"

"Very nice. If you'll excuse me, I need to speak to Alice."

"Paul dropped in at mine not much more than a week ago. Him and Ian. Last time I saw him. You never know, do you? If I'd known it would be the last time I'd see the boy, I would have made more time for him. Invited him to stay for a meal. But I was getting the last of my things packed up for the movers coming the next day, and so I told him where to get the box and left them to it."

I'd decided I wasn't going to get the chance to politely excuse myself from this barrage of chatter, so I might as well simply walk away. I'd half turned and had one foot in the air. Instead, I froze, lowered the foot, and turned back to give Betsy an encouraging smile. "A box?"

"Yes. Books, I think. He asked Ian to keep it for him. Ian's temporarily between accommodation, having just broken up with his latest girlfriend. I don't know why Paul didn't leave this box at his mum's or even his own place."

Because, I thought, Paul didn't have a place any longer, and he might have, for some reason, not wanted to keep this box in the shop. His own mother would be likely to ask what was in it. Whereas I suspected Betsy didn't stop talking long enough to give anyone a chance to explain anything.

"When did he give you this box?"

"A few months back."

"It contained books?"

"I can't say for sure, love. I didn't look, did I? He put it down in the cellar, and my old knees have trouble on the stairs these days.

Which is why I decided, after my Freddy died, it was time to move to a bungalow. I found a lovely community not far. You must come and visit one day."

"I'll be sure and do that. Paul came to your house last week, and he left with a box he'd been storing there for some months?"

"Isn't that what I said? I told Ian Paul would have to come for his box or I'd throw it out. I was moving, and I don't have room in my new place for a lot of unnecessary things belonging to other people."

"I'd love to meet your son," I said.

Her eyes lit up. "Let me introduce you."

"That won't be necessary. I know who he is."

I found Ian in the patch of front yard, drinking beer with the men. "Hi. I'm Gemma. I've been chatting with your mum."

"My condolences," he said, taking a long drink. "Yeah, I know who you are. You used to be with Paul, right?"

"That's right. But not for some years. Your mother's been telling me about a box Paul kept in her cellar."

Ian shrugged. The other men shifted and moved off. It appeared as though I'd been tracking Paul through London by following a trail of boxes. He seemed to make a habit of asking other people to hold on to his stuff. "That box might be of some significance," I said. "You know the police are treating his death as suspicious?"

"Yeah, I know that. Me mum told me."

Ian could tell me nothing about this box. He and Paul had largely lost touch until they ran into each other in a pub about six months ago. They'd gone out drinking a few times after that, and then one night Paul asked if Ian could take care of a box of his things. Ian had broken up with his girlfriend and been kicked out of her flat, so he was temporarily sleeping on a friend's couch. He said Paul could take the box to his mother's. When his mother sold the house and began packing up, Ian told Paul he had to come for the box. Ian claimed to have never looked in it, and Paul had not told him what it contained.

"Sentimental rubbish, I figured," Ian said.

"What was the box made of?"

"What's any box made of? Cardboard, I guess."

"How heavy was it?"

"Don't know. I never touched it."

"Did he strain to lift it? Did he need a cart of some sort to move it?"

Ian shrugged again. "Not heavy. One bloke could pick it up and carry it easily enough."

Paul's office had been full of cardboard boxes. Some empty, some full. Some half-full. If he'd asked his friend to store this particular box, did that mean it was of some significance to him? Something he didn't want anyone else, such as a busy shop clerk, to accidentally come across?

Which led to the question as to where this box was now. "Thank you," I said to Ian.

"What's your rush? Have a beer."

"Another time," I said.

Under Pippa's strongly worded suggestion, as well as the belief that I was wasting my time trying to find out what happened, I'd decided last night to stop poking into Paul's death.

Unasked, unwanted, and unexpected, a fresh path had opened up in front of me.

What could I do but follow?

Chapter Nineteen

"Where do you hide a tree?" I asked Jayne.

"The main question is, why would I want to hide a tree?"

"Irrelevant. Pretend you do. Where do you hide it?"

I'd torn Jayne away from the group of women surrounding her, said our quick, apologetic goodbyes to Alice and Kate, avoided Betsy, who'd started to inquire as to if her son had asked me on a date, and ran out the door as fast as I could without attracting more attention than I already had.

We were now walking at a brisk pace, heading for the nearest tube station.

Jayne thought about trees and hiding places for a long time. "I guess the best place to hide a tree is in a forest."

"Exactly. Where do you hide a book?"

She grinned at me. "In a bookstore."

I pulled out my phone and called a recently used number. "Tamara, hi. Gemma Doyle here. Do you know if the police have taken the tape down at the bookshop?"

"Paul's father's been given the keys. He called Faye and me to tell us we can go back in if we've left anything. Mr. Erikson'll be handling whatever they intend to do with the shop. If he's going to sell off the stock at discount prices, there might be some things I'd be interested in getting, but I don't know when, or if, that's going to happen. I don't think the shop will ever open for business again, except to get rid of the contents for whatever price they can get. He'll want to pack up the new books and send back the ones that are returnable. Faye's agreed to help him with that."

"Do you still have a key?"

"Why are you asking?"

"I'm looking for something, and I think it's in the shop. I'd like you to help me with the search. Do you have time now?"

"Not really. But this sounds so intriguing, I'll make time."

* * *

Tamara beat us to Trafalgar Fine Books. We knocked and she opened the door immediately, her face alight with curiosity. "What are you looking for?"

"I won't know until I find it. You know the stock, Tamara. Some of those used books look like they've been there for a long time."

"Which they have."

"I'm not looking for a specific book, but something tucked into one. I suspect Paul hid something, likely a letter or a photograph, in the pages of a book. He'd been keeping this . . . whatever it is . . . at a friend's place, but he had to collect it a few days ago. If he didn't have any fresh options, it's possible he slipped the book onto the shelves here to hide it, rather than wherever passed for his home these days or even in the office where it would stand out. The book we're looking for will be new to the shelves, placed there within the last few days. If nothing's obvious to you, we'll have to check them all."

She shook her head. "I don't pay a lot of attention to what we get in fiction. The nonfiction I usually browse in case there's anything that might help with my paper. Nothing comes to mind now."

We climbed the stairs to the upper level, and I looked at the shelves, jammed with books of varying ages and conditions.

On the way here, I told Jayne what I was thinking. The only reason Paul would keep one small, light box in his friend's mother's cellar would be if he didn't want it to be found. If he'd kept it in the usual places, such as his own bookshop, then it might be located by person or persons he didn't want to have it.

He could be hiding a book, and if so, he'd had that book for some months at least. But that made no sense. Paul was broke. He needed money now; he'd be trying to sell this find, whatever it was, now. At the time he'd taken the box to his friend Ian's house, he hadn't known I'd be coming to London for Pippa's wedding. I could think of no reason he'd keep this book hidden waiting for me to see it. I'm not a used book buyer, and I'm not all that much of an expert, although I have some knowledge. Any rare book he'd be trying to sell wouldn't be kept under wraps. He would have sent out feelers to the sort of people who were buyers and experts at that level, but no one had heard rumors of anything coming onto the market. No one Grant or I had spoken to, at any rate. Furthermore, before putting in an offer for a potentially valuable book, buyers would insist on examining the item. Yet Paul hid it in a cellar in an old duplex in Hounslow?

If it was a rare or valuable book, and for some reason he was keeping it out of sight, Paul would have known better than to store it in a cardboard box in a damp London cellar. Therefore, I had to conclude, he was hiding something the value of which wouldn't be reduced by exposure to a bit of humidity for a short while.

Not a book, and not an old document.

"We're in no hurry," I said, "so let's try not to make too much of a mess. Jayne and I will take the books off the shelf, give them a check to see if anything's concealed inside, and put them back. Tamara, watch us and let us know if you spot anything that shouldn't be there. I'm initially only interested in the used books, but if we don't find anything, we can go downstairs and do the same with the new ones."

"I can do that," Tamara said, "but remember some of these used books have come in by the caseload. I have nothing more than a vague idea of what's where."

"Good enough," I said.

One at a time, Jayne and I took books down from the shelves and flipped the pages. Jayne sneezed steadily. The staff had dusted the front of the books, but many of them had not been moved for a long time, and the shelves behind them were thick with dust and the occasional desiccated insect. Occasionally, Tamara said, "I don't recognize that one," so I pulled it out and checked inside with additional care, but they all ended up back where they'd started.

Jayne began at the top left shelf, and I took the top right. We were about to meet in the middle, and I was beginning to fear I'd wasted everyone's time, when an image of Paul flashed into my mind. The last time I'd seen him. In the hotel lobby, lying in wait for me to leave my sister's wedding. It had been raining out and he wore a loose beige raincoat. A coat with big pockets. He had a book in his hand. As he rose to greet me, he slipped the book into a pocket. Mentally I focused on the image. *Farewell, My Lovely*. Raymond Chandler.

I stepped back and studied the shelves. And there it was. Bottom shelf, neatly lined up with books of similar genre and age. I crouched down and gently pulled the book off the shelf.

"Is that it?" Jayne said.

"I think so."

I knew as soon as I had the not-too-bad-condition paperback copy of the mystery classic that something was inside it. I got to my feet as Jayne and Tamara gathered around me. I cradled the book in both hands, and it fell open to reveal a single sheet of paper, folded. "What have we here? I'd prefer not to get my prints on it until I know if it's significant or not. Jayne, can you grab a pen out of your bag?"

She did so. I didn't worry about getting my fingerprints on the book itself—this was a bookshop after all—as I carried it to a table in the center of the room. Jayne handed me a pen, and I used it to edge the paper out from between the pages of the book. I then slipped the closed end of the pen into the paper and flipped it open. The paper was still white and crisp, the writing in ballpoint pen, the words legible. We leaned in and read.

"I do think," I said when I'd finished, "Pippa will want to see this."

Chapter Twenty

"I suspect," I said to Jayne and Tamara, "if you reveal the contents of this to anyone, you'll find yourself incommunicado for a long time indeed."

"I don't even know who those people are," Tamara said.

"Just as well."

"I do," Jayne said. "But my lips are sealed."

"By Pippa," Tamara said, "I assume you're not referring to Pippa Middleton, sister of the Princess of Wales."

"I am not."

"Now that I've read the names, I can look them up. I promise not to do so on one condition only."

"You're not in a position to make demands," I said.

She grinned at me. "You cannot leave me in permanent suspense. If you can, when you can, will you let me know who killed Paul? Presumably for possession of that letter. It doesn't mean anything to me, but clearly it does to you and other people. People Paul shouldn't have been messing with."

"I'll do what I can," I said. "Thanks for your help. For the moment, I'd prefer if you don't tell Paul's father, or anyone else, what we've been doing here today."

"Not a problem. To be frank, Gemma, if I can't work it into my dissertation, I don't much care. Someday maybe, but right now, I have far more important things to concentrate on."

With the aid of the pen, I slid the letter back into the book and then I stuffed it into my bag. We went downstairs, and Tamara locked the door behind us.

Standing on the pavement while commuters and tourists swirled around us, I texted Pippa: *Found item of significant interest to you. Where are you?*

Pippa: *Out of office. Come straight to this address. Do not take public transit. Take precautions.* The address she sent me was close to Guildhall.

"Should I leave you to it, Gemma?" Jayne said.

"Only if you want to. You're involved so you might as well see it through. It's not far to where we're to meet her. Let's go." We hurried to the Strand. Traffic was heavy and moving slowly. I waited on the pavement and then darted out to dash between two cabs, causing cars to screech to a halt and the driver of a panel van to yell unprintable words at me. No one, other than Jayne, appeared to have followed me.

"Close one." Jayne patted her chest. "If we have to take this letter to the hospital with us, Pippa won't be pleased with you."

I put up my hand and hailed a free cab. It pulled up to the curb, but I waved it away as though I'd changed my mind. The driver gave me a disapproving shake of the head. I beckoned for the next one, and we jumped in. I gave him the address Pippa had sent to me.

I tried to watch the cars and trucks and vans and scooters behind us, but I didn't see anything that appeared to be sticking close. Not that I'd be likely to notice if we were being followed in a coordinated attempt.

My phone buzzed with a text.

Ryan: *At Stanhope Gardens. Had great time. Where are U?*
Me: *Paid condolences on Paul's mum. Going to Pippa for quick chat. Back soon.*
Ryan: ♥

Beside me Jayne was also checking her phone and typing.

"Andy?" I asked.

"Yes. The happy fishermen are back and he's wondering what dinner plans are. I think it's fair to say we don't know yet."

"That it is."

As we approached our destination, I didn't bother to get out prematurely or to tell the driver to circle the block a few times. If anyone followed us this far, they'd know I was going to meet with Pippa.

I paid the driver, and we got out on Gresham Street. The buildings were all tall and cream colored, with thin windows and heavy doors. Trees, their leaves yellowing, lined the street. The door of the address we'd been directed to was painted a solid black. I checked for CCTV cameras. I couldn't see any, but I had no doubt our every move was being watched. A small bronze plaque, polished to a brilliant shine daily, announced that this was the offices of R & R Richmond and Associates. Next to the plaque was a discreet buzzer. I pushed it, and the door swung open almost immediately. A man stepped back with a nod. He wore a well-cut gray suit, a stiffly ironed white shirt, and a gray and blue striped tie, perfectly knotted.

"Ms. Doyle and Ms. Wilson," he said. "You are expected."

"Thank you," I said.

"Please, follow me."

We did so. The carpet was thick, the lights strong but not too bright. Pleasant landscape paintings hung on the walls. Closed doors led off the hallway. The only sound was the rustle of Jayne's bag. I felt the weight of the book in mine.

"I would have thought there'd be some sort of security, if this is a government building," Jayne whispered to me.

"There is. Believe me, there is."

Jayne sucked in a nervous breath, and her eyes darted around.

The man opened a door, gestured to us to go in, and we did so. He closed the door behind us. It was a conference room, much like any other. Wide, mass-produced wooden table, various communication and projection devices set into the center of the table; eight ergonomic chairs; credenza containing a pitcher of water, empty glasses, and nothing else; a 72-inch TV, turned off, mounted on the wall opposite the head of the table. No windows. No doors but the one we came through. No paintings or pictures on the walls.

My sister was the only person in the room. She sat at the foot of the table, facing the door, her phone and a small notebook and pen on the polished surface in front of her.

She did not bother to exchange friendly greetings. "Have a seat, please, and let's see what you have."

"Hi." Jayne cautiously dropped into a chair.

Pippa smiled at her. "Jayne, how are you? I hope you're enjoying your visit to London."

"It's been interesting, I'll say that."

"I trust Gemma told you about the special visit we've arranged to Hampton Court Palace tomorrow. Private tour."

"I was saving that as a surprise." I gestured to the room around me, taking in the entire building. "Is this where you have your office?"

"No. I was attending a meeting in a more secure facility, not far from here, and I decided this would be convenient. Water? Or I can call for tea?"

"No, thank you. Let's get to it, shall we?" I sat down. Goodness, but this chair was comfortable. I might ask Pippa for the name of the supplier so I could get one for my own office. Then again, unlikely I could afford it. "I believe we've found what Paul died for." I opened my bag and took out the book.

"Raymond Chandler?" Pippa said. "I must say, that comes as a surprise."

"Not the book, but its contents." I explained what I'd learned at Paul's mother's house, the thought process that led to us going to the bookshop and searching the used stock on the shelves.

I opened the book and revealed the letter tucked inside. I will confess I put a bit of a flourish into it. Not often I got a chance to show off to Pippa. "Ta-da," I said.

"How did you get into the shop?" my sister asked.

"I phoned one of the clerks, and she met us there and let us in."

"Her name?"

I told Pippa, and she jotted it in the notebook.

"And yes, before you ask, she read the letter at the same time as Jayne and I did. I told her, for what it's worth, not to discuss it with anyone."

"More like Gemma put the fear of the law, or perhaps more to the point, of you, into her," Jayne said.

The edges of Pippa's mouth curled up ever so slightly.

I slid the open book across the table. Pippa took a pair of tweezers out of apparently nowhere and used them pick up the piece of paper and unfold it.

I watched her face as she read.

"Not the errant son, Lawrence, but the father," I said.

"The father's misdeeds caused by the son. Thank you, Gemma. I'll have the handwriting confirmed, but I've little doubt it's that of Alistair Denhaugh."

The letter was handwritten, dated eight years ago. From Alistair Denhaugh to a teacher at a highly prestigious private school, asking the teacher not to reveal that Lawrence Denhaugh and another boy, unnamed, had been caught cheating on their exams. It would appear this was not the first instance such had happened, but this time it would be the last. If it was disclosed. Meaning Lawrence would be expelled and would not graduate. In not quite so many words, Alistair suggested that in exchange for a suitable amount of money, the matter need not be reported to school officials.

"Foolish to commit that to paper," I said.

"He might have thought it worse to use electronic communication," Pippa said. "Foolish to agree to the idea in any event. I assume the bribe was paid, and considering Alistair had been notified before the matter was brought to the attention of the school authorities, such was the original intention of this teacher in contacting Alistair."

"Would this be enough to ruin Alistair?" I asked.

"Unlikely, but this is not a good time for his reputation to be under question. Lawrence did finish at that school, barely, and he went on to uni. Where he didn't last out his first year. Alistair should have saved his money. I wonder if Genevieve knows about this. Irrelevant. I'd be interested to know how your Paul came into possession of this letter."

"He wasn't my Paul. Paul was several years older than Lawrence, and he didn't go to that school, so he can't be the other boy mentioned, but it's possible the family of the other boy also got a letter from this teacher, and somehow Alistair's reply made its way into their hands. I would have thought the teacher would have destroyed the letter. He's not named, but easy enough to find out who he was, and he himself is severely compromised by its existence."

"Blackmail rarely ends with a single payment. The teacher would have had to keep the letter if he was considering using it again. Criminals tend not to be terribly smart sometimes, and he might have simply had too many irons in the fire and lost track of it. Or it was stolen, which is also entirely possible. Another boy is mentioned although no name given. We can assume the other boy's family received a similar request for payment to keep the matter undisclosed. This teacher, and you can be sure I'll have him looked into, has put himself in danger of being blackmailed because of this sort of thing. He would certainly lose his position over it."

"Regardless of how this letter came into Paul's hands, he intended to use it. It makes me sad to realize he was reduced to doing such a thing. The Paul I knew might have been lazy and he might have been a philanderer, but I never thought he was dishonest."

"Why do you think he was intending to blackmail Alistair?" Jayne asked me. "He had the letter, but he hid it."

"He kept it under wraps at his mother's neighbor's house, yes, but then he was told he had to move it. It's possible he'd forgotten about it, but reclaiming it reminded him. And then, in one of those coincidences that make life interesting, he saw mention of Alistair. Alistair's been in the news, hasn't he? About his consulting on the business of the Australian freighter."

"He has. The Foreign Secretary was at her own home in York when the incident first happened, and she went to Garfield Hall to consult with Alistair. Reporters met her at the gates as she was leaving, and she mentioned that Alistair's assistance would be vital in establishing effective communication channels with the parties involved. The following morning, Alistair, along with Genevieve and Lawrence, traveled to London for my wedding that afternoon."

"Paul must have heard that news item. He realized he was in possession of something which Alistair Denhaugh, Earl of Ramshaw, would not want to be made public. He intended to use it all right. He was waiting for Alistair at your wedding dinner, not me. He had the letter with him, tucked between the pages of *Farewell, My Lovely*, as proof."

Pippa nodded.

"I speculate he'd stuffed the letter into the bottom of a drawer in his office when he reclaimed it. He didn't know what to do with it, but he didn't want to throw it out. But now that he was using it, or hoped to, considering that the guilty run where no one pursues, he was afraid Alistair would send thugs to the bookshop to get it. After getting back to the shop Saturday night, he hid it in the forest."

"A forest? I thought this shop is on Villiers Street?"

"She's speaking metaphorically," Jayne said.

"I do wish she wouldn't do that," Pippa said. "Complicates everything."

"Paul must have found out that Alistair would be at your wedding, and he thought a public venue would be a great place to confront him, tell him what he had, and make the initial demand. And then who pops up but me, leaving early."

"Why did Paul tell you he wanted you to see a book then?" Jayne asked.

"He needed a reason to explain his presence at the hotel, but mainly, if I may be so vain, he genuinely still had feelings for me. He couldn't talk to me right there. Not only because I was leaving, but because he was waiting for Alistair, and he didn't want me to see them together. On the spur of the moment, he thought of inviting me to see a book the next day. There never was any book."

"Are you saying Alistair killed Paul?" Jayne asked. "To get the letter?"

"If so, that would be most unfortunate," Pippa said. "Unlikely Alistair, if he wanted to, would have done the deed himself. He's not a young man. No, I don't see it. I'd say it's more likely people who want Alistair compromised were after the letter."

"They killed Paul, but they didn't get it," Jayne said.

"No. Because he'd hidden it as Gemma says. Maybe they didn't have time to search the entire shop. Maybe they intended to ask Paul to hand it over, but something went wrong and he died. I do not know." Pippa pressed a button under the table. She stood up.

The door opened, and a young woman in an immaculate business suit stood there. Her hair was folded into a knot at the back of her head, and her makeup was so subtle as to be unnoticeable. She looked several years older than she had at Pippa's wedding.

"Hi," I said cheerfully. "Nice to see you again. How's your mother? Millicent, isn't it?"

She gave me a barely disguised look of fury. I assumed she'd been reprimanded for letting herself be spotted at the wedding. Maybe opening doors to visitors was a punishment.

"Thank you for bringing this matter to my attention," Pippa said.

"What happens now?" Jayne asked.

"I earlier asked Gemma to ensure this matter didn't involve my office in any way. Unfortunately, it would seem we are forced to get involved. I'll see that this letter is handled properly. If certain people who wish to impede the negotiations Alistair is involved in were attempting to get blackmail material, they need to be discovered and steps taken. Cheryl will see you out."

Chapter Twenty-One

"That was . . . interesting," Jayne said when we were once again standing on the pavement in front of R & R Richardson and Associates. "I'm glad we've solved the case without getting ourselves in any sort of a pickle."

"Solved it? I'm not so sure. Alistair Denhaugh wasn't the only guest at the wedding." Once again, I phoned Pippa.

"What is it now?" she said.

"I've had a thought. When I left your wedding reception, Paul was in the lobby of the hotel. He was sitting not far from the front doors, which is a highly public place. We chatted briefly. I took my leave, he stayed. We assumed he was waiting for Alistair, but it's entirely possible he wanted to talk to someone else."

"Who?"

"I have an idea, but it's only a guess at the moment."

"You always say you never guess," said Jayne, listening in.

I ignored her. "The hotel would have CCTV coverage of the lobby, and mostly likely the corridors by the meeting and banqueting rooms as well. It's not been a week since Saturday evening, so they should still have the tapes. Check it. See who Paul met with. Other than me."

"As much as I hate to admit it, that is a good idea, Gemma."

"If you see the person I suspect, I want to know. You'll know who that is."

* * *

When Jayne and I got in from meeting with Pippa, while Jayne and Andy had a joyful reunion, and Donald tried to tell everyone about his exciting day, I took Dad, closely followed by Horace, and Ryan into the conservatory and closed the door. The conservatory is at the back of the house, with wide windows and doors opening onto a small terrace, surrounded by a low stone wall with two steps leading down to the garden. A scattering of yellow leaves covered the grass, and the large iron pots, which my mother fills with plants in the summer, had been emptied and cleaned in preparation for winter.

I told Ryan and my father what I'd been up to and what we'd discovered.

"I don't know your mother's cousin all that well, but I'm surprised he would put himself in a position to be blackmailed like that." Dad turned away from the windows. "Putting a bribe down in writing?"

"People act in panic," Ryan said. "All they want is for the problem to go away as quickly as possible. But, as we know, blackmail rarely ends with one payment. Once they have their hooks into you, they don't let go."

"True. Admittedly, there's rarely a limit to the things we'll do for our children," Dad said with a fond smile at me. "You and your sister might have given Anne and me a few sleepless nights over the years, but we never had to consider going to such extremes."

"Only because we were never found out," I said.

Ryan laughed. "I can believe that."

"Sadly," Dad said, "it would appear Alistair's efforts to protect Lawrence from his own folly were a waste of time. The lad's academic career proved to be less than stellar."

"In this case," I said, "the original blackmailer, the teacher, appears to have been satisfied with one payment. As far as we know, at any rate. The letter remained unused for eight years, but then a new blackmailer appeared on the scene. Paul had possession of the letter, but we have to consider he was acting for someone else, willingly or otherwise. Pippa suspects what we might call 'unfriendly governments' are hoping to sabotage Alistair's reputation and thus throw a spanner into the delicate negotiations going on over the Australian freighter business."

"I heard about that situation on the news," Ryan said, "International tensions are increasing, and more and more countries getting involved to their own ends, but what does any of it have to do with your cousin? Or Pippa, come to think of it."

I explained about Alistair and what I suspected about Pippa's involvement.

Ryan let out a long breath. "Wow! I figured Pippa's at a way higher pay grade than she lets on, but I had no idea how much higher."

"Remember your Sherlock," I said. "In the Canon, Mycroft Holmes is described as 'the most indispensable man in the country.' I wouldn't go quite that far, but Pippa does have her role."

"Which is never to be discussed outside this room," Dad said.

"Okay," Ryan said. "Back to the immediate matter. I have two questions. One, I'd be interested in knowing how your Paul came into possession of that letter."

"He's not my Paul," I said, "and I'd like to know that too, but it's possible we'll never find out."

"Second question, how would these unfriendly governments know to contact Paul, if that's what happened?"

"Again, I can't say, but it would appear Paul owed money to people he shouldn't. His shop clerks told me unidentified men of an unsavory appearance paid a couple of calls on Paul, and they didn't seem to be interested in the buying or selling of books. Paul might have mentioned something about it to them, trying to convince them he'd soon have their money, and they passed the word on. But that's all speculation. I'm out of it now. Pippa told me to end my involvement, and I am happy to do so."

"Shall we join the others?" Dad said.

"Can you give us a few minutes, please," Ryan said.

Dad smiled. "Of course." He called to Horace, and they left us alone.

* * *

At nine PM, we were gathered in the formal dining room at Stanhope Gardens. The table was covered in the remains of Indian takeaway, and I was eying the last spoonful of lamb korma and half a naan, wondering if I could possibly fit it in. Before I could make up my mind, Andy said, "Anyone want the last of that?" We chorused, "Help yourself," and the temptation disappeared.

Earlier, over predinner drinks in the library, we'd been entertained by an incredibly boring recitation of the joys of fishing in Derbyshire. Not just the fishing but the eating of the fish, as prepared by the chefs at the hotel, was discussed in great detail. Jayne was smiling adoringly at Andy, clearly delighted he'd had such a great time. I might have similarly been smiling at Ryan. He and my dad got on extremely well, and I was pleased about that. My parents had never approved of Paul.

Only proving, once and for all, they were wiser than I.

Speaking of adoring, Horace hadn't moved from his place by Dad's side since he got home. Dad's free hand rested on top of the dog's head, occasionally providing a light scratch between the ears.

Once talk of the intense battles to land the fish and the details of the cooking methods later used to prepare them wound down, Donald leapt in to relate the details of his day in the company of the London Sherlockians. We were all shifting restlessly, everyone searching for a polite way to change the conversation when Mum's phone rang to tell her the food delivery had arrived.

Dinner over, Mum put aside her napkin, rose to her feet, and reached for the empty bowls. Jayne and Andy leapt to their feet. Jayne said, "Let us do the clearing up, please. You've made us so welcome here."

Horace's ears pricked up, he barked, and a moment later the doorbell rang. Mum and Dad exchanged glances. "Late for a caller."

"I'll get it," Dad said.

I heard the front door open, followed by my sister's voice and the sound of her heels on the tiles in the hallway. A few seconds later, Pippa came into the room, carrying a laptop. "The gang's all here, I see."

Donald rose to his feet and gallantly offered Pippa his chair.

"Drink, love?" Mum asked.

"No, thank you. I won't stay long. I have something to show Gemma." She put the laptop on the table in front of me. "Donald, please sit. I'll stand."

"Can we all see what you have?" Ryan asked.

She hesitated and then said, "I don't see why not. The footage I'm about to show you was captured in a public place." She opened the lid and typed in her password. It might have only been a coincidence that she placed her body in such a position I couldn't see the movement of her fingers across the keyboard. "There's nothing else on this computer, Gemma. Don't bother trying to hack in if my back is turned. This one is wiped clean every night."

"Perish the thought," I said. "I assume this is CCTV footage from the wedding dinner venue. You found it quickly."

"Not difficult," Pippa said, "nor time consuming when I knew the location and the precise time frame we're interested in. The police had it anyway. I got this from them."

"In England, people can just ask the police to show them evidence?" Andy asked. "And they get it?"

"I can," Pippa said.

Andy opened his mouth to reply, but Jayne said, "Don't ask."

"I can never help but speculate," Donald said, "as to what Sherlock Holmes would have done had he had access to this plethora of data and images. Would it have helped or hindered his intensive observation of—"

"I'd be delighted to hear your thoughts, Donald," Mum said. "But perhaps that's a topic for another occasion. It's late and Pippa must be anxious to get home."

"I'm starting the tape at 9:40," Pippa said. My friends and family gathered in a tight circle behind my chair, and we watched the jerky, grainy, black-and-white footage on the laptop.

"That looks like the lobby of the hotel where Pippa had her wedding dinner," Donald said.

"So it is," Pippa replied.

The camera was mounted high on the wall opposite the reception desk. It showed the desk, part of the lobby, the front door. At that time on a Saturday night, numerous people walked across the screen. The doorman opened doors; the night clerk went into a back room and came out again, someone stopped at the reception desk to ask a question. I felt a pang of sadness, grief for what might have been, as a clearly recognizable Paul Erikson entered the frame, coming in from the street.

Ryan, standing next to me, put his hand on my shoulder and gave it a tight squeeze. I turned and smiled up at him. Never mind what might have been. What I had now was all I wanted.

"At quarter to ten, Paul enters the hotel," Pippa said. "He takes a seat in the lobby. He pretends to be reading his book, but he's clearly anxious and waiting for a particular person or persons." Pippa pressed keys, and the image jerked forward as people began rushing about and the clock in the bottom corner ticked rapidly as in a movie indicating the passage of time. "I've seen the intervening footage. No one approaches him, and he appears to pay no attention to anyone in particular until . . . now."

A woman came on-screen. Not just any woman. Me.

"That's Gemma," Andy and Donald said at the same time.

"Did that coat really look that bad from the rear?" I asked.

"No," Ryan said.

"No," Jayne said.

I peered closer. I watched Paul stand up. I watched myself come to a sudden halt. He put the book in the pocket of his raincoat. We spoke. He faced the camera, my back was to it. "Can you zoom in on Paul's face?" I asked.

Pippa stopped it, backed the tape up, and did so. The image got grainer. Paul's lips moved. He spoke to me, but occasionally his eyes darted over my shoulder.

"I must have been extremely tired," I said. "I failed to notice at the time. He's watching for something to happen behind me."

"Yes, he is," Pippa said. "What I find significant is that you are not the focus of his attention."

Somehow, that made me feel better. Paul hadn't been lying in wait, hoping to see me again, desperately wanting to spend time with me. Maybe even hoping I'd love him again. He'd been at my sister's wedding venue to see someone else. And likely for nefarious purposes.

Pippa pulled the image back. On-screen, I walked away from Paul. The doorman opened the door for me, and I disappeared into the rainy London night. Pippa hit fast-forward again. I saw a few people I recognized as wedding guests leave. No one so much as glanced at Paul. His leg twitched nervously. He didn't take the book out again.

"At 10:17, he moves." On-screen, Paul leapt to his feet, as alert as Horace when he hears Dad's key in the door. He walked out of view of the camera, and Pippa said, "I'm switching to the camera watching the hallway."

I saw the corridor outside the banquet room, leading to the loos and the kitchens. A man dressed in a suit, jacket off, tie askew, came out of a side door, hesitated, checked both directions, clearly looking for the men's room. Something caught his attention, his head swiveled, and a moment later Paul came into view. Paul stopped in front of him. The two men spoke.

"Not who I was expecting," I said.

"You thought Genevieve," Pippa said.

"I did."

We couldn't hear a word, and I couldn't read their lips, but it was obvious they were not having a polite, casual conversation. Lawrence Denhaugh faced the camera. His expression tightened, his shoulders straightened, his hands formed fists at his side. Eventually, he threw up his hands, turned, and walked rapidly away. Paul hesitated and then also turned, and he headed back toward the lobby.

The image froze on Paul's face. He was not smiling.

"Lawrence Denhaugh," Pippa said, "then went into the men's loo. We do not have footage from there."

"Glad to hear it," Andy mumbled.

"He emerged more than five minutes later and returned to the dining room. I'm trying to put a trace on his phone to determine if he placed a call while in the loo, but that sometimes proves to be difficult."

"Even for you?" I couldn't resist saying.

She did not dignify that comment with a reply, so I continued. "It's likely, possible even, he was attempting to compose himself before rejoining his parents."

"About ten minutes later, he and Alistair and Genevieve leave the reception, gather their coats, and leave the hotel. The doorman hailed a cab for them, and they got in together. As for Paul, he walked straight out after the encounter with Lawrence. The police are attempting to trace his movements after he left the hotel, but that is a good deal more difficult. The streets were crowded, and the rain disrupts the images."

"He probably went straight to the shop," I said. "Leaving us with the question of who followed him there. Lawrence after seeing his parents home?"

"The police can find no evidence of Lawrence and Paul meeting again. Lawrence has been questioned about what they discussed. He claims he and Paul are casual acquaintances. Paul asked him for money and he refused. He says he has no idea why Paul would have accosted him at the hotel at that time of night, other than it must have been a coincidence. Paul saw him and took advantage of the opportunity. The police have no reason, as of yet, to bring Lawrence in for further questioning."

"Where is this Lawrence now?" Ryan asked.

"Unknown. He is not under suspicion, therefore not under surveillance. I believe the letter Gemma found, and the fact that Paul approached him at the wedding, now places Lawrence very much under suspicion."

"Have you told the police this?" Ryan asked.

"Not until I determine definitively it is not a matter of national security. I have attempted to contact Lawrence, but he's not answering his phone. Not to me at any rate, but I don't read too much into that. Many people these days don't answer numbers they don't recognize."

"I saw him Sunday when I left the bookshop in the police car," I said. "He was on the pavement, on the other side of the Strand, close to Trafalgar Square. I assumed—that horrid word again—he was either part of the demonstration going on there or he wanted to be an observer for some reason."

"What time was this?" Ryan asked.

"One o'clock, maybe? Shortly thereafter. We got to the shop at noon. Found Paul, called 999, waited for the authorities to arrive, and Patel sent us to wait for her at the station."

"Paul died long before you arrived, you said."

"That's definitive," Pippa said. "While asking for the CCTV footage, I also requested a copy of the autopsy results. Paul Erikson died sometime between midnight and three AM. He had not eaten for several hours, but he was, to put it mildly, plastered."

"Meaning drunk," I said.

"Yes. He'd consumed a substantial part of a bottle of whiskey in the hours before his death. He was strangled, most likely by a scarf or similar length of cloth. The police have searched extensively for whatever was used, but no sign of it. It's likely in the river, burned, or otherwise disposed of by now. People watch far too much telly these days. They know all about forensic evidence and the like."

"They think they know," my dad said. "Not always the same thing."

"Point taken," Pippa said. "Paul's body showed no signs of resistance. He was asleep or more likely passed out when he was attacked, too slow to react, unable to fight back."

I took a deep breath. Ryan's hand rested on my shoulder. My mother laid her hand lightly on mine.

"When Gemma saw Lawrence in the vicinity of the store at one o'clock," Ryan said, "he can't have been coming from killing Paul."

"It's not a myth," Dad said, "that amateur criminals often return to the scene of the crime. They want to either reassure themselves that what happened, happened, or they want to enjoy the fallout."

Pippa looked at the faces watching her. "If Lawrence Denhaugh did kill, accidentally or otherwise, Paul Erikson, that's a matter for Scotland Yard."

"Surely, you can't strangle someone accidentally," Donald said.

"I'm being generous," Pippa said. "If Lawrence followed Paul to the shop and inadvertently witnessed anything that might provide evidence as to what happened, that is also a matter for the police. These tapes show nothing other than two men talking. Proof of nothing. Gemma thinks she saw Lawrence—"

"I saw him," I said.

"If you say you did, you did," Pippa said. "The police, however, need more evidence than your word, and even if he was in the vicinity of the bookshop at one o'clock in the afternoon, that proves nothing. Donald was there at that time."

"I was," Donald confirmed, "but—"

"Simply making a point, Donald," Pippa said. "The death of Paul Erikson is a police matter. If, however, it can be determined that third parties are involved in an attempt to take advantage of the blackmailable material for subversive reasons, then the matter remains under the auspices of . . . other agencies."

"Huh?" Donald said.

"What does all that mean?" Andy asked.

"It means," my mother said, "we are not to discuss this with anyone outside of the police, in the event they have further questions about the death of Paul. I have to say, Pippa dear, I'm surprised you've shared this much with all of us."

"As is her annoying way, Gemma has managed to place herself directly in the center of a matter that should have absolutely nothing to do with her."

"What can I say," I said. "Trouble finds me."

"And don't I know it," Ryan said.

"Rather than beating about the bush," I said, "you've told my friends if they blab, I'll be in trouble."

"I never beat about the bush." My sister shut the laptop.

"Would you like me to have a quiet word with the officers in charge?" Dad asked. "I can ask if they've come across any reason to suspect this third-party involvement. Rumors circulating in the underworld, for example."

"That would be helpful, thank you. Silos do exist and not everything is shared with me. Now, I must take my leave. I have to travel to Yorkshire tonight. I fear I'm going to have a difficult conversation with Alistair."

"The first train doesn't leave until quarter to six in the morning," Donald said in an attempt to be helpful.

"I do not intend to travel by train," Pippa said. "Fortunately, the lawns at Garfield Hall are expansive enough for a helicopter to land. Good night, all. Gemma, you may walk me to the door."

"I may, may I?" I said.

"This is all way, way over my head," Andy said. "I'm just a cook trying to enjoy his vacation. Jayne, honey, do you know what's going on?"

"Enough to be totally confused," Jayne replied.

Mum stifled a fake yawn. "Andy, dear. You haven't had the chance to tell me about your restaurant. Gemma says it's one of the best in your town."

"I say it is the best," I said, as I left the dining room after my sister.

Pippa opened the front door. Outside, a black car was parked at the curb. The streetlight above shone down on it, revealing one person in the driver's seat.

Pippa stared into the night and spoke to me. "Two lines, at least, of investigation are open here. If you interfere in a national security matter, I'll have you thrown in jail. I've been known to lose keys to jail cells."

"Of that I have no doubt. But the other line?"

"If Lawrence killed your Paul—"

"He wasn't my Paul."

"If Lawrence was involved over nothing more than a shady piece of blackmail, you're free, as far as I'm concerned, to poke your nose in as much as you like. In that regard, I'll let you know what, if anything, I find out when I arrive at Garfield Hall."

"Thank you."

I watched her walk down the steps. She got into the back seat of the black car and it drove away.

Chapter Twenty-Two

I was woken by Ryan shaking me.

"Wha? Wha?"

"Your phone's ringing, Gemma."

That got my attention. I keep my phone on do not disturb overnight. Only Uncle Arthur, Jayne, Pippa, Ryan, and my parents can override that.

The phone was on the nightstand, the screen illuminated, the sound indicating it was an actual phone call. I grabbed it. "What? What?"

"So sorry. Did I wake you?"

"Of course, you woke me. What time is this to be calling?" I looked at the screen. Ten past two. Outside all was dark, the streets quiet.

Ryan sat up and switched on the light at his side of the bed.

"The time is pertinent," Pippa said. "Rain over Halifax delayed my departure, thus the lateness of the call. I'm at Garfield Hall and will be returning to London shortly. Alistair and I had a pleasant chat. He confessed to paying the teacher to keep Lawrence from being expelled, but he says he's heard nothing more of that matter since then."

I struggled to sit up. Ryan placed a pillow behind my head, and I threw him a smile. "Do you believe him?"

"I do. As this has the potential to be a security matter, he can be trusted to be forthcoming."

"Okay. So?"

"So, would you agree that the death of Paul Erikson did not have the hallmarks of professionals?"

Ryan pointed to the phone and then to him.

"Okay if I put this on speaker so Ryan can listen?"

"You may," Pippa said.

I did so. "I don't know what makes a murder professional or not."

Ryan's eyes opened wide. I shrugged.

"Can you take a guess?" Pippa asked.

"I can. The bookshop was not searched thoroughly. Not even Paul's office. Unless the killers went to the time and trouble to put everything back, which I find difficult to believe. Those sort of people aren't likely to, far as I am aware, accidentally kill their suspect before they get around to asking what they want to know. Paul would have given up the letter instantly to anyone who waved a gun in his face, as would any sensible person. By which I conclude the killer or killers were not after the letter. Thus, it was more likely to be a personal reason or a random theft that went wrong."

"Or . . . ?"

"There's an 'or' in this?"

"Or," Ryan said, "the killer was after the letter, but they hadn't the slightest idea of how to go about asking for it. Because they're not a professional and they haven't done this sort of thing before. They intended to act threatening, and when that didn't work, because they aren't tough, they didn't know what to do and killed Paul. And then, rather than taking the time to search for the letter, they fled in panic."

"You think this person might have been Lawrence?" I said into the phone.

"The possibility is there," Pippa said. "The first line of inquiry, as to if third parties wanted to get hold of the incriminating letter to disturb Alistair's work, will continue to be investigated at my end. But I have no interest in why Lawrence might, or might not, have killed your Paul. And so, because I know you like to solve these little puzzles to your own satisfaction, I can tell you where Lawrence is at the moment. You can have a little chat. In a public place, naturally, to keep everything on the up and up."

"Where?"

"He has a favorite nightclub. Expensive, exclusive. Far beyond anything he should be able to afford. To his parents' despair. He should be arriving right about now."

"How do you know this?"

"No spy craft involved. Genevieve called him earlier to remind him they're scheduled to meet with the estate manager first thing in the morning to go over the finances for the quarter, and Lawrence said he wouldn't be back from London in time. Genevieve is attempting to get Lawrence to show some interest in the family business. Waste of time, but that's up to her. He told her he wouldn't make it because he was going out with his friends later tonight, and they had an intense argument. She relayed that conversation to Alistair, in my presence. The nightclub Lawrence prefers doesn't truly get going until the early hours." Pippa rattled off an address.

"If this place is so exclusive," Ryan said, "they're not going to let a wandering American cop in. Probably not Gemma either."

"They'll let you in. Tell the doorman your names are Jayne and Donald. One more small matter, before I go. Alistair confessed to me that he arranged for you to be followed when you left Garfield Hall, to and on the train and once you arrived in London. As he wasn't entirely sure he believed what you said about why you were involving yourself in this matter, he wanted to ensure you weren't intending to make contact with possibly unfriendly, or even criminal, forces. His people reported that you were acting shifty, you might like to know.

But you did return to Stanhope Gardens without any obvious detours. Other than to treat yourselves to a gelato. Good night." Pippa hung up.

I looked at Ryan. Ryan looked at me. "You were followed?" he said.

"So it would appear. They must be better than I'd thought. I didn't spot a tail on the train itself."

He shook his head. "Pippa could have called earlier than this."

"Pippa likes to play games with me. On the other hand, when Pippa's working, time has little or no meaning for her."

"Are we going?"

"Up to you," I said.

"Why not? All part of the genuine London experience. An exclusive club frequented by royalty and maybe gangsters too. We're going so you can talk to this Lawrence guy in a public place. That's all, right? You're not going to follow him to the top of a cliff or chase him out to sea in a stolen boat?"

"I suspect that if this place is as exclusive as Pippa suggests, frequented by the sons and daughters of the most privileged in Europe and beyond, there will be adequate security."

"To protect you or Lawrence?" he asked.

We dressed quickly and tiptoed down the stairs, not wanting to wake the rest of the house.

We found Jayne and Donald waiting by the front door.

"What are you two doing?" I asked.

"I might ask the same of you," Jayne said. "Except it's obvious you're sneaking out to work on the case without us."

"Did Pippa call you?"

"No. Donald did."

"What?"

"My room's adjacent to yours," Donald said. "I was unable to sleep and was reading when I heard your phone ring. Naturally a call at two AM attracted my interest. I . . ." he coughed in embarrassment, "listened in the event assistance would prove to be necessary. As proved to be the case." He wore his Ulster cape and carried his ever-present black umbrella. Ryan and I had put on the clothes we'd worn to Pippa's wedding, in some attempt to look as though we belonged at an exclusive London nightclub, although I hadn't wanted to take the time to do much with my hair and makeup. Jayne was in jeans, T-shirt, and a cardigan, trainers on her feet, and her long blonde hair tied back in a high, tight ponytail. That shouldn't matter. She was pretty enough that in those circles she'd be allowed to dress however she liked. Donald just looked eccentric. The English like eccentric.

"Andy not coming?" Ryan asked.

"Andy is not a light sleeper," Jayne said with a wink as she pulled her large leather bag over her shoulder.

"Let's go, then," I said. "I called an Uber and it's arriving now."

* * *

Ryan gave the Uber driver the address of our destination. Traffic was light at this time of night, and we soon arrived in Soho, the center of London's nightlife.

It was approaching three AM, and there was no line outside the club. The sign over the door was discreet, and sounds of revelry did not leak from inside. A man stood next to the door. Good suit, white shirt, thin black tie, polished shoes. About two hundred pounds of solid muscle. The strong light from the bulb over the door shone on his bald head. Small black eyes sized us up as we approached. He said nothing, but the look of barely disguised contempt gave me the feeling he was fully intent on turning us away.

"I'm Donald." Ryan pointed to me. "This is Jayne. The others are with us."

"Very good, sir, madam," the man said. "Enjoy your evening." He opened the door with a small bow.

"I intend to," I said.

We stepped onto a dark, narrow landing. A brightly lit staircase led down, and the sounds of music and laughter drifted up.

"'Once more unto the breach, dear friends,'" Donald said.

"Shakespeare?" I asked. "Not a Holmes quote?"

"A suitable one didn't come instantly to mind."

We descended the stairs. Jayne sucked in a breath, and Donald said, "Goodness. I was expecting something reminiscent of the opium den in 'The Man with the Twisted Lip.'"

A vast room opened below us, packed with revelers. Walls of mirrors ran along three sides, reflecting laughing, dancing, gyrating bodies. Glass balls hung from the high ceiling, throwing flashing rainbows of green and blue onto the floor and the dancers. Bartenders, clad in white shirts and black bow ties, flipped bottles and shook cocktail shakers. The glass shelves behind them contained possibly hundreds of bottles of colored liquid. Wait staff, also in white shirts, black trousers or skirts, black bow ties, ferried trays piled high with drinks to patrons seated on the low platforms along the walls, outlined in hundreds of small flashing white lights. Plush banquettes in red and purple and deep wingback chairs surrounded tables, each of which contained a single flickering electric candle.

The sound of music and people talking and laughing was deafening.

"I feel . . . old," Donald said.

"So do I," Jayne said.

Almost everyone in the place, customers as well as staff, were in their twenties. Attire ranged from crop tops under big jackets over leggings or fashionably shredded jeans to three-piece suits and cocktail dresses and jewels.

No one paid us the slightest bit of attention, not even the wait staff.

The place smelled of too many people packed too closely together, overlaid with tobacco, liquor, and excessively applied perfume or aftershave. Most of all, it smelled like money. The jewels looked real;

the clothes, designer. Even the ripped jeans would have cost a bundle at the best clothing shops in London.

More than a few people, men as well as women, looked completely out of place and were not attempting to hide it. Dark clothes, short haircuts, earpieces in ears. Bodyguards and drivers. I recognized at least one movie star, sitting at a table surrounded by sycophants and shot glasses. A not-minor royal and his entourage were at another table. The royal was the same age as most of the other people in the place, but the movie star was considerably older than even us. She didn't look as though she was having a great deal of fun. It's hard work, desperately trying to pretend one is keeping age at bay.

"How on earth are we going to find Lawrence in this madhouse?" Donald bellowed into my ear.

"We look," I said.

"What?" Jayne and Ryan yelled.

"Look for Lawrence!"

"If he confesses to murder, we're not going to be able to hear a word," Ryan said.

"We'll have to suggest we step outside. There must be private rooms in here someplace." A wide sweeping staircase led up to the next level. Next to it was a closed door.

The constantly flashing lights and the booming noise were starting to give me a headache. A man leered in my face and said something unintelligible. Ryan growled at him, and he wisely moved off.

"Hey, darlin', love love love that coat." A young woman, all bleary eyes and streaked makeup, smiled at Donald. "It's so retro, it's absolutely adorbs. Can I have it?" She hiccupped and exhaled a wave of liquor-saturated breath.

"What?" Donald said.

"You can buy me a drink." She dragged Donald away. "And then we'll negotiate terms for the coat."

This might not have been the most optimal place to find and question Lawrence. Oh, well, we were here now. If we lost Donald, he should be able to find his way back to Stanhope Gardens. With or without his cherished Ulster cape.

"Wanna dance?" A handsome young man approached Jayne. Thick stubble on his chin, a lock of bright yellow hair falling over one eyebrow, a small hoop in his right ear, leather jacket, tight black jeans, black and white boots with two-inch heels. Blindingly white teeth and a silver ring on every digit on both hands. I struggled to remember where I'd seen him before, then I had it. Smiling down from a huge poster advertising a reality TV program in the tube station.

Jayne threw me a panicked look. Ryan took her arm. "She's with us," he said.

The TV presenter shrugged and walked away. For a brief moment, I was insulted that he hadn't asked me to dance.

I just wanted to find Lawrence and get out of here. I went first, shoving and pushing and excusing my way through the crowd. Ryan kept hold of Jayne's arm and they followed me. I decided to do one sweep of the main room looking for Lawrence, and if I didn't see him, I'd have to ask. If this was, according to Pippa, his favorite hangout, the staff should know him.

The wait staff crossed the room with laden trays, deftly maneuvering between dancing and/or drunken bodies and people who didn't bother to look where they were going. I did my best to imitate them and managed to avoid most, although not all, collisions.

It wasn't long before I spotted my quarry. A group of dancers, gasping and laughing, broke apart and a view to the far side of the room temporarily opened up. Laurence sat at a banquette table on a low platform overlooking the dance floor. He was with four other people, two men, two women, all about his age, all clearly well into their cups. Once again, I noticed something familiar about one of the women. She was barely old enough to be allowed into the club, with long hair she was constantly tossing around her head and an excessive amount of makeup, even for this place. Lawrence said something, and she threw back her head and screeched with laughter. The people at the table next to them watched us approach. Suits, short hair, earpieces. Absolutely not smiling.

American secret service. You can spot them a mile away. I looked at her again, and then I remembered where I'd seen the young woman. On the news, getting into a helicopter next to her smiling and waving parents.

"Isn't that—" Jayne said to Ryan.

"Looks like it," he replied.

I stopped at the table. "Hi," I said to Lawrence. "Remember me?"

"Ryan Ashburton," Ryan said to the secret service agent who'd risen to his feet. "West London, Massachusetts. My friend is a relative of Viscount Ballenhelm."

The agent nodded, but he didn't take his eyes off me.

Lawrence peered up at me and blinked. His eyes were very red. If he'd only just arrived here, it hadn't been his first stop of the night. "Gemma. Hey, what's up? Everyone, this is Gemma, my cousin. Sorta. And . . . her friend. Hi, Jayne."

"Hi," Jayne said.

"Can I have a minute, Lawrence?" I said. "I need to speak to you and it's somewhat noisy in here."

He looked at his friends. They shrugged, not much caring. The younger woman waved her hand in the air to summon a passing waiter. Her protection detail didn't look too pleased at her asking for another drink.

Lawrence picked up his glass and wiggled out of his seat. "Be right back."

The American woman was not, I guessed by the uninterested look on her face, Lawrence's date. Perhaps his much older minor royal didn't care for the atmosphere in this place. More likely, she didn't care for the publicity her appearance might generate.

I led the way to a comparatively quiet corner and arranged us so Lawrence's back was to the wall. Ryan stood next to me, Jayne slightly behind, hemming Lawrence in.

"Wha's up?" Lawrence asked.

"I need to talk to you for a few minutes."

"Talk about what?"

"The death of Paul Erikson."

The drunken blur began to disappear from his eyes. "Who?"

"Don't give me that, Lawrence. I know you knew Paul, and I know you spoke to him on Saturday night, not more than a few hours before he died. I also know the police have questioned you in that matter."

"What's it to you?"

"I represent parties other than the Metropolitan Police." That wasn't a lie. I represented myself. Ryan and Jayne too. Even Donald, whom I hadn't seen since he'd been dragged away by the young woman who liked his coat.

Lawrence's eyes darted around. All around us, the party continued. No one was paying any attention to us, not even the secret service detail. "I told the cops what happened," he said finally. "Paul asked me for money. I barely know the guy. I told him to get lost. I wouldn't give him money even if I had it. Which, as you know from my dear parents, I do not."

"What about the letter?"

His attention snapped back to me. "What letter?"

"You know full well what letter. The blackmail letter. Paul didn't give it to you that night, likely because you didn't, or couldn't, pay. Did you go around to his shop later and demand he hand it over? Did you kill him when he refused? Or did you not even bother to wait for him to refuse, but decided to get rid of him then and there, when you found him passed out at his desk?"

Lawrence started to sweat. It was extremely hot in this room, but he hadn't been sweating a few minutes ago. "You're talking rubbish."

"I'm not and you know it. I also know you went back to his shop the following afternoon. I saw you there myself. Did you hope to get your hands on the letter, but Paul had been found by then and the police called so you walked away?"

"I was at Trafalgar Square Sunday afternoon, yeah. I had . . . I was meeting a friend for lunch near there."

"What happened to Paul, Lawrence?"

"Nothing happened! Yeah, okay, he came up to me at your sister's wedding dinner. I'd never even seen the guy before, but he told me he had this letter my dad wrote years ago. He wanted me to pay him to give me that dratted letter. I told him I couldn't, and he said he'd phone me in the morning to ask again. If I wouldn't pay, he'd release the letter to the gutter press. I went to his shop the next day, hoping to talk some sense into him. By the time I got there, the cops were all over the place. So I left. The police saw the CCTV footage of us meeting at the hotel and they called me. I told them all of this."

"You told them you spoke to Paul Saturday night, but you didn't say anything about a blackmail attempt. You didn't think they might consider that to be important?" Ryan said.

"Everything okay here?" One of the men who'd been sitting at Lawrence's table pushed his way between Ryan and Lawrence. He was a big guy, nose broken more than once, scar over his right eyebrow, scraggy goatee, rapidly receding hairline. He was at that stage of early drunkenness to be both aggressive and dangerous. He spoke to Lawrence but looked at Ryan.

I felt, as much as saw, Ryan brace himself as he gently moved Jayne to one side.

"Yes. I mean no," Lawrence said. "These people are bothering me, Reggie. They got in under false pretenses. They don't belong here."

"Is that so?" Reggie put a meaty hand on Ryan's shoulder. "In that case, you'd better be on your way, mate."

Ryan plucked the hand off his shoulder as though he were removing an ant that had lost its way. He spoke calmly and clearly. "We're not causing trouble. My friend's having a nice chat with her cousin."

"The way I see it, her cousin doesn't want to chat with her."

Ryan's eyes flicked toward me.

As soon as Ryan's attention wavered slightly, Reggie shoved him, hard. "So get lost, mate." Ryan dropped back and bumped into Jayne, knocking her against a passing waiter bearing a tray heavy with fresh drinks.

"Watch it!" the waiter yelled. Jayne made a wild grab for the tray, her hand collided with his, and he lost his grip. The tray tipped; glasses and liquid went flying. Someone laughed, some people cheered and clapped. A man yelled in anger.

And then, before I knew what was happening, everyone was wading in. Security guards surged forward to prevent the melee from spreading.

Too little, too late.

Reggie threw a punch at Ryan, but Ryan saw it coming, stayed on his feet, and managed to dodge the blow. He ducked and came up ready to strike back. Reggie swung again, and Ryan retaliated. Reggie was big and he looked as though he was no stranger to bar fights, but Ryan was a cop. And, most importantly, Reggie had spent his evening drinking and Ryan had not.

Figuring Ryan could take care of himself, I looked around for Jayne. Before I could move toward her, Lawrence grabbed me by the shoulders and shook me until my teeth rattled. "You stay out of what doesn't concern you."

Rather than me rescuing Jayne, my friend charged toward us, let out a mighty yell, swung her hefty bag, and hit him solidly on the side of the head. "Let go of her!"

Blind rage filled Lawrence's eyes, and he started to turn on Jayne. She danced nimbly to one side, still gripping her bag. Ryan saw what was happening and moved to intercept, but Reggie took advantage of his change of attention. He punched Ryan hard enough in the jaw, I heard the snap as it connected, and Ryan's head went flying back. But he didn't go down, and he shifted smoothly into a defensive position. "You don't want to do this, pal."

Fearing Lawrence would go to the aid of his friend, I grabbed his arm and pulled him away, yanking him off balance.

All around us, women were screaming and trying to get out of the way, while some men, and a few other women, ran forward to join the fight. Chairs overturned; glasses smashed on the floor. The music cut out in midnote.

"You leave him alone!" The daughter of the American political figure charged me, all streaming hair and wild eyes. She kicked me, hard, in the shins, and I lost my balance. I grabbed a chair in panic; if I fell, I could be trampled in this melee. I managed to hold on. One of the secret service people grabbed the daughter and hauled her away, shouting into the mic tucked into his lapel. She screamed in protest and kicked wildly. Her stiletto heels went flying, and one of them connected with the cheek of a man calmly standing on the side, beer in hand, simply observing the action. He let out a roar of pain and shock. Recognizing that he'd be in serious trouble if he tried to punch the owner of the shoe, he took his anger out on the man standing next to him. The political daughter was carried from the field of battle like a rag doll, still kicking and screaming. The other agent threw me a very nasty look indeed, as though this was my fault, and followed them.

A woman grabbed Jayne's hair and pulled hard. I went in low from her side, and kicked high, getting the assailant in the right knee. She screamed and released Jayne, but rather than retire from the fight, she charged at me, long red nails extended. I grabbed her right hand and twisted. She yelped in pain but didn't back off; instead she reached toward my face with her free hand. Those nails were like eagle's talons. I held on as best I could, wondering how long I could keep her away. Then she dropped like a stone and hit the floor. Jayne stood over her, legs apart, breathing deeply. Another combatant felled by Jayne's trusty handbag.

Jayne and I exchanged a brief glance. I'd swear my friend, hair tumbling around her face and shoulders, blue eyes gleaming, breathing heavily, was grinning.

I searched the crowd for Ryan. About ten people were between us, grabbing and swinging at each other. He was fighting someone different now, the two of them grasping at each other, pulling at jackets, trying to land a blow, but neither was able to get a good swing in the crowd surrounding them. Before I could move toward Ryan, another man came up behind him. He was so lanky he didn't look as though he'd be able to stand straight in the face of a strong breeze, but that didn't matter now. He held a bottle by the neck end, lifted it high, and swung it directly at the back of Ryan's head. I screamed a warning, knowing he wouldn't hear it over the racket in this place.

And then the man with the bottle was on the ground, floored by a rolled-up black umbrella. Donald Morris waded into the fray, his Ulster cape streaming behind him, wielding his brolly like a sword.

I checked for Jayne. The woman who attacked her lay face down on the floor, arms and legs spread. Jayne sat on top of her while combatants swirled around them. "I'm good here," she called to me. She poked the back of her adversary's head with her index finger. "We're good here, right?"

The woman moaned.

I headed toward Ryan and Donald. The bottle holder had dropped his weapon and was making a rapid escape on his hands and knees. Donald was swinging his umbrella in an arc around himself and Ryan shouting, "Back off. Everyone, back off! I am qualified in baritsu. Challenge me if you dare." Baritsu is the form of hand-to-hand combat Sherlock Holmes excelled in. I doubt very much anyone in this room other than Donald and I knew that. But the expression on his face was fierce, his stance determined, and no one was truly invested in the fight at any rate. Besides, the big American next to him looked like someone who could do some damage if he was so inclined. Several men slipped away.

Lawrence, however, was also under attack. Neither he nor his opponent were much good at this fighting stuff, and they stumbled across the room, gasping and grunting and gripping each other's shirt.

I hesitated, wanting to intervene, but unsure how to accomplish that without getting a punch in the face. Before I could decide, another man arrived. Heavily built, face marked with memories of bar brawls in far less refined places than this, and definitely meaning business, he grabbed Lawrence around the waist and lifted him off the ground, much like the secret service agent had earlier done to his charge. Lawrence's opponent straightened, a mean gleam came into his eyes as he realized now was the time to take advantage of his adversary being incapacitated, but one growl and an intense stare from the new arrival had him reconsidering his options and slinking away.

Sir John Saint-Jean gave Lawrence a good shake and said, "You going to behave yourself now, sunshine?"

Lawrence nodded rapidly.

With the help of Donald and his trusty brolly, Ryan had cleared most of this section of the floor of fighters. Bouncers and security guards were grabbing shirt collars and hauling miscreants to their feet or shoving them toward the door. A scattering of secondary fights, threatening to lead to tertiary eruptions, had broken out, but they were soon quelled.

I held out a hand and helped Jayne get off the woman she had pinned under her. The woman didn't move, and I peered closer at her, wondering if she needed assistance. Another woman arrived. Stark black hair shaved to the scalp on one side, rivers of black eyeliner running down her cheeks, red lipstick staining her teeth. Ignoring Jayne, she screamed at the woman on the floor, "What on earth do you think you're playing at, Maise? Get up. I'm leaving, and I'm not going to wait for you. If the cops find me here again, I'm done for. I'll be cut off."

Maise groaned, shook her head. Cautiously, watching for signs she was going to renew the attack, Jayne stepped back. Maise staggered to her feet with the help of her friend. She didn't spare Jayne and me another look as she limped away. She and her friend pushed their way through the crowd of onlookers and disappeared from sight.

"You lot, out of here now." A middle-aged man, short and weedy, greasy hair, watery pale blue eyes, pencil-thin mustache, dressed in a dark suit, stood in front of us. His face was red with indignation. "Before I call the cops."

"We didn't—" I started to say.

"I don't care who started it. Out. And you," he swung toward Lawrence, who'd taken a seat at the single chair still upright at a small round table, "are banned. Permanently. I've had enough of you."

"You can't—" Lawrence said.

"He can do whatever he wants in his own place." Sir John grabbed Lawrence and hauled him to his feet. "We'll go. Quietly and peacefully, right?"

Jayne, Donald, Ryan, and I chorused, "Right."

"You, laddie?" Sir John shook Lawrence as a terrier might a rat.

"Okay," Lawrence said.

"Call me," Sir John called over his shoulder as he shoved Lawrence across the floor, "and we'll discuss settling up. After I've done with this waste of space here."

"I'll do that," the thin man said.

The pounding music started up again, the lights began to swirl and flash. Bartenders resumed their places, wait staff lifted their trays, and the remaining patrons surged toward the bar or the dance floor.

The thin man, who I assumed was the owner or manager of this establishment, scurried around us and led the way to the door beneath the staircase I'd noticed earlier. He opened it, we passed through, and he slammed it shut behind us. We were in a brightly lit corridor. Closed doors I took to be offices and storage rooms led off it. Without a word, we walked down the corridor, climbed the stairs at the end of the building, and pushed open the fire door to emerge into an ill-lit alley.

"I'm guessing," I said, "your timely arrival wasn't a coincidence."

"No," Sir John said. "And you can be glad of it. I managed to convince Albert there not to call the coppers to have the place cleared out."

"Albert?" Ryan said.

"Old SAS buddy. He's a lot tougher than he looks."

"He'd have to be," Ryan muttered. He touched his jaw and winced.

"Pippa gave me a call. Said you lot were headed down here and might need a hand," Sir John explained.

"Thanks," Ryan said. "Nice work with the umbrella, Donald."

"Thank you." Donald preened and twirled his umbrella. Jayne leapt out of the way to avoid having an eye taken out. "I've been practicing. After the incident the previous time we were in this city, I thought I might have need to improve my skills. I don't actually know baritsu, although the art seems to be regaining some popularity these days, but throwing it out there added a touch of authenticity to my combative persona."

Somehow Jayne had lost one shoe. She carried the remaining one in her right hand and bounced on her toes, punching the air with her fists. "That was exciting. I've never been in a bar brawl before."

"You have no idea," Ryan said. "Please do not make this a habit."

"You people are nuts, all of you," Lawrence said. "You've managed to get me banned from my best place. What's Marie going to say when I tell her we can't come here again?"

"I don't much care what Marie, or anyone else, has to say," I said. "You and I have a conversation to finish."

"Don't think so," he said. "I'm outa here."

Before he could move, a strong light appeared at the end of the alley, and a woman called, "Gemma Doyle?"

"Here."

The jerking light moved closer. DI Patel held a flashlight. A uniformed officer came behind her, carrying his own light.

"You're late for the party," I said.

"So it would appear." She studied us. Most of Jayne's hair had escaped its ponytail, and she was missing one shoe. Ryan's right sleeve hung by a couple of ragged threads. His shirt was half untucked, and a bruise was rapidly forming under his right eye. I took steps to straighten my own clothes. I doubted this nice dress would be suitable to be worn again.

Lawrence, nose bloody, shirt not only torn but spotted with blood, didn't look any better.

Donald, still immaculate in Ulster cape, black trousers, Harris tweed jacket, and white shirt, beamed at the detective and proudly showed her his weapon of choice.

"What brings you here in such a timely fashion?" I asked.

"Your father called me," Patel explained. "Unfortunately, I was indisposed and didn't get the call until a half hour ago. Whereupon I came down."

"Does no one trust me to act on my own?" I said to Ryan.

"No," he replied.

"All this has nothing to do with me," Lawrence said, his voice muffled as he attempted to staunch the flow of blood with another of Jayne's tissues. "If you're not going to arrest this lot for drunk and disorderly, I'll be on my way."

"DI Patel, you might want to ask Mr. Denhaugh here to clarify precisely what he and Paul Erikson talked about the night Paul Erikson died," I said. "He might not have been entirely truthful when you interviewed him earlier."

She looked at Lawrence. He threw me a thoroughly nasty glare. Not, I thought, of fear but more of annoyance. *Interesting.* "Yeah, okay. Whatever. I wasn't exactly going to come out and tell you Erikson was threatening to blackmail my father, was I?"

"You didn't think that might be pertinent to my investigation into his death?" the detective asked.

"My father's a very influential man, highly connected. He doesn't need past indiscretions tarnishing his reputation."

Patel reached into her own cavernous cross-body bag and pulled out a notebook. She gave it a good shake, the book flipped open, and she found the page she was looking for.

I sucked in a breath. Ryan and Jayne threw me questioning looks.

Patel consulted her notebook. "When advised of the CCTV footage from the hotel where you were attending a wedding, you admitted Mr. Erikson spoke you to that evening. At that time, you told me, he asked you for money, you refused, and he left. You claim you did not see him again. Is that still correct?"

"Yes."

"You said he asked you for money. You neglected to mention any blackmail attempt."

"It wasn't any of your business."

"It is my business now, and I don't conduct interviews in dark alleys behind nightclubs. Let's go to the station and have a proper chat."

"Are you arresting me?" Lawrence asked.

"Not at this time. A chat, like I said." She nodded to the uniformed constable, who stepped forward and put his hand on Lawrence's arm.

Lawrence looked at me. "I didn't kill him."

"I know you didn't," I said.

Chapter Twenty-Three

"You know?" Jayne said.

"Know what?" Donald asked.

"She knows Lawrence didn't kill Paul Erikson. That means she knows who did."

"Do you, Gemma?" Ryan asked.

"I have my suspicions."

"That means she isn't going to tell us what those suspicions are," Jayne said.

The police had taken Lawrence in for further questioning. Before getting into the car, DI Patel had, not at all politely, told me to make myself available for an interview in the morning. I might, or might not, do that, depending on what happened next.

We stood on the street outside the nightclub after the police had driven away. The doorman who'd admitted us earlier was still on duty. I gave him a cheery wave, but he looked straight through me. I suspected Albert had instructed him not to let us back in. A few patrons emerged, bedraggled, bleary-eyed, some of them looking quite the worse for wear. They pointedly crossed the street to avoid us.

Jayne wanted to go back inside to look for her missing shoe, but I convinced her that might not be such a good idea. "We must look awful," she said.

"As though we've been in a bar brawl," I said.

"How am I going to explain this to Andy?"

"Leave it to me," Ryan said. "Hopefully we can sneak into the house before everyone is up and it won't be necessary. Although it's going to be hard to explain this," he pointed to his right eye, "shiner, and that," he pointed to my dress, "ruined garment to Gemma's parents."

"On the bright side," Jayne said, "Andy won't notice if I never wear those shoes again."

Sir John Saint-Jean chuckled. He slapped Donald on the back with such force the older man almost pitched forward into the street. "Good man to have in a fight. Wouldn't have thought it, to look at you."

Donald beamed with pride. "My friends are worth it."

Jayne gave him a hug, and he blushed.

A car came down the street. Its lights flashed twice and it pulled up in front of us. Sir John had called us a ride. "You people take this one," he said. "I could use the walk."

Ryan, Jayne, and Donald called good night and piled into the Uber. "Thank you," I said to our rescuer.

He grinned at me and cracked his knuckles. "Always happy for a chance to practice the old skills. A chap can get rusty. You can pay me back when you find that book Paul was trying to unload."

"There never was any book."

He nodded. "I suspected as much. Unlike Pippa Doyle to care about a book, no matter the potential value. I assume it was the blackmail letter DI Patel referred to. No need for me to know what that's about." He started to walk away. Then he turned abruptly. "On my way here, the cabbie had the radio on. There's been movement in the Australian freighter dispute. If you need any further assistance while you're in London, don't hesitate to ask."

* * *

We drove through the quiet streets in silence. It was still dark, but a watery light touched the horizon to the east. Delivery trucks had started making their morning rounds, and a few yawning early-bird workers, along with yawning late-night partiers, were heading for the tube stations. Blinds were rattling and pavements swept as coffee shops and cafés opened for the day.

All was quiet on Stanhope Gardens. Except for the lamp in the front hall, the house lights were off. Only Horace met us at the door.

"What are we doing tomorrow?" Jayne gave the dog a hearty thump on his rump, and he wagged his stubby tail in appreciation. "By which I mean today."

"Pippa has arranged a special private tour of Hampton Court Palace," I said.

"About the case, I mean."

"I have to think things over," I replied.

I looked at my circle of friends. Jayne, always by my side. Donald, ready to do anything for us. Ryan, who loved me no matter how much trouble I caused him. I felt tears flood my eyes.

"Good heavens," Donald said. "Aftershock has gotten to her. I have to admit, I'm feeling a mite wobbly myself. Unaccustomed physical exertion does that to a chap of a certain age."

"I'm dead tired, but I won't be able to sleep," Jayne said. "I'll pop up and check on Andy."

Jayne and Donald went upstairs together, accompanied by Horace.

I smiled at Ryan. "Let's go into the kitchen and find some ice. You need to put something on that eye."

"Too late to do much good, I fear," he said. "When Louise asks me how my vacation went, I can say it was eventful and not offer any explanation. That'll drive her nuts." Louise Estrada was his partner at the WLPD.

Ryan took a seat at the breakfast bar while I rummaged in the freezer for the ice. Unfortunately, I'd caught a brief glimpse of myself in the hall mirror as we passed. A bruise was forming on my right cheek, which would be noticeable for several days. Jayne had a deft hand with makeup when she wanted to, which wasn't often, so I hoped she'd be able to disguise it tomorrow.

Tomorrow. Which was now today. Friday, two days before we were due to return home. An eventful vacation indeed.

I wrapped several ice cubes in a clean towel and applied them to Ryan's face. He gathered me close and we stood together, feeling the beating of each other's hearts and the soft exhale of breath.

Footsteps in the hallway, a cough, the sound of dog's nails on the floorboards. Ryan and I pulled apart, and my father and Horace came into the kitchen. Dad looked at us both, shook his head, and said, "Productive evening?"

"Partially," I said. "You told DI Patel where we were. How did you know?"

"Pippa thought you might need intervention in the event things went awry; she rang me and we conferred."

"She conferred with both you and John Saint-Jean," Ryan said, holding the ice pack to his face. "Pippa's very good at maneuvering people. I wouldn't want to play chess against her."

"You would not," I said. "She was the champion in the club at Cambridge. She gave up the game because she was getting bored with it." Ryan yawned, and I said, "Why don't you grab a few hours' sleep? I want to check into a few things on the computer. If I can find what I'm looking for, I'll let you know. I won't leave the house without telling you. Promise." I gave him my most honest smile and crossed my heart.

Ryan did not return the smile. "You'll text me as you're leaping into a speeding vehicle and consider that telling me so as to not break that promise."

My father laughed and filled the kettle. "Tea, love?"

"Yes, please," I said.

My mother was next into the kitchen, dressed in a lacy peach satin robe and fluffy slippers. She looked at Ryan. She looked at me.

She looked at my father. "I ran into Jayne creeping down the hallway like an errant schoolgirl who'd climbed in through the window after an all-night party she was forbidden to attend. I simply do not want to know. You've started the tea, Henry. How nice."

* * *

I used my father's computer, after promising him I wouldn't do anything illegal that might compromise him. If I did need to go places on the internet I wasn't supposed to go, I'd get my iPad. But I knew that wouldn't be necessary. What I needed to know would be publicly available and easy to find.

It was.

I waited impatiently until the reasonable hour of nine o'clock and then I made two phone calls. The first person agreed to meet me, the second was more cagey. "I suggest you come," I said. "Or you will be reading about it in the papers."

"I have no idea what you're talking about."

"Meet me, and I'll explain."

"How do I know this isn't some sort of trick?"

"You don't. Ten o'clock. Don't be late, now."

Jayne was in the kitchen with Dad when I emerged, the remains of tea and toast, croissants, butter, and strawberry jam between them.

"A good old-fashioned pub crawl," Dad was saying as I came in. "Every time you come here with my daughter, I have all sorts of grand plans for things you can do in London, and you end up doing none of them. Next time, ditch Gemma and come alone with your young man."

"Speaking of ditching Gemma," I said. "I'd like your help this morning, Jayne."

She'd showered and washed her hair and was once again her normal bright and perky self.

"Andy still asleep?" I asked.

"Yup. That bruise on your cheek is looking nasty."

"It's okay," I lied.

My father indicated the newspaper in front of him, folded to the front page. "The Australian freighter has been allowed to go on its merry way and all parties are standing down. Everyone claims to have saved face. A rare good result all round. What do you need Jayne for, pet? Anything I need to alert Jasmine Patel about?"

"I have her number if I need her," I said.

"Are we taking Ryan on this outing?" Jayne asked.

"Yes." Ryan headed straight for the coffee pot and poured.

"How are you feeling?" I asked.

His hair was wet from the shower and he'd dressed in fresh khakis and a clean shirt. The bruising on his face had deepened and spread, and his right eye was swollen. "I'm feeling fine." He twisted his jaw to check if it still hurt. It did.

Ryan and I could both be good liars when it suited us.

He wrapped his free arm around me and pulled me close. "If we're going out, you need to change. You look like you had quite the wild night."

"Which I did," I said. "Dad, can you entertain Donald and Andy for a while this morning?"

"The sound of snoring coming from the room next to ours is deafening," Ryan said. "I suspect Donald's out for the count."

"We'll have to manage without his trusty brolly," I said.

"Andy still hasn't gotten accustomed to the time change," Jayne said. "He won't be up before noon."

"I'll take them on a pub crawl then," Dad said happily.

"I went out for croissants earlier," Jayne said to Ryan. "There's more in the bag on the counter. Help yourself."

"I will," he said.

I poured myself a cup of coffee and took it upstairs with me while I changed and did something to make myself look moderately respectable once again. I decided not to ask Jayne to disguise the evidence of last night's fight on my face. It gave me a slightly dangerous look that might prove to come in handy for what I had in mind.

* * *

"We're going to the bookshop," I said to Jayne and Ryan as we walked down Cromwell Road to Gloucester Road tube station.

"This time, Gemma, I insist you tell me what's going on before we get there," Ryan said. "I'm not going in blind, and I'm not letting Jayne do so either."

Jayne nodded. "Right. Spill."

"You spent time last night on the computer," Ryan said. "This morning you have that gleam in your eye that tells me you've figured it out."

"And the game is, once again, afoot," Jayne said.

"That too," Ryan said. "I'm not making threats, Gemma. I'm just asking you to, for once, trust me. Trust us."

"Okay," I said.

"Okay?"

I nodded.

"That was easier than I expected. First, how sure are you it wasn't Lawrence?"

"Close to positive. Paul met with Lawrence at Pippa's wedding, not with Alistair or Genevieve. The letter would be worthless against Lawrence himself. He has no reputation to worry about. But he knows the letter could compromise his father, and he wanted to avoid that. I find his actions in that one instance admirable. At that meeting they discussed terms under which Paul would hand over the letter. Lawrence is virtually broke. He has nothing to pay Paul off with. I believe he told Paul that, and that he needed time to raise the money."

"Raise how?"

"His sister, Zoe. She's not wealthy, but we're unlikely to be talking big bucks here. Just enough to get Paul out of whatever hole he dug himself into. My impression of the Denhaugh siblings is that, if anything, her family and their reputation means more to Lady Zoe than it does to Lawrence, the heir. Lawrence might have thought he could convince her to pay to avoid scandal. After agreeing to meet again, Paul and Lawrence went their separate ways. Shortly after that, Lawrence left the hotel with Alistair and Genevieve."

"He could have changed his mind. Gone home with his parents, and then snuck out to confront Paul, and things got out of hand. You saw him outside the shop the next day, right?"

"Yes, I did. He was there, on the street at any rate, after Paul died and the police were called. Lawrence might have been returning to the scene of the crime, but I consider it more likely he wanted to go to the shop with the intention of once again discussing the letter. Maybe he hoped to talk Paul out of his blackmail attempt, maybe try to haggle the price down. Bear in mind, as we saw earlier, Lawrence is a party boy. He likely doesn't often get out of bed before noon. It's possible he followed Paul that night, but I consider it unlikely. He went home with his parents, remember. If someone killed Paul because of the letter, why didn't they then look for it? The shop was not searched, not even, as far as the police or I could tell, minimally."

"We talked about this before," Ryan said. "They panicked."

"I don't buy it. If this person intended to force Paul to hand over the letter, they would have been prepared for some resistance, and prepared to then take the necessary steps. It was late at night. A business district. No one around. No one due to come into the shop for hours yet. They had plenty of time to search. But they did not. They walked away. Turning out the lights and not bothering to lock the door behind them, I might add."

"You believe Paul wasn't killed for the letter?"

"He was killed for the letter, but not by anyone in the Denhaugh family. Two other people were mentioned in that letter. The teacher and the unnamed boy who'd also cheated. Of interest to me is that the door to the alley showed no signs of having been tampered with. Meaning, it was either left unlocked when Paul got in, which is possible considering he had a lot on his mind, or he let his attacker in, also possible, meaning it was someone he knew whom he did not believe meant him harm. Or, the third option, that person had a key."

I stopped talking as we approached Gloucester Road station. We descended the stairs and while we waited for the next train, I told them what I knew for sure and what I believed.

The rest of the journey to Embankment station passed in silence.

A "Closed Until Further Notice" sign hung in the window at Trafalgar Fine Books, and the door was locked. I could see Tamara and Faye inside. Faye was flipping casually through the paperbacks on the back shelves, selecting one, flipping the pages, putting it back, and then taking out another. Tamara paced the room. I knocked lightly on the door. Both women started, and Tamara hurried to let us in. She locked the door behind us.

"Thanks for coming on such short notice," I said to them.

"You're late." Faye slid the book in her hands back into place. "You said ten, and it's half ten now."

"Tube delay," I lied.

Jayne and I walked into the shop, but Ryan remained by the door. Tamara looked between us. "What happened to you lot? Were you in an accident?"

"You might say that," I said. "Is there any news about what's happening with the shop?"

"The police let Paul's dad in yesterday so he could have a look around and see what's what. I don't think he knows what to do with it all."

"Are the police finished here?" Ryan asked.

Tamara nodded.

"Can you tell us what this is about?" Faye said. "I have a job interview this afternoon."

"You don't expect the shop to reopen?"

"No point in trying to save it, and Mr. Erikson knows that. It's deep in debt and hasn't turned anything more than pennies in profit for years. I've offered to help him sort things out when he's ready, but that job won't last for long."

"What about you, Tamara?" I asked. "Are you also going to give Mr. Erikson a hand with inventory?"

"No. He doesn't need two of us if there's no customers coming in." She gave me a small smile. "Losing my job here wasn't my fault, so my grandma's going to give me a loan to help me get through this year. Enough time, I hope, to finally finish my dissertation, get my degree, and be on my way. Whatever on the way means for someone with a PhD in English lit."

"Works out well all around then," I said. "Faye, you'll now have the time and the privacy to search for the letter."

Faye's head jerked up. She gave me a sharp look and then allowed a blank expression to settle over her face. "What letter? I don't know anything about any letter."

Ryan remained by the front door, creating a solid obstacle to anyone who might want to make a break for it. Jayne had one hip resting against the sales counter.

"You're wasting your time flicking through those books," I said. "The letter's been found. I found it, and only because I got to it ahead of you. It was precisely where you expected it to be. Between the pages of a book. Not a rare or valuable book, just a used paperback stuffed among all the others on the shelves hoping to be sold."

"I have no idea what you're talking about. I have places to be." Faye headed for the door. Ryan didn't move.

"Get out of my way," she said.

He focused his lovely eyes, the color of the ocean on a sunny day, on her and said nothing.

Faye swung around. "Tell your hired muscle to get out of my way, or I'll have the both of you charged with unlawful confinement."

"Feel free to call the police at any time," I said. "DI Patel would have given you her number. Use it."

Faye stared at me.

"Your son, Greg, is the unnamed boy mentioned in the letter sent by a teacher at one of England's most prestigious private schools to Alistair Denhaugh. You don't want the letter for blackmail potential against Alistair, but rather to get rid of it before it can be used against Greg."

"I saw that letter," Tamara said. "You told me it was a matter of national security. Now you're saying it was about Faye's son?"

"It is both," I said. "It was an easy job finding out where Greg went to school. Lots of pictures on the internet. Photos of sports teams, all the rest, all of it available for anyone to see. Greg and Lawrence were friends at school. Greg was the other boy mentioned in the blackmail letter Alistair received from Richard Starecross, their teacher. Greg was not the initial subject of the blackmail; that was Lawrence Denhaugh. But obviously Greg would be compromised if it came to light."

"That boy's name wasn't mentioned. It could have been anyone," Tamara said. "What led you to Greg?"

"The first time I was here, moments before we discovered Paul's body in the office, I noticed Faye shaking out a book before she rang the sale through. At the time it seemed like an odd thing to do, but I assumed she was checking for dead bugs or the like."

"I'll admit this shop's getting run down," Tamara said, "but it's not infested. I do clean it now and again, you know."

"Precisely. Only when I thought it over did I realize the stock isn't in that bad of a condition. You are in the business of selling books. People aren't going to return to any store in which they bought a book with a dead insect or rats' teeth marks or droppings inside. You would have looked for those things when the used books arrived here initially. If she wasn't checking for that, what was Faye looking for? Obviously something that could be slipped between the pages of a book. Nothing bulker than a single thin piece of paper."

"Faye?" Tamara said. "Is that true?"

Faye said nothing, but the expression on her face told me I was right. In the early hours of this morning, not only had I found out that Greg Forgate had been school friends with Lawrence Denhaugh and they'd been roommates and had many of the same classes and teachers, but Greg was now rapidly climbing the ladder of the law world. It was rumored he had political ambitions, and his party of choice was looking for a safe seat for him to run in the next election. He was young, presentable but not excessively handsome, charming, successful, from solid working-class roots. Exactly the sort of fresh face the staid old political party needed.

The slightest whisper of cheating would be the end of their interest in him.

"Did you ask Paul for the letter, Faye?" I asked quietly. "Did he refuse to hand it over?"

She nodded. Her face had gone very pale.

"How did you know he had it?"

"He told me," she said.

"He told you? He tried to blackmail you? What did he think he'd get?"

"Not blackmail me, no. He didn't know about Greg. We went to the pub after the shop closed last Friday."

"I remember that," Tamara said. "He invited me too, but I had work to do on my paper. That was unusual; he didn't normally associate with the staff outside of the shop at all."

"It's never been easy for me, putting my Greg through school," Faye continued. "First that fancy school and then uni, even with all the scholarships he got. I don't often get the chance to go out of an evening. I had more to drink than I'm used to that night, so I ended up telling Paul I was looking for another job. I didn't see much of a future in this shop, and I didn't want to wait until I was out on the street." She took a deep breath. "He told me not to worry about it. Things were about to get a whole lot better. He had this letter, a letter that would compromise a very important titled individual. He'd been holding on to it for a while, waiting for the right moment to approach the person he had in mind. They'd pay, he told me, and pay big for the letter."

"You thought that was okay?"

"What do I care about some rich mucky-muck with his fancy title and his reputation and his important job? I've worked hard all my life and don't have much to show for it, do I? This job might not be the best, but it's a lot better than many. But then—"

"You realized who else was mentioned in the letter."

"Soon as Paul told me he had compromising material on Alistair Denhaugh, I knew. Greg was friends, if you can call it that, with Lawrence Denhaugh in school. For all that the boy was the son of the Earl of Ramshaw, I didn't like him. Lazy, shiftless, stupid. He was a bad influence on my lad, and I knew it all along. Greg was just happy to be invited over half-terms to a big estate in Yorkshire. They never invited me, I can tell you." The bitterness leaked out of her.

She was right about Lawrence, although I believe Genevieve would have been happy to invite her son's friend's mother, if Lawrence had asked her to. Greg himself likely didn't want to remind the aristocratic family about his shop clerk single mother. The first time she mentioned him, Faye told me Greg was so busy these days he rarely visited her. I suspected he'd left her and his working-class roots far behind long ago.

"Paul said the name. Denhaugh. And I knew. My Greg came to me when it happened. He told me he was going to be expelled for cheating. When I said maybe they'd give him another chance, he said he'd had another chance. And he'd been caught cheating again. It was that Lawrence who talked him into it. Greg didn't need to cheat, but Lawrence needed Greg to cheat for him. If Lawrence had been expelled, what of it? He'd go to another good school. But my Greg, no matter that he was head and shoulders above the rest of the students in his school, he'd lose his chance for a good education. I was beside myself with worry, but nothing happened. Greg was not expelled. He finished the year top of his class and got a good place in uni and then law school."

"Did you ask him why there were no consequences?"

"I did not. We never mentioned it again. I assumed Lawrence's family had taken care of the matter. Then, that night at the pub, Paul told me about this letter he'd found that would save the shop. Alistair Denhaugh had paid off a teacher at his son's school not to report an incident of his son and another boy cheating."

"Did Paul know the other boy was your son?" Ryan asked.

"No. He had no idea. But I knew. Who else would have been foolish enough to cheat to help the likes of Lawrence Denhaugh?"

"Faye," I said, "why did you want the letter? Paul was trying to blackmail Lawrence, not Greg."

"Lawrence Denhaugh wasn't going to pay any money to save himself," Faye said. "He's never amounted to anything worth saving. As for his father, he's retired now. He's got nothing to lose either."

I glanced at Jayne. She widened her eyes. Alistair had come out of retirement to help with the Australian freighter business. Not only Alistair, but the U.K. itself possibly had a great deal to lose if the letter had been made public. Alistair's involvement in the situation had been briefly mentioned in the papers. Paul must have seen the story and realized the time was right to use his blackmail material. Faye had told me she paid little attention to the news. Faye, poor desperate Faye, didn't know Lawrence's father was back in the game. Meaning, he was highly blackmailable.

"Once Paul realized he had no leverage against the Denhaughs," Faye said, "he'd be looking for who else was mentioned in the letter. The teacher, the other boy. Easy enough to find out who they were." She pointed at me. "You did."

"I did."

No one said anything for a long time. Poor Faye, I thought again. Paul would never have been able to figure out that her son was the other boy. The idea of searching for Lawrence's unnamed school friend likely didn't even occur to him, and even if it did, he hadn't had the investigative smarts to try to find out who the unnamed student was, much less the patience to dig deep enough. First roadblock encountered and he would have given up rather than work out a way to get around it. Even his attempt at blackmailing Lawrence wasn't all that clever. He had an old letter in which Alistair once offered to pay off his son's teacher. Small potatoes, really, in the wider scheme of things, for a peer with Alistair's long, distinguished career and background. Pippa had also been wide of the mark here, and I was looking forward to telling her that. No one in any unfriendly government would have paid a penny for it.

"Paul told you about the letter on Friday," I said. "He told you he was going to use it as leverage to get money to save the shop. The next night, Saturday, you came here intending to get the letter. You knew Paul was sleeping here. Did you ask him to give it to you? Did he refuse?"

"No." Faye's voice was voice low and calm. "I wasn't going to waste my time asking. He'd never give it to me, and he'd guess fast enough why I wanted it. I opened the door with my key. Found him sleeping it off in the chair behind his desk. He'd been drinking and that made him slow and stupid. I made sure he wouldn't be able to use that letter to ruin my Greg."

Jayne sucked in a breath. Tamara dropped into a chair. Ryan took a step closer to Faye.

"After making sure, as you put it, why didn't you search for the letter?" I asked Faye.

"At the pub he told me he hid it in a book. I did a quick search of some of his personal things in the office, but I didn't find it. I didn't want to hang around any longer than I had to at that time of night, and I was afraid of leaving traces of me behind. Even though I work here, and I go where I want. When I want. I watch all the police shows on telly. I knew no matter how much care I took, if I searched the shop for the letter that night, I'd leave some evidence behind.

Rather let the police concentrate on those men who'd come in to talk to Paul. He was in debt, and the police would find out soon enough. Let them think he'd been killed because he couldn't pay up. I knew the shop would be closed following Paul's death, but I'd hold on to my key. I'd have time later to have a proper search. I would have found it too. If you hadn't found it first."

"The book might have been sold," I said. Although the shop had been open for less than an hour that morning, before the police shut it down, it was still possible.

"I was prepared to take that chance. If anyone found it tucked between the pages of a secondhand book they bought, they'd more likely than not throw it out. Or even bring it back. That happens sometimes. Remember the wedding photo, Tamara?"

"Photo?" Tamara blinked in momentary confusion at the abrupt change of subject. "Oh, yes, I do. That old wedding picture. Someone bought a stack of books from us a couple of months ago. They found a wartime wedding picture in one and brought it back. It's still around somewhere; no one has claimed it. We don't keep track of who sold us what in the way of used books."

"Enough talk," Faye said politely. "If you don't mind, I'll be on my way now."

"I can't let you leave." Ryan took out his phone. "I'm calling the police. They'll want to talk to you."

"Why?"

"Why? Because you told us you killed a man, that's why."

Faye laughed lightly. Her smile was bright and her eyes twinkled with amusement. "You didn't believe that silly story, did you? You Americans are so naive." She turned to me. "As for you, Gemma Doyle, interfering in matters that have nothing to do with you. Bad habit, that. Don't count on Tamara being a witness. She's as fanciful as anyone I've ever met. Still chasing after that useless degree when she should be settling down and starting a family."

"Hey," Tamara said.

Faye turned again so she was facing Ryan, guarding the door. Her feet were apart, her arms relaxed at her sides. "You will let me pass. If you try to stop me, I'll resist, loudly. I'll scream my head off, and that will not look good for you in court." She pointed to the windows, through which we could see people passing by. A few even stopped to glance at the display of books. "You have the look of a copper about you, and I'm confident your employers wouldn't like to hear you've been arrested for assaulting an older woman."

"I still have the letter," I said.

She spoke without bothering to look at me. "Are you going to blackmail me? You're not the type."

"You don't know what type I am, but I don't need to use it myself. I'll give it to DI Patel."

"The Metropolitan Police don't engage in blackmail either."

"Gemma?" Ryan said.

I nodded at Ryan and waved my hand. We were three, four counting Tamara, against one. But Faye was correct. If we tried to physically restrain her, we could find ourselves in a lot of trouble. Ryan, in particular. He nodded in return, understanding what I was saying, and he reluctantly stepped to one side.

"Thank you." Faye brushed past him.

The chimes over the door tinkled as she let herself out.

Chapter Twenty-Four

"Are you going to simply let her walk away?" Tamara said. "She openly confessed to killing Paul."

"I don't know what else we can do," I replied. "Ryan?"

He took out his phone. "I'll call the police. We can tell them what she told us, but she's right that a confession like that won't stand up in court. It's not even enough to have her arrested. They'll question her about it, but if she sticks to her guns . . . nothing they can do without physical evidence."

He placed the call.

"Do you still have the letter?" Tamara asked me. "Can you hold it over her and make her confess?"

"I don't, and I wouldn't do that in any event. As you know, and are still bound to secrecy about, the letter has more significance than any minor indiscretion regarding Faye's son."

"Seems to me," Tamara said, "she killed Paul over nothing. Even if the letter was made public, who cares about some schoolboy cheating that happened years ago?"

I wasn't so sure. Greg Forgate was on the verge of becoming a rising star in political circles. The British gutter press were notoriously vicious. With a letter like that in hand, proof Greg had cheated at the fancy school where he'd been a scholarship student, even if his own cheating had been to help a friend, they'd go after him with all they had, all they could imply, and all they could make up. Yes, if the letter was released on a slow news day, he could have been ruined. Politically anyway.

"What do we do now?" Jayne asked.

"We wait for the police," I said. "Fortunately, we have plenty of reading material at hand if they're delayed."

* * *

We didn't have to wait for long. I was still surveying the stacks of books, trying to make up my mind about what to read to occupy my time, when DI Patel and her crew arrived. One by one, she took Ryan, Jayne, Tamara, and finally me into Paul's office for a chat.

When it was my turn, I told her exactly what had happened here earlier, and the thought process that led me to the conclusion that Faye had killed Paul and why. I gave a brief description of the contents of the letter, not mentioning any names. She let me talk, without interrupting, and when I finished, she leaned back in Paul's office chair and studied me.

"Anyone else, I'd think that was a whole lot of nonsense. But Henry Doyle tells me you're . . . astute."

"Praise from a parent is always nice to hear."

"I never take the word of a father about his child, so I've been in contact with the police in America. Do you recognize the name Estrada?"

"I certainly do. I trust you sent Louise my regards."

"I can't say she has warm and fuzzy feelings toward you, but she did admit you've occasionally been of help to them in the past."

"By which she means I solved cases for them. Although honesty forces me to admit they would have figured it out. Eventually. Probably. Maybe."

"She said you don't know how to draw boundaries between helping and interfering, but never mind that now. I also checked into your friend Detective Ashburton. He's got a good record and a solid reputation. He says the same as you as to what went on here earlier. As do Jayne Wilson and Tamara O'Riordan."

"Because we're all telling the truth."

"I have one question. Where is this letter everyone mentions but no one seems to have?"

"Beyond your reach. I gave it to . . . someone above your pay grade. They might not be willing to hand it over." I still had a photo of the letter on my phone, but I decided not to mention that. Let Pippa decide if the police would be allowed to see it.

"I suspected so. Tamara clammed up mighty fast when I asked her if she'd seen this letter, as did Jayne Wilson. Ashburton claims to have never seen it and only knows what you told him. Which is precious little. I'll ask my bosses to try to get it or at least have a peek at it. If they can't . . . yet another reason we'll have trouble building a case against Faye Forgate. If I can't produce it in court or even tell the jury what's in it."

"I doubt this will be the first time you know for sure who the guilty party is but can't prove it," I said.

"It won't be. Catch your flight home on Sunday, as planned. If I need anything, I know where to find you."

I stood up. "Thank you."

"One other question. Perhaps not relevant, but I would like to know. Assuming this mysterious letter exists . . ."

"Which it does."

"Buried in the depths of a vault deep beneath government offices, somewhat like the Ark of the Covenant in *Raiders of the Lost Ark*."

"Movie buff, are you?"

"I can be. Before you ask, my favorite Sherlock Holmes is Basil Rathbone. Which is, clearly, beside the point. How did Paul Erikson get his hands on the letter? He's not one of the parties involved, is he? I believe he was older than Faye's son so they would not have been schoolmates, and as far as I know, he was never a teacher. Did he meet

Alistair Denhaugh when you and he were married? And yes, Tamara did let slip that the letter we're talking about was written by Alistair Denhaugh, the Earl of Ramshaw. She immediately attempted to swallow the words, I might add. You put the fear of the powers-that-be into that girl."

"The fear of my sister, which is much the same thing. As for your question: again, I speculate, but I believe Paul simply found the letter in a book someone sold to the shop."

In my internet search for pictures and reminiscences about Greg and Lawrence's schooldays, I was able to arrive at a good idea as to the identity of the teacher who'd blackmailed Alistair. That teacher, I discovered, died about six months ago. He'd been an English teacher. Chances were he was a keen reader. Chances also were his heirs simply packed up all his books and sold them to a used bookshop for whatever they could get. Once they'd been obtained by the shop, the books had to be unpacked, sorted, their condition checked, and then put on the shelf. Had Paul discovered the letter? Had he kept it? In case he ever had the chance to use it, or only as an item of interest? And then Alistair Denhaugh suddenly became relevant again, and Paul, desperate for money, decided to try to take advantage of what he'd found. Unlike Faye, Paul was a regular consumer of the news; he would have seen mention of Alistair in reports of the Australian freighter incident.

"The night he died," I told DI Patel, "Paul said to me, 'You never know what riches can be found in old books, do you, Gemma?' At the time, I thought he was speaking metaphorically. Now I believe he was specifically referring to the letter."

"I'll be in touch," she said.

"One minor thing before I go. You might want to have another look at the fingerprint analysis of this room in particular. Faye Forgate, like the rest of the staff, could and did go pretty much everywhere on the premises and was permitted to touch everything. With one minor exception."

Chapter Twenty-Five

"So that's that," my father said. "She gets off scot-free."

"It happens," Ryan said. "It's happened to me. There have been times when I've been absolutely positive I know who's guilty, but I can't build a case. Must have happened to you in your career, Henry."

"More than I want to admit. Not to mention the times I've built an airtight case, and some fool of a sloppy detective, or a brilliant barrister, punches holes all through it, and the guilty party walks."

"More tea, Ryan?" my mother said.

"Thanks." He held up his cup. "I might get to like tea after all, if it's made like this."

"It is not," Jayne said. "Not in the sort of coffee shops you find back home. If, however, you come for tea at Mrs. Hudson's Tea Room, I'll make sure you get our very best brew."

"I might just do that sometime."

My mother poured. The tea was a first flush Darjeeling, light and floral. "By brilliant barrister, I should point out that Henry may be referring to me."

"There have been times, Anne," my father said.

"I can't believe I slept through it all." Andy slathered jam on his scone. A huge dollop of clotted cream followed. "And now, just when I'm raring to go, we're off home. Where I'll then be jet-lagged for another week."

Jayne gave him a radiant smile. "You had a nice fishing trip, didn't you? And a great day today?"

"I did," he admitted.

It was Saturday afternoon, and we'd gathered for afternoon tea at the Wolseley. Yesterday, when we'd finally left the bookshop, we found Donald and Andy pacing up and down in the library at Stanhope Gardens, both of them furious at us for bringing the case to a conclusion without them. Andy had taken one look at Ryan's black eye and the bruise on my cheek, stared at Jayne in horror and dragged her away for a full explanation. I hated to think what he'd have had to say to me if Jayne had been injured in the fight. But she hadn't been, and by now he was used to her getting involved in my schemes. Meanwhile I assured Donald that because I knew his baritsu and brolly-wielding skills wouldn't be required on this occasion, I thought it better to let him rest.

Friday night we went our separate ways. A chef friend of Andy's recommended a special restaurant in London and he wanted to treat Jayne. Ryan and I went to a less fancy restaurant, and Dad and Mum treated Donald to dinner at the Sherlock Holmes Pub.

Saturday, we agreed to meet for tea in the afternoon before heading out to get in some solid tourist time. Jayne and Andy went to Hampton Court Palace for the private tour Pippa managed to reschedule. Donald wanted to go back to Baker Street and take photographs of all the Holmes-related pictures on the walls of the tube station there. He was highly disappointed when no one jumped at the chance to accompany him. My dad stepped up and said he'd love to see it, whereupon Mum suddenly remembered some last-minute work she had to attend to. At Ryan's suggestion, he and I toured Roman London and he had a great day seeing the Mithraeum, the ancient stone walls, and the relics at the Museum of London. I had a great day watching him being so happy.

* * *

Saturday evening, the night before our return home, Grant and Pippa had us to dinner. Over pre-dinner drinks and canapés, my sister told us they'd been able to book a last-minute holiday in Majorca for their honeymoon and were leaving the next morning.

"That was short notice," Mum said.

"Life with Pippa," Grant said. "Good thing I'm flexible. More cheese, Andy?"

"Don't mind if I do."

"A minor crisis at work was satisfactorily resolved," Pippa said. "I won't be needed for a while."

"Until the next minor crisis," Dad said. "Speaking of which, I read in the paper this morning that the King and Queen are going to Vietnam at the end of the month. No reigning British monarch has previously been to that country."

"Is that so?" Pippa sipped her wine.

"Would have been awkward if that announcement had been made during the Australian freighter crisis. Would have looked as though their majesties were favoring one side over another."

"Shocking breach of protocol." Pippa stood up. "Grant, darling, can you refill Donald's glass and top up the cheese tray? I've remembered something I want to talk to Gemma about."

Grant headed for the kitchen. I wiggled my eyebrows at Ryan and then followed my sister down the hallway to the study.

She closed the door behind us.

"Not going to Vietnam?" I asked.

"On my honeymoon? Why would I do that? Besides, I was there only a month ago. Lovely country. Nice people. I have an unofficial update on the investigation into the death of your Paul."

"He wasn't my Paul. Never mind. I'm getting tired of saying that. What's happened?"

"We've agreed that the letter from Alistair can be admitted in court in camera, if the matter ever comes to trial, that is. Meaning the judge and relevant barristers will see it, but the jury and public will not. If that isn't acceptable to the court, Alistair has said he will not put up any objections to it being released in open testimony."

"So he should," I said. "A man died because of that letter. Paul wasn't an innocent, but he was desperate and he made a foolish mistake. Is that relevant, though? The police don't have a case against Faye, and our testimony about what she said isn't enough."

"A simple case of murder is normally not part of my remit, but in this instance, I had a word with the commissioner and asked to be kept informed."

"You had a word with the commissioner of the Metropolitan Police?"

"Didn't I just say that? Do attempt to keep up, Gemma. DI Patel is building herself a reputation as a determined, dogged detective. Once she got out from under the thumb, more like the boot, of the odious DI Morrison. When Paul's shop and offices were originally fingerprinted, they got hundreds of prints, as could be expected in such a place. Countless will never be identified. Obviously, the employees' prints were everywhere, and no one regarded that as significant initially. But then—"

"But then Patel said let's examine some of this again, and they found Faye's where they should not have been."

"On the zipper of Paul's backpack and on his shaving case. No employee would have a legitimate reason to go through their employer's personal items. Faye Forgate was brought in for questioning a short while ago."

"She'll find a reason for her prints being there. Maybe Paul asked her to fetch something for him."

"She can try to bluff her way through. As I'm sure you know, Gemma, once the police find a hole in a witness statement and they start to burrow further and deeper, more often than not the entire edifice of lies crumbles. Tamara O'Riordan was interviewed again early this afternoon. She told the detectives Paul instructed his staff to keep out of his things and to give him some personal privacy while, in his words, he was temporarily short of accommodation. If the case does go to court, and I'm fully expecting it will, you'll have to return to testify."

"Always a pleasure. I suspect Faye will fold as soon as she realizes what going to court will mean for her son. At the least, she won't want the letter to be released in open court, and I hope it isn't. I don't know Greg Forgate, never met him and have no desire to, but he doesn't deserve to have his name dragged through the tabloids because of a juvenile indiscretion, or because of something his mother did recently he didn't know anything about."

"I suspect you're right."

"I hope you have a wonderful honeymoon."

"I intend to, Gemma. I fully intend to."

* * *

When dinner was over and we were making our farewells, Ryan whispered to me that he'd like to go for a walk before returning to the house. A cab was called for Mum and Dad, Jayne and Andy, and Donald. After we'd seen the others off, Ryan and I walked through the quiet streets, holding hands, not saying much.

"Do you miss it?" he said to me, as we stood on the pedestrian bridge, looking over South Dock. A cold wind was blowing down the river, bringing the promise of winter soon to come. Lights from the city filled the sky and reflected off the black river. We were well wrapped in cardigans, gloves, and scarves. A woman passed us, a Labrador puppy dragging her across the bridge, and two young men ran past, shouting into the night.

"London? Dreadfully. I've lived in this city most of my life, and I can still turn a corner and suddenly realize I'm standing in front of a fourteenth-century church I've never seen before. In West London, I feel as though I know every inch of the town. But a city is just a place, and once you've seen one fourteenth-century church, you've seen them all." I lifted my hand and stroked his cheek. The eye looked considerably worse today. "I love this city, but West London is where I belong. Where I found the life I want."

He put his hand on top of mine and together we watched the traffic moving on the river below.

"Gemma," Ryan said at last, "do you think—"

My phone trilled to announce an incoming phone call. "Sorry about that," I said. "I'll ignore it."

"Better not. Who knows what might have befallen Donald between here and your parents' place."

I pulled it out and checked the display. "Ashleigh. I do have to answer. Hi, Ashleigh, what's up?"

"I thought I'd better tell you myself, Gemma, rather than you hear it through social media or get an angry text from some of the businesses on the street."

I groaned. "What's happened now?"

"The power's out at this end of town. Most of Baker Street is affected, and the business owners are not happy."

"Why is that my problem? The power will be back on soon, won't it? If it's one part of town, not further spread. We have nothing that will spoil without refrigeration. You might want to pop into the tea-room and see if they're managing, although I'm sure Mikey's run into that sort of situation before. Now, remember I'll be home—"

"Uh, Gemma?"

"Yes?"

"Thing is, it's sorta our fault. And thus people are mad. At us."

"Our fault? How is that even possible?"

"Arthur and Bunny—"

"I already don't like the sound of that, "I glanced at Ryan. He gave me a quizzical look in return.

"Yeah, well. You see, Bunny happened to find out that some of her backup band, you know from when she was a singer." Bunny Leigh was Ashleigh's long-lost mother. She'd been a major pop star in her youth. Which was many years ago, and she wasn't letting go of the fame and adoration easily. "The band, what remains of them, were in the area. Having done a gig in Boston and going on to Provincetown for some musical festival. So she thought it would be a great idea if they could hook up with her for one more show. An impromptu concert, like." Ashleigh's voice trailed off.

"And?" I prompted.

"And, well, they couldn't find a suitable venue on the spur of the moment, so she asked Arthur if they could use the store."

"My store."

"Yours and Arthur's store."

"Yes, that one. And?"

"Arthur thought it was a great idea, and he took it to the street's business association. They said yes, figuring it would get people into town in the off-season, so part of the blame is on them, right? It's a slow time of year, and the town agreed to close off the block for a couple of hours so Bunny and her band could perform on the sidewalk in front of the store. I mean, there's not enough room inside the store for a concert and an audience, right? Anyway, a van full of all this equipment pulled up into the alley this morning, and they unloaded it all. Brought it into the store and out to the sidewalk. Took ages to get it all set up."

I could see where this was going. "Did they think to check if the wiring in the nineteenth-century building which now houses the Sherlock Holmes Bookshop and Emporium could provide that much power without tripping a lot of fuses?"

"I guess not. Anyway, they lugged all their stuff out onto the sidewalk. Like speakers, amplifiers, microphones, the whole works. A real professional-looking show. Bunny was really excited, Gemma. She put on one of her sparkly outfits and had her hair done and everything. A big crowd gathered too. I guess people don't have much to do in the middle of the afternoon in October."

"It would appear not," I said. Ryan had returned to watching the river.

"One of them flicked a switch to start the show and . . . well, the power went out over half of West London. Poof. Just like that."

"I don't imagine Bunny took that very well."

"It turned out okay. She made a joke about it and sang a couple of songs without the mic and the backup music. But then Maureen came stomping over and complained, and Arthur got up to tell her what she could do with her complaints, and Maureen said she'd had enough of us; she's going to see that the store is shut down."

"That's not going to happen."

"No, but Arthur told her to go ahead and try it. I tell you, Gemma, for a moment there, I thought they were going to get into a stand-up, knock-down fight. And I don't know who'd win. One of the band members tried to get involved, and he yelled at Maureen to leave, and I quote, 'the old guy' alone, and Arthur said he didn't need some wet-behind-the-ears punk defending him. Maureen left, hurling threats behind her. She started phoning the other businesses on the street and managed to get them riled up too. Norm at the restaurant was mad because he was in the middle of dinner prep and his food was ruined. Or so he said. And Jen at the decor shop is threatening to sue you . . . us . . . because she twisted her ankle coming down the stairs when the lights so abruptly went out. I think you have a case there, Gemma. There are windows in that building. It's not that dark in the daytime, even without lights."

"Play nice until I get home, Ashleigh. If anyone complains, be very polite and say you have no idea what happened. Do not, under any circumstances, admit fault. Perhaps it's best if you send Uncle Arthur home for the rest of the day. Where is he now?"

"In the nook with Bunny and her pals, having a good laugh over what happened. He's telling the band guys about all the bar fights he was in in his early days in the navy. They seem to like that." As if to emphasize her point, a roar of male laughter came down the phone line. "I managed to persuade him not to go to Norm's restaurant to tell him he once had a steak there that was so overcooked, he should turn his ovens off more often."

"Thank heavens for small mercies. See you tomorrow." I put my phone away.

"Do I want to know?" Ryan asked.

"You do not." He slipped his arm around my shoulders and we stood together, looking out over the dark, rapidly moving river. The tide was out, and the mudbanks were exposed. In Sherlock Holmes's time, the poorest of the poor, those called mudlarks, would have been clambering down the banks, searching for flotsam and jetsam that might be of some worth. In Gemma Doyle's time, a party boat slipped under the bridge, all music and lights and drunken cheers. The tall buildings surrounding us were ablaze with lights. Pippa's building shone like a beacon, reaching up into the night sky.

"I was looking forward to relaxing back into work," I said. "Maybe going in late a few mornings, taking an afternoon off. Not gonna happen."

Ryan just laughed.

Acknowledgments

I had a fabulous trip to London in fall of 2023 with Alexandra Delany to check out locations for Trafalgar Fine Books and other places for Gemma and the gang to visit. Not everything described in these pages is entirely accurate, but the Wolseley is and we enjoyed a marvelous afternoon tea there.

Thanks go to my good friend Cheryl Freedman who always provides a keen editor's eye to an early draft, and to Sandy Harding who gently points out all of my errors and omissions. Thanks also to the team at Crooked Lane Books and to my marvelous agent, Kim Lionetti, for their continuing encouragement and support of this series.